THE UNITED FEDERATION MARINE CORPS' LYSANDER TWINS

BOOK 1
LEGACY MARINES

Colonel Jonathan P. Brazee
USMCR (Ret)

Semper Fi Press

A Semper Fi Press Book

Copyright © 2016 Jonathan Brazee

Illustration © 2016 Jessica TC Lee

ISBN-13: 978-1945743061 (Semper Fi Press)
ISBN-10: 1945743069

Printed in the United States of America

Acknowledgements:
I want to thank all those who took the time to pre-read this book, catching my mistakes in both content and typing. Thanks to Sammy Fernando for her editing. And once again, a special shout out goes to my cover artist, the award-winning Jessica Tung Chi Lee. You can see more of her work at:
http://www.jessicatcl.com/news.html.

Original cover art by Jessica TC Lee

Cover graphics by Steven Novak

In remembrance:

CT5 Harry Brose, USN, Vietnam Vet

RIP

EARTH

Prologue

The cell was stark, bare except for the table and two chairs bolted to the floor. The walls were padded, the two ceiling lights recessed. Three prisoners were in the room. In an ineffective act of defiance, they ignored the table and chairs and were huddled on the floor, up against the far wall.

Hannah Lysander, wife of General Ryck Lysander, leader of the Evolution, sat easily, knees up, forearms resting on them. Esther Lysander, Hannah and Ryck's daughter, sat next to her, staring at the ceiling. Noah, Esther's twin brother, sat on the other side of his mother.

They'd been held in captivity for nine months, picked up as they'd tried to flee the homeworld at the onset of hostilities. Hannah blamed herself for that. Now they were pawns as the old government tried to put down the "rebellion," as they termed it.

Initially, the three of them had been treated as well as could be expected, living under house arrest in a condo in Brussels. It was on the 40th floor, and with armed guards ever-present outside the door, it might as well have been a jail cell. There had been no Red Cross visits, but the fabricator worked, and there was even a library of flicks and holo series that they could watch.

That had changed two weeks ago—at least they thought it was two weeks ago. The three had been whisked away in the middle of the night and stuck in this real prison cell. Hopkins Garrison, the First Minister, had personally taken charge of a renewed interrogation. Hannah knew Garrison from when Ryck had been his military aide. He was a driven, ambitious man, and she hadn't cared

1

much for him. Now, she hated him with a passion that surprised her.

They hadn't been physically tortured, but the threat of it was ever-present, a stink that all the air purifiers in the world couldn't erase. His smarmy attitude, his constant reminders that their very future was in his hands, grated on her. He inferred that he was the only person keeping the wolves at bay, the wolves who wanted the blood of the Lysander family in revenge for the rebellion.

The problem was, Hannah believed it. But not from any sense of honor or compassion. The three of them were mere pawns being played in the big game.

Esther let out a sigh, then asked, "Have we ever figured out how long we've been here?"

"I still think they're screwing with us," Noah said. "They've dimmed the lights 13 times, but I don't think they do that every 24 hours. Look, my beard is still stubble. I think they're speeding the frequency up to make us think it's been longer."

"You've never been able to grow much of a beard there," Esther said, but without her normal delight in pulling his chain.

Noah frowned, then lowered his head between his knees and closed his eyes. He'd been outwardly calm during the ordeal, controlling the rising tide of angst that sometimes threatened to surface.

They sat quietly, lost in their thoughts, when the lock on the door clicked. All three sat up straight before the door opened and the first minister strode in, looking immaculate in a blue polytwill suit with a deep yellow cravat.

"Get up," he said with the voice of a man who expected—and received—instant obedience.

"Eat me," Esther snarled, remaining seated.

The first minister walked across the cell until he was standing in front of her, examining her as if she was a piece of meat. He reached out and with his forefinger lifted a lock of her blonde hair up from her face.

With a huge force of will, Esther kept herself from flinching, staring venomously at the first minister instead.

"Eat you, dear Esther? As appealing as that might be, I think I'll pass. But a word to the wise. Be careful of glib invitations, because you might not appreciate when a vampire takes you up on one."

He dropped her hair, turned, and repeated, "I said, get up."

Esther started another retort, but Hannah reached out to place a hand on her knee, silencing her.

"Why?" she asked.

"Why? Because I told you to. But I guess it wouldn't hurt for you to know. You're leaving here."

"Oh, thanks for releasing us," Noah said.

"Noah? Actually speaking, and with sarcasm, no less. I'm impressed. No, as you know, I'm not releasing you. Can't do that with traitors and all. All four of us, well, more when you included the muscle to make sure you stay compliant, are going to the moon."

Hannah gasped, unable to keep it checked.

"To the Cube?"

"I cannot confirm that, Hannah. I can't deny it, either," he said, a self-satisfied-looking smile on his face.

The Federation and Fiji were the only two Earth-based governments that still practiced capital punishment, but the UAM Charter prohibited executions on Earth soil. Therefore, both governments carried out executions adjudged on Earth at Luna Base, at the "Cube."

"What, no trial? Is that what you've sunk to?" Hannah asked.

"Traitors don't have any rights. Certainly, you know that. Besides, we can have a quick trial on the way up, if you insist. But for now, what I insist is that you get up and come along quietly. It's either that, or I ask the hulks outside the door to drag you."

"Come on," Noah said, slowly standing. "Let's just do it."

"Smart boy."

Hannah got up, but Esther took a good 15 seconds, glaring at the first minister until she stood.

"See, isn't this better? Now, if you would follow me?"

He walked out of the cell, not even looking back. His arrogance annoyed Hannah, but it incensed Esther, who imagined creative and painful ways to kill the man. The five large guards who fell in behind the three didn't faze her at all.

They trooped to the elevator, and then rode it for at least half-a-minute. Hannah realized that they had to be deep within the bowels of the city. Two more guards were waiting for them as the elevator door opened. Now, with eleven people in the parade, they marched down an empty hallway until they reached a door, guarded by yet another two guards.

The first minister submitted to a retinal scan, and one of the guards opened the door.

It was night outside, one of the warm, muggy nights that were so different from Hannah's homeworld of Prophesy, where water was at a premium. Even after following Ryck to Tarawa, she'd never gotten used to the viscosity of the air that weighed heavily in her lungs.

"Told you," Noah muttered to Esther as they stepped out into the darkness.

Since the lights hadn't been dimmed in the cell, it shouldn't have been night, so Noah took that as proof of his contention that they'd been screwing with their time.

A windowless van awaited them at the loading dock, the back open. The three Lysanders were hustled inside, along with five of the guards and the first minister.

"Cuff them," he said as he sat on the bench seat that ran along the right side of the van.

"What, afraid we'll jump your ass?" Esther asked as she submitted to the cuff around her wrist, with the other side secured to a ring on the floor.

"I know you'd like to try," the first minister said.

No one said another word as the van lifted and silently got underway. Twenty minutes later, it stopped. A few muffled words were exchanged outside, probably between the driver and some sort of guard, and the van smoothly accelerated once more, this time driving for only a few minutes before stopping and settling onto the ground. The back door opened, revealing a tarmac. Across the landing pads, the bright lights of the terminals and commercial shuttles let the prisoners know they were at Brussel-Zaventem instead of some secret military spaceport. Their corner of it, however, was dark.

One of the guards released their cuffs from the floor rings, then attached all three to each other.

"If you please," the first minister said with fake sincerity.

Mindful of their one-meter tethers to each other, the three slowly got out of the van. Parked beside them was a black ship without markings. It had the shape of a private yacht, one able to both land on planets as well as travel between stars, but there was a sinister air about it that brought a shudder to Hannah's very bones. She feared the ship was their hearse, even if the hangman hadn't released the trap door yet.

One of the guards gave Noah a shove towards the waiting hatch on the ship. All three Lysanders walked forward with as much dignity as they could muster. An old-fashioned mobile stairway was pushed up against the side of the black yacht. They climbed it, walked past yet one more armed man in Navy overhauls, but without insignia or patches, and took the seats the man indicated.

"You can take off the restraints," the first minister told one of the guards.

Noah and Hannah, held out their hands for the guard, but Esther refused, causing the guard to jerk up the chain up roughly so that he could release the cuffs.

The first minister led them to the base of the stairway, then with a dramatic gentlemanly flourish, waved his arm to allow Hannah to go first.

The cabin of the ship was nothing extraordinary, belying the grim exterior. It could have been any commercial yacht. The three Lysanders took the indicated seats and strapped in while another non-Navy sailor prepped the ship for takeoff and got their clearance. As the ship lifted from the surface, Hannah wondered if this was the last time she'd be on Earth.

The trip to the moon was short and silent. Hannah, Esther, and Noah were lost in their own thoughts, and even the first minister restrained himself. An hour-and-a-half later, the ship settled down on the moon with a soft bump.

"And, we're here," the first minister said, his voice bright and seemingly happy.

The guards stayed on board as the first minister escorted his prisoners out of the ship and into a large, surprisingly empty hangar. Hannah looked around in surprise. She could understand the government having some secretive hangars, but this one looked pretty big, too big to be much of a secret.

The hangar bay doors were open to the lunar surface, but none of the Lysanders knew enough of the lunar landscape to recognize where they were.

The first minister put his hand on Esther's back as if to turn her towards the near bulkheads, but she snarled, knocked back his hand, and said, "Keep your hands off of me."

He laughed and replied, "Calm down little tiger. I just don't want to see any of us flatted by the tractor assist beams."

He pointed back to the ship, which was rising over the landing pad. The four moved out of the way as the progressive beams turned the ship and led it to the hangar doors. After the ship crossed the red line, its own power took over, and with a flare in the electrostatic gate, it crossed into the vacuum of space and flew out of sight.

"What now?" Hannah asked, unable to contain herself.

"Now, we wait."

"For what?"

"For whatever happens next."

And so they did. For the next two hours, the four stood around in the hangar, the first minister on his PA, the three Lysanders standing close to each other, but not speaking much.

"I wasn't sure about how this would go down, but I should have been," the first minister finally remarked.

"Sure of what?" Esther asked.

"Patience, young lady, is a virtue."

"I'm not very virtuous, you know. I come from rebel stock."

The first minister harrumphed, but didn't say anything.

Ten minutes later, another ship made its appearance outside the huge hangar doors. The landing pad took over, pulling it through the gate with its tractor assists and to the middle of the deck.

"Our ride out of here? Why didn't you just take us to wherever the first time," Esther said. "Too afraid of anyone seeing us? You should be, you know."

The ship was a good 150 meters away, and Hannah waited anxiously, wondering when their fate would be revealed. She couldn't image what the sloop was there for, but it couldn't be good news.

The stress level rose as nothing happened for one minute, then two. Finally, the hatch opened . . .

. . .and Ryck stepped out.

"Dad!" Esther screamed out, her tough exterior melting at the sight of her father.

"Stay where you are," the first minister said, his voice brooking no argument.

Esther started quietly sobbing, grabbing and holding onto Noah's hand as their father firmly marched towards them.

"Send them over!" he shouted at the first minister when he'd reached the halfway point between them.

Hannah's thoughts were in a whirl, overjoyed that Ryck was there—and scared to death that he was.

"OK, now, you may go," the first minister said, nudging Hannah in the back. "All three of you."

Esther immediately broke into a run, bounding in the lower gravity until she reached her father and collided, arms grabbing and holding him in a death grip.

"Daddy!" she sobbed into his shoulder while Ryck squeezed her tight.

"It's all right, snugglebunny," he said, "You're safe now."

Hannah didn't run, but with Noah's arm around her shoulders, there was an urgency in her walk, her eyes locked on her husband's as he looked over Esther's head.

Noah helped his mother, but he wanted to slow down, to delay. He immediately realized what his father's appearance meant, and he felt a surge of joy that he wasn't going to be executed—followed by an immediate and immense sense of guilt that he'd felt that elation. He wasn't going to get executed because his father had traded himself for the three of them, and his father would be the one to lose his life.

There was no other explanation. During their interrogations, the first minister seemed to have taken a perverse pleasure in letting all of them know that their father had been tried in absentia and sentenced to death, and when they caught their father, that sentence would be carried out.

"But you're not safe. The first minister, he said what they're going to do to you!" Esther managed to get out between her sobs.

"I'll be fine, Esther. I always am," he said as he tried to soothe her.

Hannah and Noah reached Ryck, her eyes red and puffy.

"Ryck," she said.

"I know," he replied, bringing her into the hug.

Noah put his arms around the other three, and the four stood there for a moment, a family again.

"I'm so sorry, Hannah. And Ben. . ."

"We know. They told us."

"I. . .it's my fault, I let him enlist, and now, I've dragged you into this."

"That's about all the time you have!" the first minister shouted from back along the bulkhead. "Let's go!"

"Why did you agree to this?" Hannah asked, like Noah, aware of what would happen.

"Do you really have to ask? Because I love you, all of you," Ryck answered.

"But the rebellion—"

". . .will do fine without me," Ryck said, changing what Hannah had meant to say. "And you mean more to me than anything else."

"That's time, Ryck!" the first minister shouted out again.

"Look, you've got to go. Hans is waiting for you in the ship."

"No, Daddy!" Esther shouted, hugging him tighter.

Ryck had to reach down and peel her arms from around him.

"Noah, take your sister to the ship."

Noah wanted to tell his father he loved him. He wanted to tell him he was proud of him. But the guilt that overwhelmed him for feeling gratitude that his life would be saved was a huge barrier, a barrier that he couldn't overcome. He tried, but all he could do was let out a strangled grunt. Giving up, he nodded, then put his arm around the sobbing Esther and started to the ship.

"I love you, Hannah, with all my heart. You've made me the luckiest man in the world," Ryck told Hannah as their children walked to the sloop.

"Why, Ryck? Now I have to live with this, to live alone without you. I'd rather stay here."

He embraced his wife and kissed her gently on her forehead. "Go, Hannah. Take care of the kids."

He turned her and gave her a gentle shove towards their children, and that broke Hannah's heart. She walked away, focusing on them, knowing that if she turned back to her husband, she would break down and run to him.

Esther reached the access ladder, turned around and cried out, "Daddy, I love you!"

Right inside the hatch, Gunnery Sergeant Hans Çağlar, General Lysander's long-time friend and shadow, waited. He helped Esther into the cabin of the sloop, and then turned to give Noah a hand.

"Hans, did you have to help him kill himself," Hannah asked as she came aboard.

"I'm sorry ma'am, but he was going to do what he wanted to do. And what he wanted was to save you."

Noah put a hand on the gunny's shoulder and said, "I'm glad he had a friend with him, Gunny."

The corner of the gunny's mouth was ticking, the only sign of the turmoil the big Marine was feeling.

"A friend wouldn't have taken him here," Esther said.

Noah stepped to his sister, who had collapsed in a seat, and kneeled.

"Gunny Çağlar had to, Ess. You know that. He couldn't say no to Dad."

Seeing Esther like this jarred Noah. Esther was the strong one, the fierce one. But he knew she was also Daddy's Little Girl, and that had broken her will.

The hatch closed behind them, and the gunny said, "We need to leave now. Please take a seat."

Hannah paused at the top of the ladder, turned, and blew her husband one last kiss. "Can you turn on a viewscreen?" she asked, her voice terse, as she entered the ship.

"Yes, ma'am."

Gunny Çağlar reached the control panel, and a moment later, the view of the hangar appeared on the screen. All three Lysanders moved in front of it, staring at the image of their father reached the first minister.

Esther prayed that he would jump the asshole, then come running back, but she knew he wouldn't. He was a man of honor to a fault, even if that would cost him his life.

The gunny sat in the pilot's chair, and within a few moments, the hangar's tractor assists picked the ship up and backed it.

Esther let out another muffled sob, and Noah put his arms around her, hugging her tight. Their eyes were glued on their father as he turned to watch the ship cross the hangar deck.

They had one last glimpse of him before the view-screen flared with them piercing the gate, and Gunny took control, sending the ship into the Dark.

PART 1

Jonathan P. Brazee

PROPHESY

Chapter 1

Esther

"Just be yourself," Ernie Jackson-Pohl said as he smiled at Esther.

She didn't know if that was simply part of his broadcast personality or if he was hitting on her. She looked over at Noah, who was slumped in his seat, staring at his PA. She nudged him with her foot.

"I'll be ready, don't worry," Noah said.

"That's his usual self. You sure you want that?" Esther said to Mr. Jackson-Pohl, then immediately regretting her slight slide into what could be considered as any degree of friendliness.

Jackson-Pohl was well over 60, still quite attractive through the best efforts of modern medicine—and he knew it. His reputation was that he considered himself a star, and he wooed young women and men with reckless abandon (and if the snap-holos of him were any indication, with great success).

Maybe on Prophesy he was a star, but Esther and Noah were not natives and had lived on much more populated worlds. They were only on their parents' homeworld due to the pure chaos back on Earth and even Tarawa. When their dad had left to kick the government out of office and eventually take over the Council, her parents had sent them back to their homeworld to stay with Gamma and the extended clan. Esther would have rather stayed on Tarawa, and as an adult citizen, she could have refused to go, but she understood their reasoning even if she hadn't agreed with it. Moreover, her father didn't need to have the added stress of worrying about his remaining children.

When her younger brother Ben was killed, she saw the loss in her parent's eyes. It was without remorse that she acknowledged that Ben had been the apple of her father's eye, the son who followed him into the Corps at the cost of his life.

Mr. Jackson-Pohl laughed and said, "Don't you worry your pretty head about that. Your brother is going to do fine," as he reached over to put a hand on her knee—which she deftly avoided with a slight change of her posture.

A crew member rushed up and ran a face-scanner over Jackson-Pohl's face, then immediately pulled out a spray tube, entered some numbers, and sprayed it over the reporter's face. Mr. Jackson-Pohl didn't even seem to notice the administrations. Another quick scan, and he seemed satisfied.

The makeup man turned to Esther, scanned her, and entered whatever numbers he deemed necessary.

"Look up," he said curtly before spraying her face.

Esther felt a cool mist, then a slight tightening of the skin. She wondered how different she looked.

Noah brushed off the makeup man, refusing even to look up from his PA. The man looked to the producer who had escorted Esther and Noah to the recording stage, his dismay evident. The producer shook her head, and for a moment, Esther wondered if the makeup man was going to tackle Noah and force him to accept whatever mastery the man wanted to do on him.

"So, you must have been very proud of your father," Jackson-Pohl said.

Esther had heard this a million times in the four weeks since the Evolution and her father's successful ascension to the chairmanship. Except technically, her father had taken over the position over a year before. There had only been the small problem of the old chairman not accepting that, along with half of the Navy fleet and almost all of the FCDC.

The planet had been bursting with pride that one of their own had made the chairmanship, and now that her father had suddenly resigned, questions were rampant. This was Noah's and her tenth interview since her father's resignation, so she was getting used to the line of thought. It was as if every newsie followed the same script.

Despite the intense questioning, neither she nor Noah knew why their father had resigned his position so soon after gaining it. Noah had uttered a single "Thank God" when they'd seen the broadcast. Esther, on the other hand, had been more than a little disappointed. She was immensely proud of her father, to answer Jackson-Pohl, and she'd been confident of his ability to govern the torn Federation. To have him suddenly resign and hand over power to Councilwoman MacCailín had been a shock to her. She knew he must have had a good reason, but until he arrived back on Prophesy, she wouldn't know what that reason was.

"Are we ready, Talia?" Jackson-Pohl asked with a bit of snap to his voice.

"Five minutes, sir," the producer said.

Esther wasn't sure why the producer was calling the reporter "sir." Wasn't she the boss? In the Marines, rank was evident, and there was a comforting knowledge of where people were in the pecking order.

Not that I've been around Marines much lately, Esther thought. *School's a different world.*

Where Ben embraced everything Marines since he was a toddler, neither she nor Noah gravitated in that direction. She excelled in sports and was attending the University of Michigan, back in the USA on Earth, on a full athletic ride and had her eye on a professional career in either basketball or etherball.

Noah? She looked at her brother with a loving eye. Noah, quiet Noah. She wasn't quite sure what he wanted to do with his life. A culinary career seemed the most likely choice. But neither of them even considered a career in the Marines or Navy.

". . . pride to Prophesy, something along those lines," Jackson-Pohl was saying, snapping Esther back. "Just follow my lead."

"Sure. We've been through this before."

"But not with me, I assure you," the reporter said, once again reaching out to pat her knee.

And not with such a jerk, I assure you, she thought as once again, she shifted just out of his reach. *Let's just get this over with.*

The producer finally seemed ready to start. She cued the holo-engineer, and green lights on the dozen or so small holocorders lit green. Esther kicked Noah, then sat straighter in her seat.

"We're on in ten," Jackson-Pohl told them.

Esther cleared her throat and considered taking Noah's hand to show family solidarity, then dismissed the thought as too corny. Their team of handlers had suggested it during the previous day's interviews, but Noah had resisted, and Esther had agreed. Their father might be chairman, but he was not a career politician, and his children had not been raised in that circle. With their father resigning, it wasn't as if they'd have to learn that way of life now, anyway.

"Hello, Prophesy! Ernie Jackson-Pohl here with an exclusive with twins Esther and Noah Lysander, whose father, as if you didn't know, is our very own General Ryck Lysander and until yesterday, the Chairman of the United Federation. With the general on his way back home, we wanted a chance to sit down and talk with his two surviving children to see if we can get to know the man and the legend from their perspectives."

Exclusive? It's only our tenth interview over the last two days.

"So, if I can start with Esther first. Esther is a junior at the University of Michigan all the way back on Earth. She's a star on both the basketball and etherball teams and is carrying a Nutritional Studies major.

"Esther Lysander, welcome home. I know you are proud of your father."

No shit, she thought, trying to keep an interested expression on her face.

"What do you plan on saying to him when he gets home?"

"I will tell both of my *parents*," she said, stressing that her mother was coming back as well, "how much I love them and how happy I am to see them. Both Noah and I have not been able to spend much time with either of them throughout the fighting, so it's going to be great just to be a family again."

"Missing your brother Benjamin, though," Jackson-Pohl said with what she was sure was mock sincerity and compassion. "But you must be so proud of your brother's service.

"I don't think I need to point out to all of you at home that Private First Class Benjamin Lysander was killed in action on First Step, saving the lives of his fellow Marines. The acorn doesn't fall far from the tree.

"Well, not all acorns," he continued with a chuckle. "Esther, you didn't choose to follow your father into the Marines, and you are a collegiate athlete. And Noah, you're a what? A cook?"

Noah nodded, and Esther hurried to add, "Noah's studying culinary history and how that affects humankind and our evolution."

Esther loved Noah dearly, but sometimes, his lack of ambition and refusal to stand up for himself drove her batty. Jackson-Pohl was clearly being demeaning, yet Noah hadn't bothered to take issue with that. He never seemed to care what others thought of him. Her comment about "culinary history" was probably pretentious, but she wasn't going to let others think Noah was lazy or had no drive. It was just that his priorities were not necessarily the priorities of many others.

"Well, I know the effects of my culinary history, especially if I'm eating Mexican! Whoo!" he said, laughing at his own wit.

Esther leaned back ever-so-slightly. She wasn't a prude, but in her family, joking about farts on a public broadcast wasn't a sign of good upbringing.

"OK, now. Let's get serious again. I have to ask you, why did your father resign as chairman? He led the Evolution, he gained control of the Council, then a couple of weeks later, turned it over to Michiko MacCailín."

Esther was ready for the question, and she hadn't needed their handlers to craft a response.

"My father didn't lead the Evolution to seek personal gain. His sole goal was to restore order and justice in a system that was broken. Neither my brother nor I have spoken with him since he resigned, so we don't know for sure. But if I had to guess, he realized his mission was completed, and now was the time to relinquish the position to those who are skilled in the art of governing and serving the people of our great Federation."

"And Noah, we haven't heard much from you so far. Do you agree with that?"

"Probably. But we'll know for sure after we speak with our parents."

Jackson-Pohl seemed to be waiting for Noah to expand on that, and when nothing more was forthcoming, he turned back to Esther.

"I'm sure all of our audience, both here on Prophesy and out among the stars, are waiting to hear from his own mouth why he resigned. Will he be addressing us upon his arrival?"

"I don't know. I think we'll have to wait--"

Esther's attention was caught by a man rushing up to the producer. She looked surprised to be interrupted, but she slipped out her earpiece and tilted her head to listen. Something about the two tickled something in the back of her mind, and she felt a sudden wave of dread wash over her.

"Wait for what?" Jackson-Pohl asked, oblivious to the producer who looked up at them in shock and strode forward to the set.

"Stop slinging!" she shouted.

"What's going on? I'm in the middle of my interview, and it's live, if you've somehow forgotten that!" Jackson-Pohl said.

The producer ignored him, coming to a stop in front of the twins.

She took a deep breath, then said, "I've got some bad news. Your mother and father were just assassinated. The ship leaving Earth was sabotaged, most likely, and it exploded outside of Luna Station. There were no survivors."

Esther's world crashed around on top of her.

TARAWA

Chapter 2

Noah

> *Eternal father grant we pray,*
> *To all Marines, both night and day,*
> *Who bidd'st the mighty space lanes deep,*
> *Their own appointed limits keep;*
> *For those in peril out in space*
> *Take them into your strong embrace.*

The sounds of the organ slowly faded away. Noah had always loved the ancient hymn, but now it took on a new, deeper meaning.

"Here endeth the service. May Ryck and Hannah Lysander rest in peace forevermore," Brigadier General Palcovic, the Chaplain of the Marine Corps intoned.

Noah simply stood next to Esther, looking at the portraits of his mother and father. With the destruction of their ship, there were no bodies, of course. No one would be buried in the United Federation Cemetery on the base. General Hanata, the new commandant, had assured Esther and him that a monument would be erected, but while that seemed to soothe Esther, Noah didn't care. A statue of his father wouldn't bring his mother back. She had died, too, and not many people seemed to focus on that. Only the great Ryck Lysander, hero of the Federation.

Despite his usual outward calm, Noah was in turmoil. He was angry that his mother had been killed, that his father had dragged her to Earth and put her in danger. He felt her loss deeply. He was also angry that his father had died, but he was also sad that he didn't feel his loss to the same emotional degree. He loved his father, but that had always been a two-edged sword. He knew his father the man loved him. But he was also well aware that to his father the Marine, he was a disappointment. He wasn't Ben, the child whose very breath led to service in the Corps. He wasn't even his sister, the sports star who excelled in competition. He was just quiet Noah, lost in his own universe, whose chosen interest was old-fashion cooking. Noah knew his father's feelings, he accepted them, but that didn't mean he liked them. And deep down, where he tried to hide his own emotions, he resented his father in some ways.

He'd thought he'd lost his father once, back on Luna. After his father had escaped with the help of the deep-cover Confederation team, Noah had promised to take the opportunity to forge a stronger relationship with the man. And with his father retiring, it seemed as if fate was handing Noah the time to accomplish that. But fate is a fickle mistress, and his father had been taken from him. Noah would never get that chance to impress the man. And that hurt.

"I'm so sorry for your loss," the chairman herself, Michiko MacCailín said, stepping up to him and extending a hand.

"Thank you, ma'am," he said, more rote than anything else.

"He was a good man, but I guess you already know that."

Yes I do. Everyone tells me that continually.

The chairman, the most powerful person in the Federation, had been a governor of a back-water planet only a year ago. Now, she'd been elevated to her position by his father. Noah knew that the two had an unusual relationship of some kind, one that went back to his father's deployment to her home planet. Noah didn't think there was anything romantic to it, despite some undernet rumors to the contrary.

"If you need anything, just let me know," the chairman said before stepping to Esther to offer her condolences.

I don't have your number now, do I?

Noah knew he was being petty, but he didn't care. Soon, all the VIPs would be gone, Esther would be back at school, and he didn't have a clue as to what he was going to do next.

Admiral Blankenship, the new first minister, was next, and Noah barely heard what the man said to him. The man was not a friend of his father's, but he'd been given his position as an olive branch to the former government. He hoped his mumbled responses were acceptable. The commandant offered his condolences as well, and once again, Noah was in a fog, not really listening and wishing he could just leave the chapel and get some time for himself.

That is, until Major General Jorge Simone stood in front of him. Tears welled in Noah's eyes, and he stepped forward to hug the broad-shouldered heavy-worlder. The general was a fine man with a brilliant mind, and for most of his life, Noah could turn to him for anything from advice to a scintillating conversation on almost any subject.

"I've got tears on your blues," Noah said, trying to brush them off of the general's shoulders.

"It doesn't matter, son," the general said. "I'd like to come by later, if that's OK with you, after all of this is over."

"I'd appreciate it, sir," Noah said before the general stepped to Esther, who almost threw herself into his hug.

The line of worthies stretched out, and Noah realized that he was stuck there in the front of the nave. Without a casket or urn, they hadn't even had a chance to follow them out and then have the receiving line outside the entrance. Once the chairman had started at the pew, everyone else took her cue.

"Mr. Lysander," a big gunnery sergeant said as he stepped up.

"Come on, Gunny. You can call me Noah."

Noah had known Gunnery Sergeant Hans Çağlar for most of his life. The big man had been his father's everything-guy, from bodyguard to confidant. It hadn't been clear that he'd be free to come to the ceremony—after the incident, he'd been grilled by the FOI incessantly. He'd been the last one to see Noah's parents alive, and he'd arranged for the yacht to take them home to Prophesy.

Noah rather resented the gunny, and he resented the attention his father gave the man. But he was as positive as he could be that he did not have a hand in his father's assassination. The man was too dedicated, to *worshipping* of his father to be part of a plot.

"Very well, Noah. You have my deepest condolences on your loss."

It might be more of loss for you, he thought, softening his feelings.

"I know you loved my father, and he loved you. I am glad that you've always been there for him."

The gunny sighed, then hesitated as if he wanted to say something else. Instead, he nodded and said, "Thank you, sir."

He stepped to greet Esther, but turned back and said, "He was very proud of you, sir."

Noah didn't know if it was true or not, but the tears blinded him as the next person stepped up to greet him.

Chapter 3

Esther

"Does it have those rosehips in it?" Esther asked as Noah handed her the cup of tea.

"Fab rosehips. No real ones here."

She took a tentative sip. It wasn't bad. Even with a fabricator, Noah knew his way around a kitchen. She watched General Simone take a sip of his cup and then nod his approval.

It had been a long day. After the memorial, there had been a reception at the Officer's Club, and it had been full of well-wishers. At least the press had been relegated to a few camcordermen and still holographers—no journalists to keep asking questions. Marine after Marine had come up, though, relating stories of serving with their father, and Esther had felt obligated to hear them all out. She'd lost track of Noah during the afternoon and evening, but she'd sworn that a few times, he saw him listening to the same men who'd already regaled her with their experiences.

Finally, the base sergeant major had brought the reception to a close. Esther had been exhausted, more mentally than physically, and a scheduled trip to the Globe and Laurel to honor their father's OIC[1] box was delayed. She and Noah were driven to the Wolters House, the newly re-christened visiting VIP quarters, named for Major Melissa "Missy" Wolters, the only Marine to be awarded two Federation Novas before her father was awarded his second. A few of the old salts thought the re-naming was bowing to political correctness now that women were being allowed to serve in the Corps again, but did the old name, "The Blue House," have any historical significance? The Marine Corps loved tradition, and the new name not only carried that, it was a not-so-subtle reminder that women had served admirably before.

---

[1] OIC: Officer Indoctrination Course

She'd just wanted to shower, get in a fuzzy robe, and collapse in one of the overstuffed chairs that adorned most of the common rooms, so she'd been a little upset that Noah had invited the general to join them. But she couldn't stay that way for long. The general was an old family friend, and he was a comforting presence.

"Do you want something to eat?" Noah asked. "Just fab food. There's nothing in the cooler."

"You don't have to go to any trouble. I can call for something," General Simone said.

"Trouble?" Noah said with a huff. "Like I said, it's fab food. I'll just dial it in and press the start button. No trouble at all."

"Wait, Noah. Take a seat. I wanted to talk to you, and with General Simone here, I might as well get his opinion, too."

Noah took a seat, folding his legs up underneath him as the general looked up waiting for her to go on.

"It's about the future. My future."

"You've got another two semesters at the university, right?" the general asked. "I think that with your, uh, background, you can have your choice of almost anything. The chairman said she's there for you, and I believe her. If you want any position in the government, I think she can swing, say, an internship anywhere. After that, it would be up to you, of course, but you've got the talent in you to achieve what you want."

"She wants to be a professional etherball player," Noah said.

"Really? I know you're good, but that good? But I would imagine a few calls could get you a tryout, if that's your goal."

"It's not that," Esther said, marshaling her thoughts. "I'd like to play professionally, but to what end? I get a few years, if I even make a team, then that's it. Etherballers are not known for longevity on the pitch."

Noah looked up in surprise, and that gave Esther a sense of satisfaction. He usually knew what she wanted to do before she did herself.

"With dad, I mean, we had Ben, but he, you know. Dad really loved the Corps. And now, no Lysander in uniform—" she started rambling.

"You want to enlist!" Noah said, his mouth dropping open.

"Maybe. Yeah. I think so."

"But you've never wanted to be in uniform."

"I'm thinking now I might want it."

"Well," the general said. "I'd like to say I'm surprised, but really, I'm not. You have too much of your father in you. Your mother always saw it. Even I saw it. I think, with what's happened, that it's only now surfacing."

"Are you sure?" Noah asked her.

"Not completely, no. I still have school, for one."

"You could wait until after graduation and then see how you feel," the general said in an even tone.

"If I do it, I want to do it now. Why wait?"

If she did wait, she was afraid something would come up and she'd never actually take the step.

"Are you doing this for you or for Dad?"

"I don't know," Esther said, trying to figure that out for herself.

"It's kind of important, Ess. Dad's dead. He's not going to care one way or the other."

"Noah's right, Esther. I'd be proud of you if you enlisted. So would many people. But that's not a good reason. You have to want to be a Marine. It has to be in your blood."

"And not just Dad's blood flowing through your veins," Noah added.

"If you want, I can make some ca—"

"No! I mean, I don't want any help. It'll be bad enough with my father's ghost hanging over everything I do, I don't want some general making calls for me."

"Ess, don't make an emotional decision. Lord knows we've got enough emotions running around right now. Why don't you finish school? Get your degree. And if you still think you want to enlist, heck, I'll drive you to the recruitment center myself."

Esther knew that was good advice. But when the idea hit her, it had grown stronger within her. The more she thought about it, the more she knew this was the right step. But small doubts nibbled at her consciousness. Was she reacting to the emotions of losing her parents? Was she doing this for her father?

"What about you?" she asked Noah. "What are you going to do now?"

"I was thinking about going back to Prophesy," he said.

"Prophesy? Why? You hate the place."

"It might not be paradise, but I think I want to get to know the family. When mom left, I think that created an unintended wall between them and us. I'd like to bridge that wall and see just who our people are."

Esther wasn't terribly surprised. For such a nerd, Noah cared about people, and with their mother and father gone, it made sense that he reach out to create bonds with whatever family they had left.

She shifted her gaze to the general, who'd been sitting quietly and listening.

He caught her eyes and said, "That makes sense to me. Get your degree and then decide."

She felt a small weight lift off her shoulders. The advice was sound, she knew. If she still felt this way after graduation, she could enlist, wait for the etherball draft, join a corporation, or even get a position in the government.

"OK, I'll do that," she said with conviction. "And, I guess I am a little hungry after all. Do you think the fab in this dump can whip up some decent shepherd's pie?"

PROPHESY

Chapter 4

Noah

Esther finally came through arrivals, pulling what looked to be a brand new duckling. She immediately saw Noah waiting beyond the small barrier and raised a hand in greeting, a huge smile plastered over her face.

She navigated past the other passengers, cut through a reunited family, and threw her arms around his neck.

"Oh, it's good to see you, little brother."

Noah smiled at her familiar phrasing. She'd been born nine minutes before he was, and in the 21 years since then, she hadn't let him forget it, despite the fact that he had a good 15 kilos on her.

"Good to see you, too. I'm still surprised that you wanted to come back here for this. You could have done it on Earth without spending a small fortune."

"Yeah, I could have. But then how could you drive me?"

"Ha! You're right. Earth would be a grubbing long trip just to keep my promise to my old sister."

"I'll forget the 'old sister,' but 'grubbing?'"

Noah could feel his face reddening. "Grubbing" was his father's go-to word, one the two of them thought rather backwoodish even if a bit endearing at the same time.

"It's a Prophesy saying, you know. I guess after almost a year, the place is rubbing off on me."

Esther pulled on his hand and made a show of inspecting his fingernails before saying, "I don't see any farmer's dirt there, so I guess you haven't totally acclimated."

Noah yanked his hand back and said, "There're lots of different uses for 'grubbing,' you know. But you're my sister, and this is a public place, so I'll refrain."

"Oh, you love me. You know you do," she said as she gave him a big kiss on the cheek.

"So, is that all you have? One duckling? Who are you and what have you done with my sister?"

Esther was a clotheshorse, and together with her ever-present athletic gear, she usually maxed out with three large bags wherever she went. Hovering a few centimeters above the deck, the single mid-sized duckling couldn't possibly hold enough for a normal person's visit, much less Esther's.

"I don't plan on staying long."

"I think Gamma might take issue with you on that, Ess. She's already got dinners planned for a week, and you're the star attraction."

"Yeah, I figured she would, and that's exactly why I won't be staying long," Esther said.

Noah looked sharply at her. Sometimes, she could be a little abrupt and self-centered. "Focused," she called it. The entire extended family had felt the loss of their parents, and this was the first time since they died that they'd be able to see her. This might be a pain in the ass for her, but the family needed it.

"We'll see about that. Let's talk back at the farm. You know, you really need to spend some time with them."

"Like you have?" she asked with more than a hint of sarcasm.

"Yes, like I have. They've been good to me, you know."

"Well, that's you. I don't need a bunch of people I barely know beg me to tell them stories about Mom and Dad."

Noah shook his head slightly, then to change the subject, said, "Let's get out of here. It's a good two hours to the farm."

"Lead on, oh little brother of mine," she said, but not before flicking the duckling's eye on him and pressing the imprint.

"Too heavy for you?" he asked as he started off, the slightest tug confirming that the bag had imprinted on him and was obediently following.

He led Esther—and the duckling—out to the lot where he'd parked the hover, opening the trunk and loading the bag inside.

"Not too shabby," she said, admiring the Hyundai Aster.

"Uncle Barret gave it to me," he said as he got into the driver's seat.

An Aster wasn't a luxury hover, but it was far too expensive for an out-of-work young man to own.

"He 'gave' it to you? As in it's yours?"

"No, but it's mine while I'm here."

"I guess it's nice to have a rich uncle. I might have to look into that."

"Navigation," he said, activating the autodrive. "Take us to—"

"Wait, Noah. How far is it to the government center?"

"They still call it 'Corporate Center,' here. And from the farm? Driving? Still probably two hours. When it's time, I think we can drive to Bounty, then take the maglev into Jacob Station. That will save us an hour."

"I mean from here?"

"Here? The spaceport? I don't know. An hour or hour-and-a-half? Why?"

"Because I'm thinking about going there now. I mean, why wait? I came all this way to do it here, so I might as well get it over with?"

"Really, Ess? Gamma's probably got a feast laid out for lunch, and Auntie Lysa and some of the cousins will be there. And you want to go do it now?"

She shrugged, tapped her forefinger on the window, and then said, "I specifically asked for no reception, Noah. I can't be responsible for that. I came to do this here because, well, you know . . ."

"Because this is where Dad enlisted."

"Well, yeah. It just seemed right."

Esther put up a good front. She was the tough one, the one who could handle anything. But Noah knew she was still daddy's little girl, and she missed him. He still thought her enlisting was to please their father, so it did make sense on some levels.

But she was also set in her ways, and if he wouldn't take her, no doubt she'd get out of the hover and take the spaceport line downtown.

"OK, if you want, we can go to the Corporate Center now. I'll call Gamma and ask her to delay lunch until . . ." he paused, blinking up the time on the Hyundai's windshield display. "Two. I think we can make that. Deal? Straight to the farm after?"

"OK, deal. Straight to the farm after," she said, and as he gave the autodrive their destination, muttered, "I still don't know why I couldn't stay at a hotel."

Noah kept the conversation neutral during the drive, mostly on her last year at school and sports. Esther could talk for hours on almost anything if she were interested, so he mostly listened, adding in a few "uh-huh's" when he thought it necessary.

He was getting a little nervous himself, which surprised him. There wasn't any reason for that. An hour after leaving the spaceport, the Hyundai pulled up into the Corporate Center passenger drop-off.

The twins got out of the hover, and Noah instructed it to, "Park and stand by."

He was anal enough to want to park it himself, to make sure it was in a good spot, but within the downtown loop, all parking was automated. He was tempted to pull the hover up on his PA and watch it, but he knew Esther would ride him mercilessly if she caught him.

It was mid-morning, before the lunch rush, but several food-trailers were setting up, and the aroma of cooking filled the square. Food-trailers, which mostly served natural foods, had become a fad on Prophesy lately—only about 15 years after they'd made their comeback on Earth, Hiapo, and Initiation—and this was one fad to which Noah could heartily support. Fabricators were the choice of the masses, and they produced excellent food out of the algae and other bases, but Noah subscribed to the theory that not only was natural food better, both in taste and for health, but mankind couldn't lose the knowledge of how to prepare food.

He caught sight of Hammal's, regarded as the best joh-eun gansig trailer on the planet. Noah personally thought that Morning

Calm, over in Robbyville was better, but the thought of Hammal's kimchi and bulgogi-pouches set his mouth watering. He didn't get into Williamson that often, and it would be a shame to pass up a chance to have one of those exquisite pouches of heaven

Maybe just one after we're through here wouldn't spoil my appetite. Gamma doesn't have to know.

"Uh, mission control to Noah? You there? Which building?" Esther asked.

"Oh, sorry," he said, snapping back to the here and now. "I was just thinking. Uh, that's the Federation Administration Building over there."

There had been talk of re-naming the building as The Ryck Lysander Building, but for now, the old, generic name remained.

"That's the problem, then, you thinking," his sister said, looking pleased with her wit.

He bumped her with his shoulder, saying, "Excuse me? I didn't see you there."

What did you say?" she asked sweetly as she suddenly stepped back onto his foot, putting all her weight on it.

He laughed as he pushed her off. It was almost as if the last dozen years had been peeled away, and they were young pre-teens again, teasing each other. Instead of another retort, he pulled her into his embrace, giving her a huge hug.

"What's that all about?" she asked, but her arms crept up around his back as she returned the hug.

People milled about, flowing around the two young people as they stood there, holding each other.

"Well, enough of that, little brother," she said after a few long moments. "Let's get this over with."

The two walked up the broad esplanade, past the fountain, and got in line to the Federation Building. The war had been over for a year, but still security was heightened. It took almost 20 minutes to get to the head of the line, then it was full body-scans to get inside the building. Noah knew that hidden scanners were also in play, and as always, he felt more than a little self-conscious.

In addition to the normal kiosks, the Federation Building had a real person at a large, round reception desk. Without hesitation, Esther marched right up to it.

"I'd like to see the Marine recruiter, sir," Esther announced.

"Do you have an appointment, ma'am?" the elderly gentleman asked.

"Not for today. Tomorrow. But we're in town now and thought we might be able to take care of this now."

"I understand, ma'am, but you should have called. All the recruiters are in an admin stand-down today. I don't think anyone is available for walk-ins."

Esther tilted her head back and lowered her chin at the same time.

Grubbing hell! She's going to go off on the poor guy, Noah thought, recognizing her trademark gesture.

To his surprise, she clamped down on whatever she was going to say, waited a moment, then asked, "And will anyone be available this afternoon, after lunch?"

"I'm sorry, ma'am, but according to the POD,[2] all of them will be in required training. I think it's best if you just come back tomorrow for your scheduled appointment," the man said.

"Uh, Mr. Patterson, is it?" she asked, looking at his name tag. "I understand what you are saying, but could you at least take my name and let the head recruiter know I stopped by?"

And Noah began to see the method to her madness.

"Certainly, miz. I'd be happy to. May I have your ID?"

Esther held out her wrist, which the receptionist scanned.

"OK, I'm forwarding it now, Mz Lysand—" he started before looking up in surprise. "Esther Lysander? As in Ryck Lysander?"

"Well, the general was our father, so I guess yes."

"I . . . let me call Master Sergeant Sukarho. Wait a second, please."

Esther leaned nonchalantly on the desk, looked back, and winked at Noah as the receptionist hurriedly punched something on his display screen.

---

[2] POD: Plan of the Day

Noah could hear him mumbling before he looked up and said, "The Top will be here in a few moments. If you could just wait?"

"Oh, I didn't want you to go into any trouble. I don't want any special privileges!" she said sweetly.

Like hell you don't, Noah thought.

It was a little funny, though, to see the receptionist fret. On one hand, Noah felt for the man. On the other, it was somewhat surreal. Neither Esther nor he was their father. They were not Marines. They were just two civilian kids.

Within two minutes, a large, barrel-chested Marine master sergeant strode down the hall, feet clicking on the stone floor with each step. He had most of the look of a heavy-worlder, lacking only the short neck. He could just be a weight-lifter, Noah realized.

"Ms. Lysander, I'm surprised to see you today. I wasn't expecting you until tomorrow."

"Yes, sir. But I just got in, and I wanted to see if we could get this done today, if possible."

"Well, I don't see why not. The major wanted to see you, but we're in the middle of an admin stand-down, and he's not in. Still, if you want, we can get the ball rolling."

"I don't want to put anyone into any trouble," Esther said in her I-know-what-I'm-saying-but-don't-believe-me tone of voice.

"Oh, no trouble, Mz Lysander, believe me," he assured her. Lowering his voice in a conspiratorial tone, he added, "Believe me, no trouble. You're getting me out of a gender neutrality seminar, and I should thank you for that. Boring!

"Not that I am prejudice against women in the Corps," he hurriedly added, his expression changing to one of concern as he seemed to realize that not only was Esther female, but it had been their father who had changed the policy to allow women to serve again. "No problem with me on that!"

Esther nodded, placed her hand on the master sergeant's arm, and said, "I know that. And I just appreciate you taking the time to help me out on this. So, where do we go?"

"Oh, to the second deck. If you can follow me?"

As both Noah started to follow, the master sergeant said, "If you can wait, sir, Mz Lysander can call you when she's finished."

"This is my brother, Noah, and I'd like him to accompany me, if that's OK?"

"Oh! Sorry, I didn't realize who you are. Of course, if you want, you can come up to the office. Of course!"

With Noah walking behind them, the master sergeant regaled Esther with tales of boot camp, of what she could expect there, and how proud the Corps would be to have her among its ranks. Noah noted that nowhere did he touch on the 27% drop- rate of recruits overall, nor the 34% drop-rate for women. When their father had opened the Corps to everyone, it had been done under the stipulation that there would be no lowering of standards, period. While women were integrating far easier in the Navy and now the FCDC,[3] fewer women passed the entry qualifications for enlistment into the Marines (which wasn't surprising, as few men did as well), and of those who made it to boot camp, a lower percentage of women graduated than men.

Noah had no such worries about Esther. She was smart, physically fit, and more than that, mentally tough. Esther would make it through boot camp without breaking a sweat. But he thought that for transparency, the recruiter should mention all facts, good and bad, instead of painting book camp as some sort of frat party.

The three passed the Navy Liaison Office, the waiting room empty and dark. The Navy was still the main power player in the Federation, but with first their father, and now Chairman MacCailín, that was two chairmen in a row who had not come up through the Navy ranks. From some of the various talking heads on the holos, the Navy wasn't pleased with this and was already maneuvering to restore all that is right in the universe by getting one of their own in the position after the current chairman stepped down.

The lights were on in an office further down the hallway, but the flag of Greater France outside the door threw Noah for a

---

[3] FCDC: The Federal Civil Defense Corps: and all-purpose federal police-slash-army force.

moment. Then he realized it wasn't the Marine Corps office, but that of the Legion. Esther didn't seem to notice it, but Noah felt a ghost's touch sweep over him. Over 30 years ago, his father had marched into that office, determined to join the Legion. Somehow, he'd enlisted in the Corps instead, putting events into motion that would eventually lead him to being awarded two Novas, become the commandant, lead the Evolution, and become chairman.

Begetting Esther and him in the process.

If he had joined the Legion, neither one of them would be standing here today. That was a simplistic view, he knew. If he hadn't become friends with their uncle, Joshua, his mother and father never would have met. If battles had gone slightly different, his father would have been killed.

If, if, if.

Standing here, though, as the master sergeant scanned open the door to a much smaller office, it just hit him stronger at how capricious the universe could be.

"Oh, the major just zapped me. He's on his way," the master sergeant said, looking at his PA.

"He's coming in on his day off?" Esther asked.

"He has to. You need an officer to swear you in. He'll be here in about 40 minutes. It'll take that long to get the paperwork done. Luckily, you've already taken your aptitude tests back on Earth, and your physical is noted. You did extremely well, I might add, although that could be expected, I guess, considering your pedigree."

That was the master sergeant's first overt reference to their father. Noah knew that just getting in today was because of that, but the recruiter hadn't actually acknowledged any special privileges or considerations.

"So, I've asked Chastity—she runs most of the admin—to come on up, and we can get this going.

"Mr. Lysander, if you can wait here, we'll be stepping back into the office to get these things done. We won't be too long."

Noah took a deep breath. He still wasn't sure if this was the right thing to do, and he almost backed out.

"No, I'd rather come back with you, Master Sergeant."

"But that's only for official poolees, sir," he said, clearly getting flustered. "I mean, I guess I can make an exception, considering your father, but this is against regs."

"You can wait, Noah. Like the top says, it won't be long."

"I don't want any special privileges, and I don't want you to break regulations."

"I don't understand."

"Oh my God," Esther said, bringing her hands up to cover her mouth in surprise.

She always did understand me before anyone else.

"I want to enlist, too."

The master sergeant's mouth dropped open, then he shifted his gaze from him to Esther and back to him.

"Really?" he asked.

"Yes, sir. I'm ready."

"Well! Well! This is great. I need to pull someone in for the tests—"

"Already done. You can look them up," Noah said, offering his wrist.

The clearly flustered recruiter scanned Noah, then pulled up his records. Noah leaned in to retinally give the master sergeant permission to view them.

"Yes, here they are. Good scores," he said, the professional recruiter coming out. "No problem there. And I see your physical. You had that done at St. Theresa's, so it's good enough for a temporary acceptance.

"You'll have to get another physical at a Federation facility, and if there's a health issue, your enlistment will be voided, but I don't see a problem with that.

"No, everything looks good on this end. Sure, we can get both of you sworn in when the major gets here."

"How long have you had this planned," Esther asked quietly.

"Six months. Maybe longer."

"Glad you could fill me in," she said, her displeasure evident.

Noah hadn't told Esther because he wasn't sure he was going to go through with it. There were a million reasons why this was a bad idea. There was only one reason why it was a good one. Despite what he'd told Esther back on Tarawa, that she should enlist only if it was something she wanted to do for herself, he was ignoring his own advice. It didn't make any kind of logical sense, but that one reason trumped all the reasons against enlisting.

Noah was enlisting to please his father and finally gain his approval.

TARAWA

Chapter 4

Esther

"Recruits Lysander, E. and Lysander N., fall in on me."

Esther immediately jumped off the rack where she was stowing her gear, and took off to the DI, beating Noah by at least five seconds.

Staff Sergeant Mallinka Hoteah, their senior DI, stood by the front hatch, glowering at them.

"Recruit Lysander N., why did Recruit Lysander E. beat you here by half a day?"

"I . . . no excuse, Senior Drill Instructor!" Noah managed to get out.

Come on, Noah, buckle down, Esther thought.

"You're starting out on a bad foot, recruit. You'd better get yourself an attitude adjustment.

"Now look, you two. The battalion commander wants to see both of you. Why he cares about two slimy-ass recruits is beyond my military mind, so help me, but we're going across the grinder to the CP. We will go in where we will stand at parade rest until the sergeant major calls your weak-ass bodies into the CO's office. You will center yourself on the lieutenant colonel's desk . . . do you know what that means?"

"Yes, Senior Drill Instructor Hoteah," the twins said in unison.

"Thank God for small favors," he said with mock sincerity. "You two will center yourselves on his desk and listen to what he has to say. If he asks you have anything to say back to him, the only answer is 'no, sir!' Is that understood?"

"Yes, Senior Drill Instructor Hoteah."

"Let me make one thing exceptionally clear. You two may know half of the generals in my beloved Corps. The Chairman of the Federation Council might be your best buddy. But now, in this series, your asses belong to me. There is no one higher than me, and no one can make your worthless lives as miserable as I can. So you can forget all about your high and mighty friends, because they don't mean shit here. I own you!" he said, and then with a forefinger punching into each of their foreheads in beat with the words, asked, "Do . . . you . . . understand . . . that?"

Despite her best efforts, Esther flinching each time his left forefinger hit her forehead. She thought she understood the score, that she knew the mind games of boot camp, but the drill instructor seemed angry, angry enough to actually cause her harm. For the first time since their arrival at midnight some nine hours earlier, she felt a degree of uncertainty.

"Yes, Senior Drill Instructor Hoteah," she stammered out, half-a-second behind Noah.

"Just remember that. Now, on my ass," he said as he spun about and pushed through the hatch.

Esther and Noah marched at attention, their eyes locked on the senior drill instructor's back, and they left the barracks and crossed the flat grinder. The sun was just climbing into the sky, a warning of the heat that would come with the afternoon. Esther would welcome that kind of heat—being on their senior's shit list not even ten hours into their training was far more worrisome.

The three of them entered the large, ornate doors into the battalion CP. Holos and plaques covered the bulkheads of the passage—not that Esther dared look at them. She followed their senior until he pointed at a spot along one of the bulkheads while he growled out something she couldn't make out. Hoping she was correct, she came to parade rest, Noah doing the same beside her.

"Don't move," the senior said before he disappeared into an office.

"What do you think—" Noah started to whisper beside her.

"Shh!" she hissed, wondering if he really could be that stupid.

A few moments later, a Marine came out of the same office into which the senior disappeared. He strode to them, gave them the once over, and asked, "Did Senior Drill Instructor Hoteah tell you that you will only answer direct questions. Unless he's asking you your freaking birthdays or your maiden aunt's name, the only answer is 'Yes, sir' or "No, sir?'"

"Yes, Chief Drill Instructor," Noah said.

How did I forget him? Esther wondered, glad that Noah, at least had.

She'd never been great with faces, but the gunnery sergeant had "welcomed" them to the platoon right after their heads were shaved and they'd changed into their recruit overalls. And keeping her head rigid and eyes to the front, she'd never really gotten a good look at the man.

"I asked you a question, Recruit," he said again, moving to stand right in front of her.

"Yes, Chief Drill Instructor!"

"Gunny Duluth, send in the recruits," a voice called from down the passage.

"Atten-hut! Right face!" the gunny hissed. "Center yourself on the CO's desk.

Esther was tempted to remind the gunny that they hadn't been trained in drill yet, but realized that was a bad, bad move. Both she and Noah had seen enough parades in their lives to know what to do.

A captain, a lieutenant, and a first sergeant were coming out of the CO's office. All three stood and watched as Esther and Noah marched down the passage. The captain looked like he was about to say something, but he held back.

The first sergeant, though, hissed, "Say nothing!"

I know, I know. We're not allowed to talk.

Esther completed a credible right turn (at least she thought it was credible) into the office and marched up to a large desk, behind which stood a tall, pleasant-looking lieutenant colonel. Esther immediately noted his Silver Star. That was nothing compared to her father's awards, but it wasn't too shabby.

She came to a stop, wondering if she should sound off immediately. Instead, she waited for Noah to come alongside her. Only, he stepped too far, and had to come back one step so that they were even.

"Recruit Esther Lysander, reporting as ordered, sir!" she said, almost, but not quite in unison with Noah.

"At ease, recruits," the CO said.

Esther wasn't quite sure what that meant from a practical standpoint. She slipped into a parade rest, thinking that was safer.

"I'm Lieutenant Colonel Sung," the CO said, "and I'd like to welcome you to the Third Recruit Training Battalion. I don't normally welcome each recruit, but as you can imagine, the two of you present a rather unique situation that merits not only my attention, but the General O'Leary's as well."

Esther knew of the general. He'd served with her father with some distinction, but she hadn't realized he was the depot's CG. Regardless, she wasn't sure just why the Noah and she presented any issues.

"Normally, we wouldn't put siblings in the same company, much less series, but there is quite a bit of media interest in you two."

Really? Esther wondered, rather surprised.

"This puts a strain on our manpower here. The depot is run lean and mean, and we don't have the personnel to deal with the media and government attention."

He must have noticed the confusion on either Noah's or her face, because he snorted and said, "Do you know I got a call today, from the Chairman herself, asking if you two had arrived safely and were 'fitting in,' she said."

Oh, shit, just what I need.

The CO had asked them a question, but mindful of their senior's warning (as well as the chief's and first sergeant's), she kept quiet.

"So, yes, there is attention on you; attention we can't ignore. And to minimize your impact to the running of this depot, you've been put into the same series.

"So now, some ground-rules. While you are a recruit, you will talk to no one outside of your official duties without expressed permission from your DIs. If someone calls out to you to ask you something, anything, you are to ignore them. Is that understood?"

"Yes, sir!" the twins said together.

"If you receive any correspondence other than from family, you will inform your DIs. Is that understood?"

"Yes, sir!"

"I know, with your background, I really don't have to remind you of these things, but it's better to get it into the open. We don't need anything to interfere with the training here. It wouldn't be fair to the other recruits, and it wouldn't be fair to you. Recruit training is hard enough as it is, and you don't need any further pressure added to you.

"I will say, though, that we are proud to have you in the battalion. I never had the honor to directly serve with your father, but his legacy lives on in the Corps, and I don't mean you two. I shouldn't say this, but with the divide within the Federation, any good news needs to be both embraced and exploited.

"So how does that concern you? You are good news. Your journey through boot camp is being followed, and the Sixth Minister's office has listed your experiences as a Cat 2 interest. Do you follow me?

So we have to make it through training, Esther realized. *Can't have us failing and spoiling the fairy tale.*

"So, if you're having any problems—*any* problems—I want you to come see me. My door is always open to either of you."

Esther thought the CO looked like he had swallowed poison and was trying to force out the words.

"If you are having trouble adjusting, if you aren't keeping up, come see me. And if I'm not here, the duty officer will be able to reach me.

"But I know none of that will be necessary. You're General Lysander's kids, right? You were born to this.

"Do you have any questions now? Any concerns?"

"No, sir," the two answered.

"Remember, I'm here if you need me," he said again.

"Staff Sergeant Hoteah, enter!" he said in a raised voice.

The senior must have been waiting right outside the hatch. He immediately entered and marched to stand beside Noah.

"Staff Sergeant, take these two recruits back to their series and carry out the remainder of the training day."

"Aye-aye, sir," the senior said before turning to the two and in a low voice, saying, "About face. Forward . . . march!"

He guided them back down the long passage and out of the CP.

"Halt," he said, then took another step, leaning forward so his head was between Noah's and hers. "All of that about the CO's hatch being open? That is no longer in effect. You will not, I repeat not, ever come back here. Am I 100% clear in that?"

"Yes, Senior Drill Instructor!"

"I don't care if God Almighty had angels carry you down from fucking heaven to grace us mere mortals with your presence, you are now nothing more than slimy worms, and I own you.

"While you were up here wasting Marine Corps time, the rest of the series was stowing gear. In exactly eight minutes, the series is marching to the Classroom 2a for their medical officer brief. You will be with the rest of the series, with your gear stored.

"Am I perfectly clear on that?"

"Yes, Senior Drill Instructor!"

"Then you better move your asses!"

For the first time since they'd left the barracks, Esther took a hesitant look at Noah, who seemed as confused as she was. How could they get their gear stored and be ready to leave in eight minutes? When the senior didn't seem ready to move, Esther, followed by a hesitant Noah, started walking.

"For all that is sacred, didn't you hear me? You've got eight minutes! You'd better double time, recruits!"

Esther immediately broke into a dead run. The CO had practically promised that they both would get through recruit training. It didn't seem like their senior had received the memo.

Chapter 5

Noah

"Come on, Fan," Noah said, slowing down to encourage the other recruit.

The series was just over half-way through a gut-buster, the exhausting "motivational runs" that were anything but. Five klicks to the Lost Lady, a tall rock formation south of Camp Charles' mainside, and back, all at a brutal pace designed to push the recruits past their limits. No more than ten or twelve of the recruits could stay up with Drill Instructor Hermanez—the rest would fall back to straggle in, and Noah was no different. Too much time spent playing games and not exercising had their effect on him.

Up ahead by almost 100 meters, even Esther was straggling just behind the first rank. She was now a recruit squad leader, the bright red tab on her t-shirt collar visible all the way back in the rear of the pack.

Noah was hurting, but Fan was about ready to die,

"I can't do it," he managed to get out between breaths.

"Sure you can," Noah said. "Here, hold on. Don't let go," he added, putting Fan's hand on his shoulder and trying to pull the recruit along.

Grubbing hell! he exclaimed as Fan's weight became an anchor dragging him back.

He kept trudging ahead, trying to clear his mind—which was difficult with Fan wheezing like a pair of old-fashioned bellows right behind him. Slowly, they fell farther and farther behind the rest of the tail-end recruits: ten meters, back, then twenty. Noah peered ahead as they made their way into the training area, hoping to see that the front of the pack had reached the obstacle course.

His lungs were burning and his side felt like it was being stabbed with a sword when a couple of figures broke away from the front to begin to make their way back. It looked like Esther joined them as well. It still took a couple of minutes before Sergeant

Hermanez, Recruits Walton and Inspiration, and Esther reached the tail-end charlies.

"You two are the last ones," the DI shouted as he reached and circled around them to head back forward. "You had better move your freaking butts, or the entire series will pay the price!"

"Paying the price" generally meant EI, or "extra instruction." Only there wasn't any "instruction" to it. Two hundred pushups or squat-thrusts were punishment, nothing more.

"Come on, Lysander," Courage Inspiration shouted. "You heard the DI. Put some effort into it!

Courage was one of the alpha recruits, good-looking, fit, and fast as a deer. Like Esther and him, he was a Marine brat, with his first sergeant father still on active duty. He seemed to like Esther, but he also seemed to find Noah seriously lacking.

"Noah, what the hell?" Esther said as she closed in on him. "We're Lysanders, and we don't finish last."

At least she had the courtesy to be breathing heavily, not like Super Recruit Inspiration.

"Fan, why are you even here?" she asked as she dropped back a step, putting her hands on Fan's shoulders and trying to push him along—which almost made him fall.

"I'm trying!" Fan protested. "I'm not used to all this running."

"What did you think the Marines were? *Altoon Attack*?"

Noah rolled his eyes. *Altoon Attack* had long been his favorite game, something of which Esther was well aware. She might as well have been attacking him directly.

Esther had been openly supportive of Noah enlisting, but he had a sneaking suspicion that on one level, she almost resented his presence, as if he was leaching from her part of the righteousness of what she was doing.

Courage followed the DI, his nose so far up the sergeant's ass that Noah thought it would break off if the sergeant suddenly stopped. But Klepper Walton stayed behind with Esther, pushing Fan while Noah pulled.

Ahead, the rest of the back-of-the-pack straggled into the finish. Recruits who had completed the run stood, hand on their knees, a few puking that good Marine Corps chow they'd had for lunch into the sand. One of the recruits yelled something out, and most of them straightened and slowly jogged back to the stragglers, yelling their encouragement.

"So help me, Noah. If you've earned us EI, I swear. . ." Esther told him.

Noah bit back a retort. No, he would not have finished up with the rabbits without Fan, but somewhere in the middle of the stragglers, most likely. But he wasn't going to let Fan struggle on alone.

At least ten minutes after the rabbits finished, the four recruits reached the stairway to heaven on the O-Course, the unofficial finish line. Fan fell to the ground where he started puking. Noah wanted to join him, but he managed to keep standing, hands clasped on top of his head as he took in huge gulps of air.

Sergeant Hermanez came back to the four, looking like he hadn't even run a hundred meters yet.

"Good job," he told Klepper and Esther. "That's how you look after your fellow recruits."

Noah felt a pang of annoyance, only somewhat alleviated by the look of Courage's face when he didn't receive any praise.

Any hope, though, that his comment meant they would not be punished evaporated, though, when the DI shouted out, "That was extremely poor, recruits. You've been here six days, and you've still got that nasty civvie poison in you. Some of you barely walked on that little jog we just had. So I'm going to have to try and sweat more of that fat poison out of you. EI time, recruits. Two-hundred squat thrusts. Starting position. . .move!"

Civvie poison running through their bodies or not, they'd already learned not to groan when given EI. Ninety-seven recruits, eleven fewer than who'd started boot camp, immediately came to attention. Even Fan, with vomit still on his chin and on his t-shirt, managed to stand.

"Ready. . .begin! One-two-three-one, one-two-three-two. . ."

No one said anything, but Noah could almost feel the waves of hate emanating from the other recruits.

Chapter 6

Esther

"Freemont just quit," Rosalee Barrent-Hyde said under her breath as she took a seat on Esther's rack.

"It was only a matter of time," Uri Weis said. "We knew she was about to pop a molt and DOR."[4]

Of the 108 recruits in Platoon 9055 that started A-1, 82 had lasted until T-8. Three admin days and eight training days had knocked out 26 of them. Twenty-one of the initial recruits had been female, and a full twelve of them already had been dropped. Two had been recycled due to stress fractures and would join a later series after a couple of weeks, but the rest has either DOR'd or been found "not suitable for further duty."

"So, that's nine of us left," Esther said as she continued to clean her combat harness.

"And I'm not giving d'Lane much of a chance. I heard her crying last night after lights out," Uri said without looking up from her cleaning.

"Shit, Uri, half the guys cry here, too," Tanya Nguyen said.

"I'm not saying the boys aren't crying," Uri said. "Let those sorry asses get kicked out, too. You need to be the best to become a Marine."

Esther looked up from her cleaning at Uri before dropping her gaze again. This was gear maintenance time, not free time, and while they could sit where they wanted, they weren't supposed to be chit-chatting. The DI's would let a little slide, but they couldn't go overboard.

Uri was a rock-stud. A jujitsu black belt of some lofty number of degrees that Esther didn't quite grasp, there was little doubt that she could kick almost anyone's ass in the series, male or female. She also brooked no excuses for weakness. You had to

---

[4] DOR: Drop on Request—a recruit asking to quit.

make the grade to fight in the ring or earn the title of Marine. Still, she socialized, if anything that recruits were allowed to do could be considered socializing, with the other women.

The Sisterhood of Ten—no, Nine, now with Freemont gone, Esther corrected herself.

It wasn't as if they excluded any of the guys. They couldn't, not and make it through to graduation. It was just that a bond was forming between them.

And she's right!

When her father opened up the military again to women, it was with the strict guidelines that no standards would be lowered. This wasn't the Navy where anyone with enough brains could serve—or where many women were proving to be superior pilots. This was the Marines where physical fitness and capabilities were paramount. And given the facts of life, without genetic modification, most women were not as strong as men, nor could their bodies take the same amount of abuse. Only 30% or so of the general male population had the needed entry qualifications, and that number dropped to about 10% of the female population.

There were no "PC" changes in the training, no "diversity adjustments." The Corps turned a blind eye to gender. What mattered was if a Marine could do the job or not.

The standardized requirements were a little tougher on Esther than she had expected them to be. She was fit and probably could have played pro e-ball. But many of the men were just as athletic, just as fit when compared to others. And that made them physically more capable than she was. Uri was Uri, a freak. And Jama Boutou ran like lightening, but those were the only two who were at the top of the fitness pecking order. Esther was solidly in the next level.

And that frustrated her to no end. She had to be the best at anything she did, and second-best just wasn't going to cut it.

But she wasn't second-best in all ways. She didn't have to look; with her peripheral vision, she could see the red tab on her breast pocket, signaling her position as one of six recruit squad leaders.

She was immensely proud of the small red piece of cloth. The DIs saw something in her that made her worthy of the responsibility. There were only two positions higher: platoon guide and series guide, and she knew in her heart that she would achieve series guide by graduation and earning the meritorious promotion that came with the honor.

She snuck a glance across the squadbay where Recruit Gaston Nunci was cleaning his boots with a brush.

Watch your ass. I'm after you!

Esther had nothing against Nunci. He was a good recruit, and Esther would be happy to serve with him as Marines. But he was the current guide, and nobody was going to stand in her way.

"Speaking of crying boys, have you decided what to do about, you know. . ." Tanya asked.

"About who?" Uri asked.

Esther glared at Tanya, trying to use telepathy to tell Tanya to shut up, but her friend didn't look up and said, "She doesn't want Noah in her squad. She thinks it makes it hard to come down on his ass."

All five of the other recruits looked to her as one.

"Are you trying to invite a DI here? Look at what you're doing," she hissed. "And no, Noah hasn't been crying. But, you know, you've seen him on the runs. I want to ream him, but, you know. . ."

"So what are you going to do?" Uri asked, a slight bit of excitement evident in her voice.

"She's going to ask the senior to move him to another squad," Tanya said.

Shut the hell up, Tanya!

"That's a good idea," Uri said.

Esther wasn't completely sure about that. Noah would take it wrong, she knew. But maybe it would be for the better. He was twice the recruit of most of the others, but he always seemed to be with the walking dead.

She looked to where he was, two racks away, where he was actually cleaning that negat Fan's assault pack.

Come on, Noah. Take care of your own shit, first!

That settled it. Someone, and not his sister, had to push him in the right direction.

"I'm doing it," she said.

"OK, then go for it," Uri said. "The shack is open."

Esther thought there was a bit of a challenge in Uri's voice. That didn't matter, though. Now was as good a time as any.

"Watch my gear," she said as she stood and straightened up her blouse.

She marched down the center of the barracks to the front where the DI's shack was just off to the left. As usual during scheduled maintenance time, there was only one DI present. This time, it was Senior Drill Instructor Hoteah.

Esther wanted to sound professional and in complete control. She took several calming deep breaths.

"I hear you out there, Recruit!" Senior Drill Instructor Hoteah. "Don't waste my time dawdling. Enter!"

Esther came to attention, then marches smartly into the office, centering herself in the middle, and looking up where the overhead met the bulkhead.

"Recruit Squad Leader Lysander, E., requesting permission to address the senior drill instructor!"

With her peripheral vision, she watched the senior DI spin his chair to look at her for an unbearably long ten seconds before he said, "What do you want, Lysander?"

"After some consideration, I think it would be best if Lysander, N., be transferred to another squad, Senior Drill Instructor!"

"After some *consideration*?"

"Uh. . .ye-yes, Senior Drill Instructor."

"And why, pray tell, did you decide that, 'after consideration?'"

This wasn't going as Esther had imagined, but she had committed herself, so she charged on, "It is my belief that with the two of us being so familiar with each other, it might make it awkward for me to be, well, jumping on his case when he screws up," she got out in a rush.

"Very well. Consider it done. You won't be his recruit squad leader anymore."

Whoa! That was easy!

"Hand it over, Recruit Lysander," he continued.

"Uh, I don't understand, Senior Drill Instructor. Hand what over?"

"Your recruit squad leader tab, of course."

Esther felt as if she'd just been sucker-punched.

"My. . .my tab?"

"Of course your tab. If you cannot lead a Marine, for any reason, then you should not be in a position of leadership. I would think that would be obvious."

"But—" she started before the staff sergeant stood up.

"But nothing, Recruit Lysander." He hesitated for a moment, then went on, "I shouldn't have to explain that to you, and frankly, I'm surprised. A leader, even a recruit squad leader, has to lead his or her Marines no matter what. Do you think the Corps is going to let you pick and choose who is in your unit just to make it easier on you? True leaders rise to the top, overcoming any obstacle.

"Your father understood that."

This was the first time during training that any DI had made direct reference to her dad.

"He ordered his own brother-in-law to his death."

Esther dropped her gaze from the overhead to stare at the staff sergeant in shock. Although she had never discussed it with him, she knew the story well. In the first action against the capys, then Lieutenant Ryck Lysander had ordered her uncle, Staff Sergeant Joshua Hope-of-Life and two other Marines into a suicidal blocking position to hold the capys off long enough to load the civilians aboard aircraft and escape.

"You've shown some promise, Recruit, and we were holding out hope for you. But it's now pretty evident that you are not your father's daughter after all."

Esther was stunned. She didn't know how to respond.

"Your tab."

Numbly, she reached up and pulled the red tab off of her collar, held it out, and dropped it into her seniors extended hand.

"You're dismissed, Recruit."

"Recruit," not "Recruit Squad Leader."

She performed a barely acceptable about-face and marched out of the office.

Chapter 7

Noah

"Hey, Noah, you want my pumpkin surprise?" Leto asked.

"Nah. Give it to Boris."

Leto was a little overweight, and he made it a habit of offering Noah his desserts. Boris Franks, on the other hand, was skinny as a rail and constantly hungry. It made sense to give it to Boris, but Noah wasn't even tempted this time. The dessert bar was a cloying, sickly sweet orange square, chock full of the calories and nutrients the dieticians thought recruits needed to function.

Leto, Boris, and a few others had started making it a habit to sit with Noah during chow, something that he appreciated. He'd tried to bring Fan into their little group, but there had seemed to be some tension, and Fan had drifted away.

Noah had never been an A-lister in school. He'd had friends, of course, mostly other gamers, but he'd been closer to Esther than anyone else, not surprisingly.

He looked over to where Esther was sitting with Uri and Tanya. She'd been pretty upset to lose her recruit squad leader's tab two days ago, and Noah had tried to be supportive of her, but his sister had inexplicably cut him off. Esther didn't take failure well, but she used to be able to confide in him when she was troubled. Now, she seemed almost angry at him.

She'll get them back, he told himself.

Their father had lost his squad leader's tab as well, for letting one of his recruits sink or swim on his own—sink, in this case. Noah even remembered the name of the recruit: Calderón, who had ended up graduating and having a successful career.

Taking care of his subordinates had been a lesson his father had learned and then passed it on to his children. And it hadn't been too expensive a lesson. He'd been able to regain the billet before his class graduated. Esther could too. She was taking to recruit training as if she'd been born to it, which maybe she had.

Their younger brother had graduated as the series honor-man, after all. The Lysanders had that Marine gene.

Hah! Except for me, he thought, almost laughing out loud.

"I can't wait for tomorrow," Leto said.

"Three hours free," Wyllyam "Willy" Dodge said.

Sunday morning wasn't technically free. There was early morning PT, then chow. But 0800 to 0900 was Sky-Six time, chaplain's call. And it didn't matter the religion, or if a recruit even was religious, all of them would be in the chapel, the first time during waking hours since their arrival that they wouldn't have a DI standing over them. From 0900 to 1100, they'd have their first down time, where they could call home or just relax. It wasn't completely their own time. They couldn't get back into their racks, and they couldn't wander the depot. But with only one DI overseeing, they could talk with others and basically decompress.

And Noah could use the decompression. He wasn't at the bottom of the series hierarchy, but he was pretty close. He just wasn't excelling, and in the Marines, excelling was a religion.

At least I have my friends, he told himself, watching Boris simply inhale the pumpkin bar. *This is the brotherhood Dad always told us about.*

Chapter 8

Esther

"What's freaking wrong with your brain-housing group, Recruit?" the Chipmunk shouted at the hapless Ghost. "Did you just decide to ignore the small fact that it's a squad leader's job to make sure his recruits are ready, not just take care of himself?"

Corporal Chimond's high-pitched voice left her with the "Chipmunk" moniker among the recruits in the platoon. Her voice was exacerbated with the substitute expletives the DIs employed to get around the recent crack-down of cursing in front of the recruits. "Freaking" didn't cut it, Esther thought, especially when sounding like it was coming out of a children's holo character.

What the Chipmunk was saying, though, mattered more. Ghost was one of the platoon's four squad leaders (down from six when there were more recruits still in training), and if he was about to lose his tab, that was one more body gone from between her and her climb back to the top.

Ghost tried to stammer out a response, but the Chipmunk was having none of it. She tore him a new one, telling him just what she thought about his lack of, well, everything.

Beside her, Tanya half-smothered a laugh, and Esther, slid a foot forward to stomp on Tanya's. Her friend grunted, but cut off her laugh.

Too late, though.

"So are you two under the impression that something's funny?" Sergeant Hermanez asked from where he was inspecting Leto Smith's junk-on-the-bunk.

"No, Drill Instructor," Esther said, fuming.

She knew what was coming—she just hoped it wouldn't be for the entire platoon, or worse, the series.

"Good. I'm glad you don't think that another recruit's troubles are humorous," he said, his sarcasm evident. "But just because I'm in the mood, why don't you two drop and give me 50."

Esther managed to kick Tanya hard in the shin as she dropped to pump out the pushups. The girl just wouldn't learn. She thought boot camp was a joke, and "just good enough to get by" was fine with her. She'd already taken quite a bit of shit from the DIs, but the problem was that the shit often splashed on the rest of them.

She whipped out 40 pushups, then slowed down slightly to get out the last 10. As she got up, she managed to make sure she stepped on Tanya's hand as she got back into position.

"What was that for?" Tanya whispered when she finished and got back up.

Esther ignored her. She liked Tanya; she really did. As a friend. But she couldn't afford to be tarred by association with Tanya's happy-go-lucky attitude. She wondered if she'd have to distance herself from her, which hurt because Tanya was her best friend in the series. She'd been the one of the few to console her about losing her recruit squad leader billet, and she'd been the only one who'd given her moral support in working to get the billet back.

She brooded through the rest of the junk-on-the-bunk, not even mollified when Sergeant Hermanez hadn't dinged a single item in her inspection.

It sure was easier, she noted, when it was just her. This was a cakewalk. It was more difficult when she'd been dealing with 15 other recruits, mother-henning them along. Still, she wanted that responsibility again.

Finally, the inspection was over.

"What was that all about?" Tanya asked as soon as the DI's left.

"You really have to ask? Laughing at a DI?"

"Well, she's pretty fucking funny," Uri said as she came over, then in a high-pitched whine, "Recruit, you are so freaking in trouble. I'm going to tell your mommy!"

"Stop that!" Esther said, looking around to make sure no DI had snuck up within range to hear.

"What's she even doing here?" Uri asked. "Chipmunk voice, and not much bigger than a chipmunk, either. She's supposed to train us?"

Esther looked at Uri in amazement, her mouth dropping open.

"Really, Uri? You don't know?"

"Know what?"

"Have you looked at her blouse?"

"Yeah, kinda tight around here," she said with a laugh, pointing at her belly.

"How the hell do you know enough to wipe your ass, Uri? I mean her ribbons."

"So she's got three of them. Big deal. Senior's got six."

Esther couldn't stop herself from rolling her eyes.

"Hoteah's got a BC2, which isn't too shabby. But what's Chimond's got?"

"I don't know."

"Holy shit, Uri. You're in the Corps now. You need to know this stuff. Chimond's got a Silver Star. And that next one is a Purple Heart—with a silver "R" for regen."

"Really?" Tanya asked. "The Chipmunk went through regen? I wonder what for?"

"For getting her ass in a sling, probably when she earned that Silver Star," Esther said.

"What'd she do?" Uri asked.

"I don't know. But something big. The Corps doesn't give those out like candy. Chimond might be small, and she might have a weird voice, but she's paid her dues."

Sisterhood of the Ten or not, Esther could be more than a little frustrated with them.

How can they be so dense?

Part of her knew she was being a little tough on them. She'd been raised in a military family. Uri, Tanya, Rosalee—all of the remaining women except fellow military brat Kai-yen—had come from various backgrounds, half of them using the Corps to escape situations that offered little chance of improving their lives. Tanya had even been an indentured, using her enlistment to get her contract paid off by the government.

They'd already had two classes on Marine Corps history and three on customs and courtesies, but nothing yet on military awards, so maybe she needed to cut her friends a little slack. Or teach them.

"Recruit Squad Leader Hapshik, report to the DI shack!" the Chipmunk shouted out.

"Oh, shit. Ghost is getting busted!" Tanya said, not sounding at all sorry.

She was right, Esther knew, though. He'd just lost his billet. She felt a small degree of compassion for him—after all, she'd had hers taken only three days before. She watched Ghost take the long walk to the front of the barracks where the Chipmunk was waiting for him. The slump in his shoulders was proof enough that he knew his time as a squad leader had come to an end.

The compassion she'd felt for Ghost was still there, but it was now counterweighed by the satisfaction that she was one more step closer back to redemption.

Chapter 9

Noah

Noah wiped the last bit of water off the urinal. The thing positively shined. Absently, he wondered about the white porcelain fixture. It was function over form, barely changed over the centuries. Oh, this one had a molecular cushion and air flow that whisked away everything put into it, but still, anyone from four or five-hundred years ago who was thrust into today would have no problem recognizing its function.

"Hey, Noah, we need more Delta-Blue," Kellen said.

Noah smiled. The urinal might whisk away every last drop, but the deck under it didn't, and recruits didn't always have the best aim. Delta-Blue was the disinfectant of choice at Camp Charles.

"No problem. I'll get it."

"Three bottles, OK?"

Kellen had been the recruit squad leader for five days now, which was a record—and which probably was driving Esther crazy. Noah knew his sister had taken losing the billet hard, but he also knew she was anxious to get another chance. She didn't have to regain Third Squad's billet—she could take over as squad leader for any of the four squads in the platoon, but to see Kellen last very long in the billet, someone who had seemingly no fire in his soul, would be frustrating for her.

He was still concerned that Esther was ignoring him. Maybe she wanted to get through boot camp on her own. But it wasn't as if he was helping her with the DIs. They barely knew he was alive unless it was to yell at him for some screw-up.

Not for the first time, he wondered if he should have enlisted under an assumed name. Ben had used their mother's maiden name, Hope-of-Life, to distance himself from their father's legacy. Now, everyone knew who he was, and he was sure everyone knew of the CG's interest in Esther's and his training. It didn't matter to his fellow recruits, he knew, but with the DIs, it could be good or bad—and he suspected bad.

He dropped his scrub-pad into the bucket and stood up, checking the urinal one last time. Most of the recruits hated head duty, but he didn't mind it. The rote cleaning cleared his mind as well and gave him a brief reprieve from the stress of training.

The gear locker was up in the front of the barracks, across from the DI shack. With the heads in the back, he had to make his way up the length of the building. Other recruits were mopping the deck, though, so he scooted to the side and walked in the small gap between the racks and wall-lockers and the bulkhead.

". . .always last in every run," he heard as he reached his platoon area.

With the double bunks and the wall-lockers between each rack, he couldn't see who was talking, but it sounded like Leto.

He's not always last, he thought. *And he's getting in shape.*

He didn't think it was fair to make fun of Fan like that, and he was about to step out to where they were mopping the center of the barracks when the next statement stopped him in his tracks.

"Just because his father led the Evolution, he thinks he doesn't have to give a shit," Boris' voice reached him.

With a shock, he realized that they were talking about him, not Fan.

Part of him rose in anger. He came in last because he was helping Fan, not because he wasn't trying. He almost stepped out between the racks to tell them that, to force them to admit it, but he knew nothing good would come out of a confrontation, and he'd get blamed for it.

"Shit, he's probably back there in the head now, happily licking the pissers. The guy has no heart," Leto said, the scorn evident in his voice. "Who the hell volunteers for that?"

"Think he'd make it if he wasn't the general's son?" a voice Noah didn't recognize asked.

"Hell, no. You saw what happened, on A-1, when he and his sister were called up to the CG. He's going to graduate only because he's General Lysander's son. Otherwise, he'd be out already."

"His sister, too?"

"Nah, she's good-to-go. You've seen her. She's a hard-ass."

"A nice ass you mean," someone said in a lower voice, as if trying not to be overheard.

"Yes indeedy, a nice one. But she's like a cobra. Beautiful, but deadly. You don't want to go be messing with that," Leto said.

"So if he's such a negat, why do you guys hang with him?"

"You have to ask? Like I said, he's got the CG's ear. What if I need some help? If any of us needs help? We just go to our best-buddy Noah and ask him to intercede for us. He calls up the CG, the CG waves his magic wand, and poof! Our troubles vanish."

"Not just here, you said," Boris reminded him.

"Oh, yeah. Once we get out in the fleet, who knows what Lysander can do to help us? So my advice to you, Donelle, is to befriend the guy. It's not hard. He's like a fucking puppy dog, I swear. Make him think he's your best buddy, and then cash in when you need it."

Noah felt betrayed. He'd opened himself up to these guys, and now he knew their motive. Once again, he almost stepped out from behind the wall-locker. He wanted to confront them; hell, he wanted to punch the smug Leto in the face.

Fuck them, he decided. *It's not worth the EI I'd get.*

Instead, he quietly moved forward, hugging the bulkhead. With his head even with the top bunks, he knew that if they bothered to look up, they would be able to tell who he was.

It took only a few moments to reach the gear locker and grab the Delta-Blue. He started to return via the same way along the bulkhead, but instead, he served and marched right down the center of the barracks.

He didn't change his course when he reached the newly mopped area, walking straight through the wet deck.

"Hey, Noah! We're mopping here!" Leto called out as Noah tracked through. "Can't you see us?"

Noah ignored his erstwhile friend, and kept walking, breaking into a wry smile when behind him, Leto said, "Now we have to hit that section again."

He gave Kellen two of the bottles and took the third with him. Dumping the highly concentrated blue disinfectant in his bucket, he waited for a second as the acrid fumes rose. Dipping his scrubbing pad into the liquid, he moved to the next urinal.

No matter his disappointment, the field-day still had to be completed.

Chapter 10

Esther

"Lysander, E.   Lysander, N.   You two are on deck!" Staff Sergeant Hoteah shouted out.

"Come on, Bester!" Vance Eatherd shouted, pounding on her shoulder pads. "Kick his ass!"

She ignored him. She was still amazed that he'd been given the squad leaders' billet, but it didn't matter. He'd be gone soon enough, she knew, taking with him the stupid nicknames that he'd given each of them. This was her fight, not his, and she didn't need his "ooh-rah" excitement to motivate her.

She looked over to where Noah stood with Third Squad. His buddy, Fan, was already on his ass and being checked by the corpsman. Rosalee had put him down within 20 seconds. No one was paying Noah much attention. Part of that was because Lamont Jonas from Third was facing Eisner Kong from Fourth in the fight that was about to get underway, but still, Noah look, well, lonely.

For a moment, Esther wished she wasn't facing him. With five DOR's from Fourth, Esther and two others in the platoon had been shifted to the squad. Esther was pretty sure that was so she could take over the squad when Vance inevitably lost the billet, so she hadn't minded. It had the consequence, though, of pitting brother against sister.

The pugil stick competition closed off Phase 1 of training. It also counted a full 10% to the final honor platoon and honor series standings, and the DIs embraced it to the core of their very being. First, the squads would face off against each other, First versus Second, and Third versus Fourth. The winners would face off against each other, and the winners of those bouts would represent the platoon against their counterpart in the lead series. They would each fight until a single company champion was crowned. Each win, whether from squad against squad or series against series counted as one point, and all those points went into squad, platoon, and series honor standings.

If Esther had stayed in Third, she wouldn't have faced Noah. But as the recruits were paired up in alphabetical order, she matched up with her brother.

If she had a suspicious mind, she might have thought the DIs rigged it that way. Both of the other recruits transferred to Fourth with her had last names that came before hers alphabetically. If Uri Weiss, for example, had come over from Second instead of Paul Gandy, the pairing would have been different.

The roar of the platoon let her know Jonas and Kong had begun. She didn't bother to watch as she tried to call forth her inner warrior.

Beating Noah wouldn't be easy. He outweighed her by a full 20kg now, and he was much stronger. On the other hand, she was fitter, and she thought she was quicker. She also had a long history of competition, where unless it was gaming, Noah didn't have much. Calling up her inner warrior was something she'd done thousands of times before thousands of matches.

There was one more thing, and Esther almost hated to consider it. Noah had always been her protector. When they were younger, Esther's bark had sometimes been bigger than her bite, and it had been Noah who had to constantly step in to save her little ass.

A memory forced itself on her: on Luna base, when her father's ship had touched down, and him walking out to give himself up to the old Council, in exchange for both their and their mother's lives. She had broken down, unable to accept what was happening. It had been Noah who put his arms around her shoulder, Noah who had led them to the waiting ship to take them away to safety.

Snap out of it, Ess! Focus on the fight!

Noah still considered himself her protector, she knew. And because of that, she didn't think he'd go full berserker on her. She could take advantage of that.

She felt a little guilty about that, but maybe he needed the stark realization of what it took to win. Noah was smart—probably smarter than she was. He was bigger and stronger. But he didn't have the killer instinct to succeed. He was simply too nice.

Esther had set her goals high—*extremely* high. And she couldn't let personal feelings get in the way of that.

Besides, he cost me my squad leader's tab, she told herself.

She'd been reminding herself of that repeatedly, and she was finally beginning to believe it.

A combined moan from 40 throats told her that someone had been hit hard. She heard a few more muffled thuds, then cheers erupting from some, catcalls from the others. She didn't bother to look.

A few moments later, the senior called out, "Lysander, E. Lysander, N. In the pit! Moudin, Padre, on deck!"

Vance came rushing back to lead her forward, saying, "OK, we lost that last one, so we're down two to three. You need to win this one for us."

She ignored his babble, ignored the hands slapping her back as she stepped into the sawdust filled pit. Sergeant Hermanez grabbed her by the faceguard and gave her helmet a twist.

"You ready, Recruit?" he asked as he pushed and pulled on her chestpiece, and then gave her groin protector a smack.

"Yes, Drill Instructor!" she yelled out, staring across the pit to her brother who was getting similar treatment from Chimond.

Normally, the close combat TDIs would run the bout, and three of them were present, keeping hawk eyes on the proceedings, but by tradition, and maybe because of the impact on honor standings, the series DIs ran the competition.

"Take your weapons!" Hermanez yelled, holding out the pugil stick.

She jammed her gloved hands under the protected handles, and Hermanez gave it several hard yanks. He stepped back and gave Hoteah a thumbs up. It took Noah a few moments longer, but finally, Chimond stepped back and gave her thumbs up.

"Recruits, Ah. . .TACK!"

On the command, Esther rushed Noah, who took an inadvertent step back and barely blocked her buttstroke. Esther knew that with the power she put into the stroke, she was vulnerable to a counter-stroke with the red-painted "blade" end of the stick, but she was pretty sure Noah would be on defensive.

Esther barely heard the laughter as Noah retreated, she barely heard the cheering. She tuned them out and focused on the attack. Two, three more times, she swung with all her might, the techniques hammered into them in a morning of training forgotten as she was in full amok-mode.

Noah kept backpedaling, easily blocking her strokes but not launching his own. And that pissed her off.

How dare he toy with me!

She wound up as if the stick was a baseball bat and swung for the fences. Noah stepped back, and Esther missed him, the momentum twisting her until the padded end of her pugil stick hit the deck, leaving her back exposed to him.

He started forward and lifted his stick to end it, when he hesitated, not delivering the blow. Esther unwound, using legs, back, and arms to generate power to reverse her swing, raising the padded end from the deck to head level just as Noah started forward again. He started to lower his stick to block, but he was a fraction of a second too late. Esther's stick caught him alongside his head.

He staggered to his left, then went down to one knee. Esther rushed him, stick raised high when the green-shirted TDI who was the referee stepped in front of her, blocking her from any more attacks.

"You won, Recruit, so calm down!" he told her.

Esther tried to push past him, but that was an exercise in futility.

"I said calm down! The bout is over!"

"Winner, Lysander, E. Fourth Squad!" the senior shouted out to both cheers and jeers.

Noah was getting up, shaking his head as the corpsman rushed up to check him out. Esther turned to see her squad, shouting out their approval.

"Are you with us?" the TDI asked.

"Yes, Drill Instructor," she said, taking a few deep breaths as her mind regained control.

"Good fight, Ess," she heard from behind her.

She didn't respond to her brother as her mind shifted to her next opponent.

Chapter 11

Noah

"Hey, Noah, can you help me with this?" Fan asked, holding out his combat harness. "It's kinda screwed up."

For a moment, he just wanted to scream at Fan, telling him to take care of himself for once. It took an effort of will to force that back down. Surprisingly, it seemed to work, and his flash of anger dissipated. With a resigned sigh, he left his own preparation and took Fan's harness.

"Grubbing hell, Fan," he said. "Look. You've got the right side connected to the H-slot, the left to the J-slot. No wonder it won't hang right. Let me show you."

He thumbed the release, pulled the left-side connectors free, and then reconnected them in the H's. He shook the harness a couple of time, then handed it back to Fan.

"Now it hangs straight. How did you even screw that up? I haven't even disconnected mine at all since it was issued."

"I don't know. I was just fidgeting with it, and it let loose. I tried to shove it back, but I didn't know about no H or J whatever. Thanks, Noah."

Fan had already defied the odds, in no small part due to Noah, he realized without any sense of accomplishment or pride. Most of their fellow recruits hadn't thought he'd last a week, much less make it through Phase 1. Now, with Phase 2, their field training, starting in the morning, the grunt-stuff would start in earnest, and some of that training imposed risk. Fan was willing, but was he able? Would the DIs continue to carry him if he was a danger to himself and others?

"No problem, Fan. Just be careful with your gear, OK?"

"Sure thing, Noah. And thanks."

Noah went back to his list. Everything was going to be inspected before the 30 km hump to Camp Lympstone, where the Phase 2, Field Training, would be conducted. He looked forward to the change in scenery. Phase one hadn't been horrible. Some of it, like the Marine history classes with Dr. Berber had been interesting. Dr. Berber had taught his father the same classes so many years ago, only now his father was part of the curriculum.

The RCET[5] was pretty fun, too. Noah considered himself somewhat of a games connoisseur, but nothing he'd played before even approached the sophistication of the huge trainer.

Overall, though, Noah was more along the lines of just wishing it was over. The constant haranguing by the DIs, the physical toll, and more than that, his emotional toll were draining. It was just not Leto and the rest. What hurt most of all was Esther's distancing herself from him. During their pugil stick fight, he'd seen something in her eyes that he'd never seen before. He'd tried to hold back in the fight, but she looked like she wanted to kill him.

Noah was sure he could make it through recruit training, even without the battalion COs inference that they would put him through no matter what. But what if he DOR'd? He could, right now.

Was he really meant to be a Marine? He was confident he could perform adequately as a rifleman. But beyond that was another question. He just wasn't a hard-charging gung-ho kind of guy. He wasn't sure he could lead anyone.

As he got back to his gear checklist, he could feel eyes boring into him. He looked up to see the Chipmunk looking at him. When she caught his eyes, she motioned him over.

What now?

He pulled down on the bottom of his utilities blouse, then double-timed up to her.

"Come with me," she said in her high-pitched voice.

Noah followed, his eyes on her back, but that wasn't enough to keep him from seeing Leto lean out as the Chipmunk passed, making a fist and rotating the spot between his thumb and forefinger around his nose.

I'll grubbing brown-nose you, asshole.

---

[5] Realistic Combat Environment Trainer

Noah hadn't told Leto and the rest that he'd overheard them in the head, and he sure as hell didn't want to put up with any of their shit.

Noah followed her into the office and was surprised that she closed the hatch. With all the recent cases, most of the DIs were gun-shy about being alone with a recruit without witnesses. They might lament the passing of the "Old Corps," but they weren't going to jeopardize their own careers with a real or imagined case of abuse.

"Stand at ease, Recruit," the DI said.

Noah came to a parade rest, wondering what this was about.

"How're you holding up?" she asked.

Noah almost choked. DIs simply did not ask recruits that.

"I. . .this recruit is fine, Drill Instructor Chimond!"

"I'm not really too sure about that," she said in a casual voice. "I've been watching you. I may not be a doc, but I think I recognize depression. Do I need to send you to sickbay to get checked out?"

Oh, shit, that's all I need!

"No, Drill Instructor Chimond. This recruit is fine. Ready to excel!"

She moved in front of him, staring up at his face. Noah began to tremble.

Finally, she nodded, then said, "You're a good recruit, Lysander. I've watched you with Recruit Lueng. You could have left him to figure out what was wrong with his combat harness. You could have left him when he falls back on runs, but you don't."

"Recruit Lueng is doing fine, Drill Instructor! I just, well, I just encourage him a bit."

"And the other recruits? Smith? Mamoud? Vasilakis?"

She'd just picked Leto, Boris, and Mouse.

At random? he wondered.

"They, uh, they are. . .*friendly* with this recruit."

"Yes, I'm sure they are," she said with what sounded like a small snort of contempt.

"Look, Lysander, I know when a recruit is wavering, when he is thinking about DOR'ing. And you've got that look."

"I'm not a quitter—"

She held up a hand, palm out, stopping him.

"I'm not saying you are. But DOR'ing is not necessarily a bad thing. Some people just aren't cut out for service."

"So you think I should quit?" Noah asked surprised, forgetting protocol.

"Not at all. You see, I think you belong in the Corps. Not because of your father, but because you care. You care about others; you care about your unit. When combined with competency, with military skills, that makes a hell of a Marine.

"Don't, well, how should I say this? Don't be concerned if you're not the most testosterone-laden recruit out there. Learn your craft, but never forget your fellow Marines. OK?"

Noah stood there silently, taking it in. He had been concerned that he wasn't joining in the maneuvering to be the alpha wolf. He frankly didn't care who was in the limelight. He took pride in a job well done, but his pride was focused inwards. But that was giving him his second thoughts. It didn't seem to jibe with the accepted picture of being a Marine.

But if Drill Instructor Chimond thought he was doing well, maybe he should just take that at face value.

"Thank you, Drill Instructor. I appreciate your insight."

He waited, wondering if that was all.

She seemed to hesitate a second, then said, "Dismissed. Get your gear ready for tomorrow."

"Aye-aye Drill Instructor!"

He started to turn when she said, "Wait."

"Do you know where I earned my Purple Heart?"

Noah's eyes drifted down to her chest. The deep purple ribbon with the small silver "R" for regen was between her Silver Star and her Combat Mission Medal, the campaign ribbon with the Gold "E" for serving during the Evolution. His dad had been awarded two Novas, but Noah was still impressed with her ribbon bar.

"No, Drill Instructor."

"I was on First Step. With 2/3."

Noah took a step back. He immediately knew what she was going to say.

"Yes, you understand. But what you might not know was that I was in the path of the Armadillo that your brother and Yale Haerter took out. We were firing everything at it, but nothing had any effect. If your brother and Yale hadn't, well, you know. I wouldn't be here today."

"But you. . ." he said, looking at her Purple Heart again.

"I got zapped after that, covering the retrograde."

Noah nodded, then came back to a position of attention. He didn't know what to say, so he kept silent.

"I don't know why I told you that, Recruit. Maybe I just wanted you to know how selfless your brother, he and Yale, were. They cared more about us than for themselves. Your sister is a hard-ass, and I know she'll go as far as she wants in the Corps. Some of the other DIs think she's like your father.

And I'm not, I know.

"I never met the general, so I can't say. But I knew Ben, and I see him in you. If I'm right, then the Marine Corps can't ask for a better Lysander to carry on.

"Now, it's lights out in 20, and I didn't see you even close to being ready. You'd better get moving. Dismissed!"

As he turned and started out, she added, "I'm going to ride your ass hard, Recruit, so stand the fuck by."

"Aye-aye, Drill Instructor Chimond!" he shouted as he double-timed back out into the barracks.

He was smiling as he sprinted back to his rack, noticing Leto as he tried to give him a ration of shit only long enough to give him the finger.

Fuck him and his games!

"You about done, Fan?" he asked as he picked up his camelbak. "Lights out in 20!"

Chapter 12

Esther

"Assignments are in!" Uri shouted as she darted to their table.

Esther took one more bite of mystery meat, then stood up. Finally, she'd know where she'd be spending the next three years. She'd put down 2/3 and 2/9 on her dream sheet. Two-three was her father's battalion, the one he'd commanded. The Third Marines, and the entire First Marine Division, for that matter, were based right here on Tarawa, and being under-the-flagpole, any battalion in the division was considered one of the Corps premier units. Two-nine was her father's first battalion, right out of boot camp. Third Marine Division was headquartered on Alexander, which might not be as prestigious as First, but still, it had a long and storied history, and her father's connection to it resonated with her. Esther wasn't superstitious, but she thought either battalion would be a fortuitous start to her career.

Along with most of the series, Esther rushed to return her tray, the food only half-eaten. Once outside the messhall, she had to restrain herself from sprinting across the grinder to the barracks. Double-timing was allowed and even expected, but full-out sprints were frowned upon.

By the time she reached the barracks, a crowd of recruits had gathered around the posting. If recruits were allowed PAs, it would have been a simple thing to promulgate, and Esther chaffed at not being close enough to read the posted plastisheet. If she were shorter, she could worm her way in, but as it was, she had to wait.

"One-one," Vance shouted in front of her, happy with his assignment.

One-one, "America's Battalion," due to its patron being the U.S. Marine Corps, considered itself the premier battalion in the Corps. The rest of the Corps might vehemently disagree, but that didn't stop them—and they had a proud history that could make that claim legit. If Esther hadn't wanted 2/3 or 2/9, then 1/1 might have been a good choice.

Tanya turned from where she was at the front, not looking too happy.

"One-thirteen," she mouthed to Esther.

Oh, sucks to be her!

The Thirteenth Marines were stationed on Aegis 2, the "Asshole of the Federation." A valuable source of rare earths and other minerals, the planet was barely terraformed, had horribly hot weather, and an almost complete lack of social amenities. On the "Egg," it was pretty much stick to the bases or try the mining camps during their free time. The 13th Marines had a pretty good professional history, but their quality of life might be the worst in the Corps. Heck, most of the Outer Forces had a lower quality of life than the Inner Forces.

Esther slowly pressed forward until she was close enough to read the list. She scanned down until she could see "Lysander, Esther. 1/16."

Her heart dropped.

How the hell did that happen? I put down 2/3 and 2/9!

The dreamsheet was just that, a dream. The Corps did not have to follow those preferences. But Esther thought her case was different, and the attention she'd received from the battalion CO and even the CG should have made this a slam dunk. And now, she was going to Wayfarer Station?

The 16th Marines, the "Limitanei," was the farthest-stationed regiment from Earth, deep within the Far Reaches. While both the capys and the Klethos had invaded from the opposite side of human space, the regiment, along with the Navy's Task Force Deep, was still considered the first line of defense against a threat coming from the galactic center. Except for during the War of the Far Reaches, the regiment had only minor participation in the various wars since the Federation's founding, with putting out brush fires and fighting piracy being their main actions.

With the "war" with the Klethos under control, and no huge immediate threats on the horizon, the 16th Marines perhaps offered Esther a better chance of a skirmish or two in which she could get blooded in combat, but the problem was the regiment was so far out in the Dark that it was usually out of the public's eyes.

One-sixteen wasn't even with the regimental headquarters. It was located in Wayfarer Station, a multi-purpose station deep into empty space. Esther didn't know that much about the station, but her dad had visited the battalion once, and he'd noted the lack of space for proper training.

No, 1/16 wasn't her idea of a good first duty station, and she was considering how she should approach the CO to see about getting that fixed. She looked up once more at the list, as if it could have changed in the last ten seconds. Her eyes then went down a line to "Lysander, Noah." To her surprise, his assignment was to 1/16 as well.

She ran an eye through all 68 names on the list. There were a few recruits going to 2/16 and 3/16, but no one else to 1/16. This just wasn't right, and she had to address the orders with someone high enough on the ladder to do something about it.

She turned around, pushing back through the other recruits.

"Who'd you get?" Noah asked her from where he was standing behind the mass of recruits.

"One-sixteen," she said, noting the tiniest narrowing of his eyes as he heard her. "Don't go thinking you made out over me, Noah. You're going there with me."

At that, he gave a shrug nodded.

"Not that this is going to last long. I'm on my way to Colonel Sung's office now, and if he can't help, I swear I'm going to the CG himself."

Noah put a hand on her shoulder, stopping her from pushing past him.

"Uh, I might want to rethink that, if I were you."

"Why not? The CO said he had an open-door for us," she said. Then after seeing his puppy dog expression, another thought hit her, and she said, "Look, we came to boot camp together, which was probably a mistake. But we can't be connected at the hip as Marines. We have to go our own way. *You* have to make your own way."

Noah seemed to brush off her statement and said, "Think, Ess. Think of what Colonel Sung told us about why were in the same platoon, so that they could keep the public away from us with minimal interruptions to their operations. And this is at Charles and Lympstone, two camps closed off not only to civilians, but to Marines who aren't part of the staffs. What do you think it'll be like out in the fleet, when in an open base, or just out in town to get a pizza and beer?

"It will be bad enough tomorrow when we graduate, but what do you think it'll be like when the flick comes out?"

A major Hollybolly production about their father was nearing production, and Esther knew Noah and she would be receiving even more attention when it was released. Part of her looked forward to the attention, but she understood that her new unit might not be as welcoming.

"The Corps wants a minimal impact created by our service. And I think they want us to be able to develop without interference. Where better than on Wayfarer Station? What reporter is going to come all the way out there to interview one of Ryck Lysander's kids?"

"So you think this was planned?"

"It has to be, Ess. 'Minimal disruption' and 'easy to manage?' This was decided from on high, probably all the way to the top."

"The commandant?"

"I'd bet so. And if we fought it, well. . ."

Shit, he's right. This was all thought-out, she realized. *And even if he said "we fought it," he means if I fight it, I'll look like a whiny, self-entitled bitch.*

He looked at her expectantly, waiting for her response.

Hell, even now, he's looking out for me.

She felt a little guilty for avoiding him for the last seven months.

"OK, so I'm not going to go see the CO. I guess we're off to the Far Reaches."

A smile broke out on his face, and he pulled her in for a hug. She hesitated only a moment before returning it.

"But, so help me God, if we're assigned to the same squad, I'll call the chairman herself!"

Chapter 13

Noah

. . .and so, I send you off to make your own mark, to start your own contribution to the traditions that make us the finest fighting force in human history! *Audaces Fortuna Iuvat,*" Brigadier General Konstantinov said to the two series standing tall in front of him.

The CG looked out over the recruits, and Noah felt a sense of anticipation rising within him. It was silly, he knew, but there it was.

"Colonel Rischer, I think there's one more thing, isn't there," the CG said, toying with the recruits. "Do you want the honor?"

Noah was standing at attention, eyes locked straight ahead, so he couldn't see what the training regimental commander replied, but a moment later, the CG said, "Very well, then. Lieutenant Colonel Sung, you may dismiss your MARINES!"

There! He'd said it. Noah, and all the rest, were no longer recruits—they were Marines! He still had the 12-week IUT, Initial Unit Training, before he joined 1/16, but that would be as a Marine, not a recruit.

The battalion CO called out, "Captain Morrisy, you may dismiss your Marines."

This was repeated down the line, from the company commander to the series commanders to the platoon senior DIs.

Staff Sergeant Hoteah waited, and from down the line of recruits. . .no, Marines, the seniors of 9052, then 9053, and 9054 dismissed their platoons, and roars of new Marines shouted their elation.

"Platoon 9055, dis. . .MISSED!"

Noah felt a surge of joy as he stepped once to the rear, did an about-face, and with 29 throats yelling in unison, shouted to the heavens.

A fist pounded his back, and he turned to hug Fan.

"We made it, Marine," Fan said, his face flushed. "And thanks to you, bud. Thanks to you."

"Ah, bullshit. You were always going to make it."

Whatever else Fan was going to say was lost as Leto crashed into them, an arm around each of their shoulders.

"Hey, Marines! We fucking did it!"

Noah had long-since distanced himself from Leto, but if the Marine had noticed, he never let on. Still, Noah was in too good of a mood to let his petty grievances take over, so he pounded Leto a few times on the back.

"Hey, Noah, come here. I want you to meet my folks," Leto said, starting to drag Noah away.

"Wait up," Noah yelled at Fan from over his shoulder. "We'll catch a ride out tonight."

Some of the new Marines were going to hit the town tonight before the general exodus to their new divisions started in the morning.

Probably a third of the new Marines had family at the ceremony, and they were just now making their way out of the stands. Leto pulled Noah to the far left where an older couple and a teenage girl were waving.

"Moms, Pops, this is Noah Lysander, the Chairman's son. I told you about him."

Mr. Smith's eyes lit up, and he shook Noah's hand.

"It's so good to meet you, Private Lysander," the man said. "Leto's told us all about you, and we're happy you two have become such good friends. Are you going to Alexander with him, too?"

Good friends? What other BS has he told you? he wondered, but instead said, "No, sir. I'm going to Sixth Division, in the Outer Forces.

"Oh, that's too bad," Leto's mother said. "You two are so close. But please, if you ever get to Freeman's Anchorage, you simply must stop by and visit. We insist."

Noah was saved from having to respond when a corporal rushed up, saying, "There you are, Lysander. The major needs you now."

"The major" was Major Fox-Mason, the depot Public Affairs Officer. A gruff, no-nonsense Marine, he'd been grooming Esther and him for their first news conference as members of the Corps. The depot had been protecting them as recruits, but now as Marines, the major felt it was better to give the press some access in what was still a controlled environment.

"It was good to meet you," Noah said to Leto's parents as the corporal led him away.

"We're going to the Butcher Block for dinner. Why don't you join us?" Leto shouted.

Noah ignored him. Even if he considered Leto as a friend, the Butcher Block would not be his choice for his emancipation meal. The chain was designed to appeal to the senses with intricate animatronics and programming. The tables were massive, and the vibe was to overwhelm the guests with just how great the place was. But the food itself was typical fab food. Good, but not great. Their recipes were designed to appeal to the median, not the sophisticated.

Oh, yeah, and I'm SO grubbing sophisticated, Noah thought with a smile. After 294 days of messhall food, even the Butcher Block would be quite a step up.

Noah followed the corporal to where the major and Esther waited, standing in front of about nine reporters and camcordermen. At the moment, the CG was speaking in front of them. Noah slid beside Esther.

"Looking good, PFC Lysander," he said, nodding at the new PFC stripes on her sleeves.

"Thanks, Noah," she said, not bothering to hide her smile.

Esther had been appointed as the series guide just before the Crucible, and she managed to keep it through the grueling three-day culmination of training. Along with their sister series guide and the four platoon guides, she'd received a meritorious promotion to PFC.

"OK, Marines. . ."

Grubbing hell, that sounds good, Noah thought, savoring the sound of the word.

". . .just remember what I've told you. Short, succinct answers. Don't volunteer anything, don't pontificate. You'll be fine," the major said.

"And remember, this is your day, not theirs. Be proud!"

The CG carried on for a few minutes, but the media-types were looking beyond him to the two twins. Noah was still amazed that anyone really cared enough about them to send reporters to a boot camp graduation, but with the flick coming out, he figured that anything peripherally connected to their father would gather attention. It wasn't about Esther and him, it was about their father.

Finally, the CG turned and introduced the two of them.

Immediately, one of the reporters asked, "Esther, you made honor graduate and have been meritoriously promoted. Do you think your father would be proud of you?"

No, he'd be ashamed, Noah thought. *Did you really wait through an entire ceremony to ask that weak-ass question?*

Esther, though, handled it like a pro, saying, "I'd like to think so. The Marine Corps was his life, and if either Noah or I can contribute to the Corps and the Federation, then I'm sure he would have been proud."

"What about your brother Benjamin?"

What about him? What's your question?

The early word was that the flick was going to cover Ben's death in depth, so the question had to be expected, as the major had warned them, but still, what the question was vague.

"Our brother Benjamin felt he had a duty to the Federation. He gave his life for all of us, as did over 80,000 Marines, sailors, and FCDC troopers during the Evolution. We honor all of those who have made the ultimate sacrifice."

Noah could almost feel the major relax behind him. Esther had listened to his advice, and now she was on a roll.

"Noah, are you proud of your sister, becoming your series honor man?"

What is it with proud? Is that all you want to know?

"Of course I am. My sister Esther is extremely capable, and I was not surprised that she was the series guide."

"What about you," another reporter asked. "Why didn't you get a promotion, too?"

What?

"If I can interject here," the major said. "Private Lysander also performed admirably here at Camp Charles. But this is just a reflection of the super quality of young men and women who enlist. These stalwart citizens could excel in any endeavor, but they chose a life of service to Federation and Corps."

The reporters drifted back to Esther. Some of the questions they asked were ridiculous; some were reasonable. Noah was only directly questioned twice more, and that was OK with him.

He started to relax, just listening to Esther handle the questions like a seasoned pro. Let her take over; he didn't need the attention. Just earning the title of United Federation Marine was more than enough for him.

PART 2

Jonathan P. Brazee

WAYFARER STATION

Chapter 14

Esther

The door whooshed open, the cool air of the station a welcome relief from the recycled air of the ship. Esther knew that was mostly her imagination; the scrubbers on the ship were just smaller models of those that were used in the much larger station. Imagination or not, she simply felt better stepping into the large terminal area. Cramped ships had always made her feel uncomfortable.

That wasn't to say the terminal was anything like a planetary terminal. Even the bare-bones spaceport on Malika's World, where the Regimental headquarters was located, was much bigger and less enclosed than Wayfarer Station.

Three years of this, she thought without enthusiasm. *I can gut it out.*

Noah, standing beside her, on the other hand, seemed annoyingly happy.

"You four newbies, over against the bulkhead until we can find our guide," Staff Sergeant York told them.

Esther dutifully lined up on Gregori Pusht, one of the two privates from the series that graduated the week after Noah and hers. Fi Muster, the other private from that series, took his place beside her with Noah on the outside.

They'd met the staff sergeant at the regimental headquarters before they caught the ship to the station. He'd taken charge of the

12 lower-enlisted Marines newly assigned to the battalion. There was a lieutenant and a captain on the ship as well, but along with a first sergeant, they hadn't mixed with the rest of them. Already, the four higher-ups were loading aboard a small shuttle cart, ready, Esther assumed, to be whisked to the battalion CP.

"Sergeant Orinda, why don't you go check with the kiosk and see who's supposed to meet us," the staff sergeant said.

"Roger that," the sergeant said, dropping her seabag and sauntering off.

Esther had grown up a military brat, and she was used to the interaction between Marines, but after 194 days at boot camp and another 84 at IUT, the formal discipline at both schools had become embedded into her consciousness. To see such a casual response to a staff sergeant was jarring to her. Senior Drill Instructor Hoteah was a staff sergeant, for goodness' sakes. She couldn't imagine anyone casually saying "roger that" to him.

The four new Marines were standing at parade rest while they waited, eyes forward.

"Relax, boots," one of the corporals said. "You're not at the depot anymore."

Fi gave an embarrassed-sounding laugh and made an obvious effort to stand normally. Esther and the other two newbies eased into a more relaxed posture.

The station was busy, that was for sure. Wayfarer was a mid-sized station, a jumping off point for Navy patrols, prospectors, scientists, pioneers—anyone about to step off into the Dark. Home to a small four-ship Navy detachment and the Marine battalion, it also housed some 25,000 civilians and assorted government workers. Unlike the privately-owned Juliette stations, which had played an important role during the Evolution, Wayfarer was a federal property. The Federation administrator was technically in charge, but for all practical purposes, the Navy commander ran the station, with the Marine battalion CO as his right-hand man.

And like most government projects, it was barebones, nothing like any of the commercial stations Esther had seen. It didn't look inviting, but then again, it wasn't a rundown hellhole that Esther knew existed in some corners of human space.

"Battalion said to hang on," Sergeant Orinda said, returning. "They're sending a van to pick us up."

"You heard her," the staff sergeant said. "Get yourself comfortable."

"Can I pop a stim?" one of the other Marines asked.

"Didn't you attend the brief? We're on a station now. No stims unless you're in a hood or authorized space. Do you see one here?"

Esther wasn't sure why the restriction on stimsticks. It wasn't as if they leaked much into the air. Hell, a fart was worse for the scrubbers. Most commercial stations allowed them, but the government worked in mysterious ways.

"Can we sit, Staff Sergeant?" Fi asked.

"I don't care if you do or not. You can stand all day if that launches your ship. Just don't wander off. I don't want to be chasing anyone down when the van gets here. That goes for everyone," he said, raising his voice so the rest could hear.

That was good enough for Esther; she dropped her seabag and sat on it. The other three newbies immediately followed suit.

"So, what have you heard about the battalion. Any chance of action out here?" Fi asked.

"Oh, nothing since you asked that last time when we got aboard the shuttle," Esther said, trying to sound like an old salt.

But the fact was that she was extremely interested in the answer to his second question. Esther considered herself to be a sane person, and no sane person wanted to be put into combat where he or she might not only be killed, but they had the potential to have to kill another human being. Still, she felt an ache to be battle tested. Her dad had often spoken of how combat developed a person, how it brought life into perspective, and while she'd never heard a shot fired in anger, she'd looked death in the eye while a prisoner of the old government, and she thought she at least had an idea of what her father had meant.

It might not be PC, but the fact was that she wanted to go into combat, she wanted to see if she had what it takes to succeed in the most intense circumstances. She was confident in her abilities.

She was sure she wouldn't turn coward, but how could she know either until she'd been tempered by combat?

One-Sixteen was not organized for sustained combat. It had only minimal arty attached, only a platoon of the Mamba assault tanks (not the normal Marine Corps M1 battle tanks), and two Storks for airlift. But the tempo could be high in the Far Reaches, with smaller engagements with pirates and the like. With a three-year tour of duty, the odds probably favored her seeing some limited action, at least.

Noah, on the other hand, would probably relish never seeing combat. He'd never been very aggressive. For the thousandth time, she wondered why he'd enlisted, and more to the present situation, what perverse sense of humor of the gods resulted in them being sent to the same battalion together. In three years, his enlistment would be close enough to being over that he could take an early out. He'd go back to Prophesy or Tarawa or whatever, find a nice girl, and settle down with five kids and a dog.

It shouldn't matter to her, she knew. She had her own goals and aspirations, and she should focus on her career alone, not his. Still, she retained enough of her sibling rivalry to wish he was serving out his tour on the other side of the Federation.

It took almost three hours of waiting before the "van," which was nothing more than a platform that followed the embedded tracks, showed up. No one had eaten for hours, and Esther was starving. They loaded up their seabags, then clambered aboard, using the sea bags as seats. The van slowly moved out, following one of either the green, blue, or orange track lights that started out alongside each other.

"Ten on the blue," one of the corporals said.

Immediately, he had offers, and within moments, all of the more experienced Marines, along with Pusht, had covered which of the tracks the van was following. Esther didn't bet, but she couldn't help but to take interest on who was right.

Almost immediately, the orange lights veered off to the left, which resulted in both groans and cheers. Pusht had been one of those who'd put his credits on orange.

They moved slowly, stopping for foot-traffic. They'd only traveled about 100 meters over the next two minutes when they came to a fork in the track lights. Without a dog in the fight, Esther still held her breath as the van approached the fork, and she laughed when it split right to follow the green lights.

PAs came out and touched, transferring the winnings to the two now trash-talking winners, Sergeant Orinda and a lance corporal. Esther settled back on her bag, just taking in the lay of the land as the van crept along. About two minutes and another 75 or 80 meters farther, the van pulled in front of a guard post manned by a bored-looking Marine. Above the hatch behind the post was a sign where was written, "First Battalion, Sixteenth Marines" on the top, "Duty First" beneath that.

"You've got to be kidding me," Esther blurted out despite her intention of keeping a low profile. "We waited two hours to ride 200 meters? We could have walked that in a couple of minutes."

"Welcome to the real Corps, boot," Sergeant Orinda said. "And no one ever accused the Corps of being logical."

They debarked the van while the staff sergeant approached the guard post. A moment later, he came back to tell everyone to get scanned. He watched while each Marine leaned into the scanner and confirmed that they were who they said they were and that they had orders into the battalion. Each time, a small light turned green and was accompanied by a soft chime—until the staff sergeant leaned in. The light flashed red, and a three raucous "whoops" sounded.

"What the. . ." the staff sergeant said.

"Try again," the Marine on post instructed him. "The scanners have been a little wonky lately."

Staff Sergeant York frowned, but submitted to another scan—with the same results.

"Like I said, welcome to the real Corps," Sergeant Orinda quietly told Esther.

"This is bullshit. I'm me, and I've got orders to the Roos."

"Wait one," the duty said, then after checking a screen, added, "Yes, I see you've got orders here, Staff Sergeant, and the scan says you're you, but it won't clear you."

"Just open the hatch and let us in. This is a fuck-up that admin has to fix,"

"You know I can't do that, Staff Sergeant. Everyone gets cleared before entering the battalion area. I'm going to let everyone else in to report, but you need to wait until I can get your clearance."

"This is bullshit!" he repeated, this time with more force. "I'm me, and I'm supposed to be here!"

"I understand, Staff Sergeant, but you know. . ."

"Yeah, I know. I've been in for 14 years now; believe me, I know," he said sourly.

Esther was frankly shocked at the exchange. First that the staff sergeant wasn't cleared, and second that he seemed to accept it—reluctantly, but still, he accepted it.

"Sergeant Orinda, take everyone to admin and get them checked in. And get someone to unfuck this so I can spend my next tour doing something worthwhile instead of sitting on my ass in the corridor!"

The front hatch into the battalion area whooshed open, and the 12 Marines entered. Esther wasn't quite sure what to expect, but she could have been on any generic ship. On Tarawa, whether at headquarters or Camp Charles, bases were broad expanses of grass and trees, where each unit had its own buildings. The admin center for the depot was a stand-alone, two-story building. This was nothing like that. The entire battalion was mushed together in a series of corridors and levels. As the twelve Marines trooped down the main corridor, various signs indicated offices along both sides of the passage.

Esther liked the wide-open spaces. She did not particularly like shipboard life, so she was pretty sure she wasn't going to like this.

Only three years, only three years.

That had become her mantra over the last few days, and she had a feeling that she'd be repeating that to herself much more often as time went on.

Admin was like any other of the dozen or so offices they passed. The front hatch was open, leading into a small waiting area separated from the main workspace by a large counter. With 12 Marines milling about, it was pretty crowded.

"Scan yourselves," a corporal shouted from behind a desk. "I'll be with you in a sec."

Once again, Esther was surprised at the lack of basic organization. At Charles, someone would line each of them up, then give each an individual command to get scanned. Now, as the twelve jostled with each other, the organized method at boot camp made sense and was much less confusing.

But she realized that an effective unit didn't act only on orders, so maybe the micromanaging method didn't fit in well with a culture where Marines were expected to complete the mission, even if, or *especially* if, that took initiative.

The corporal stepped up to the counter just as they completed scanning, saying, "OK, I'm about to zap your checklist. You've got until COB to check in to supply to draw your gear, and then check in with sickbay, the chaplain, and the armory. Do all of this before checking into your units. Orinda and Lysander, check with me before you head off."

"Which Lysander," Esther and Noah asked in unison.

"Oh, yeah, I see we've got both here. That's Esther Lysander. Lysander, E. Check in with me."

He thumbed the send on his PA, and an instant later, all 12 Marines' PAs buzzed.

Esther looked down at hers. It indicated that she was assigned to Third Platoon, Bravo Company, and it had a large red "CHECK IN WITH ME" flashing, signed by Corporal Matise Jullien.

There were murmurs from the others as they checked their assignments.

"Ess, I'm with Charlie, First Platoon. I'll be in PICS!" Noah said excitedly.

Esther wasn't sure how Noah knew what kind of platoon he had. All her assignment notice indicated was the unit name, not its T/E.[6] Still, she felt a flash of jealousy. She hadn't bothered to check the exact T/E and T/O[7] of the battalion before leaving Tarawa, so

---

[6] T/E: Table of Equipment
[7] T/O: Table of Organization

she didn't know which companies had PICS Marines and which were straight-leg, but serving in combat armor was considered more prestigious by many Marines, and certainly by the Hollybolly establishment—and through their flicks, the broader population at large. Their father first served in PICS and started his reputation with them.

"OK, whadduyah got, Corporal," Sergeant Orinda asked as she and Esther came up to the counter.

"Sergeant, you and the boot are with Bravo's Third. The platoon is the alert platoon now, so you're to go down to the armory first and draw your weapon. Gunny Delpino's waiting for you. Then go immediately to supply. Top's got an assault kit for you. The alert ship's the *Gallipoli*—"

"Really? Our patron's the Australian Marines, and the Navy alert ship's the *Gallipoli*?" the sergeant asked, sounding bemused.

"Yeah, yeah, we all know," the corporal said with a voice that said he'd heard the coincidence a thousand times before. "Very ironic, we all get it. So if you can get beyond that, the ship's at berth A10. Staff Sergeant Czyżewski's standing by for you—"

"Wait, Staff Sergeant who? Ciz-a-what?" Sergeant Orinda asked.

"Ski. Just Staff Sergeant Ski, not to be confused with Doc Ski or Corporal Ski in Charlie. Anyway, he says he wants you there ASAP. Finally, get your AIs in the brain shack."

"What about the rest of our check-in?"

"After you come off alert. Which is in 70 hours from now."

"Balls. You mean they just went on two hours ago?"

"Got it in one, Sergeant. Can't put much past you."

For a moment, Esther thought the sergeant was going to tear the smug look off of the corporal, but she hesitated, then shrugged and said, "You heard the man, boot. Let's get it in gear."

"Where're you going, Ess?" Noah called out.

"Third Platoon, Bravo," she said as she followed the sergeant. "We're the alert platoon now."

"OK, I'll see you when you get off."

"Uh, Sergeant?" Esther asked as she followed her down the corridor, following the signs for the armory. "Can we get something to eat? I'm starving."

"You and me both, boot. But you heard that fat-ass corporal. We need to get aboard the ship ASAP."

"But surely a few moments—"

"Listen, boot," the sergeant said as she spun around and grabbed Esther's collar, pulling her down until they were nose-to-nose. "This isn't Camp Charles, and most of that drill field spit-and-polish has no place in the fleet. But one thing that we don't mess with is the alert unit. That gets our full and undivided attention. If our platoon sergeant says ASAP, then we salute smartly and beat feat. Understand?"

Esther was shocked at the sergeant's reaction. She still didn't think that taking a couple of minutes to grab a bite to eat would cause the Federation to collapse, but she wasn't about to say that.

"Yes, Sergeant," she said, trying to sound sincere.

"OK, then. Let's draw our weapons."

The armory could have been the twin to the admin paces, except that instead of a counter, a cage separated the racks of weapons from the Marines. Both Marines submitted to yet their third scan, and the duty armorer told them to wait for a moment.

"Uh, Sergeant, can I ask you something?" Esther asked, both anxious to create a better impression and out of curiosity."

"Shoot."

"What was that about the ship's name that you were talking about?"

"Hell, boot, what do they teach you in your military history classes at the depot now? You never heard of Gallipoli?"

"No, not really."

"Why doesn't that surprise me? Gallipoli was one of the seminal battles of WWI—"

"Like on Earth, in the Old Reckoning times," Esther interrupted.

"Yes, Earth. Early 20th, Old Reckoning. Well, it was a big battle between the Ottoman Empire and for the Allies, the

Newfoundland, Indian, French, but for this discussion, the ANZAC forces."

"ANZAC?"

"ANZAC. Australia and New Zealand."

"Oh, and since 1/16's patron is the Australian Marines, I see what you mean about the ship's name."

"Coincidence? Maybe, but the Aussies are pretty influential in the Federation, and not just because they're reaping in the big credits with their mining concessions in the Juarez Belt. Both countries and their settlements still celebrate April 25 as ANZAC Day."

"From that long ago? I never realized that," Esther said.

Her dad had been enthralled with history, an interest he hadn't managed to pass onto her. He'd been somewhat of a star with the Portuguese after commanding the "Fuzos," whose patron was the "Corpo de Fuzileiros." Portugal was no longer much of a Federation power, but their support of him couldn't have hurt. The Australians had much more political clout, and if they cared so much about a battle fought long ago on Earth, then they might hold the same affection for members of "their" battalion. This kind of thinking was new to Esther, but if she really wanted to succeed, she couldn't afford to turn away any potential opportunity.

Her thoughts were interrupted when the armorer called both Marines to the cage, handing each a brand new M99.

"They've been zeroed at 400 meters at one G. After you get off alert, you need to go to the range and get your personals."

The M99 was a dart thrower, firing a hypervelocity 8mm dart that was accelerated with mag rings, and capable of reaching 2,010 meters per second past the muzzle. The body of the dart was nowhere near 8mm across, but once it was fired, fins popped out for stability, and it was the fins that stretched 8mm.

No one else seemed to take issue with the "8mm" designation, but it bugged the crap out of Esther.

The "personals" they'd get at the range would be the settings for Null G, .5 G, 1 G, and 1.5 G. The factory settings were already set, and on these, at 400 meters, but each individual was different, and the weapons needed to be set for his or her shooting style.

"Thanks," Sergeant Orinda said to the armorer. She turned and told Esther, "Let's get to supply."

Supply was almost a copy of the armory, even to the cage front. Within three minutes, the two Marines were out, assault packs in their hands. They'd arrive on Wayfarer Station with their personal gear, their boots, their skins, and the skins' bones inserts. They were leaving for the ship without too much else, but still enough to go to war if it came to that. Esther was finally beginning to feel like a Marine.

Some appetizing aromas reached them as they hurried to the brain shack, and a line of Marines was entering what had to be the messhall. Esther still wanted to rush in for a quick bite, but the sergeant was pushing on, and Esther stayed on her ass. It only took a minute or so until they reached the S7, the "brain shack." This space was nothing like the armory or supply. It looked more like a Hollybolly clean room. White and spotless, this was where the civilian techs kept the processing capabilities humming.

The two Marines handed over their helmets. It wasn't the helmets themselves that the tech wanted, but the AI chip embedded in each one, the same AI chip that could be taken out and carried in a multiple of chassis, from a fighter pilot's HUD to a recon Marine's soft cover. Hopefully, this AI would be the only one Esther would ever need, updated as required, but growing with her, integrating with her over time. The AI was a vital piece of Marine Corps gear, but it took the tech less than 15 seconds each to upload the battalion pathways, check them, and hand them back as if the two Marines were both annoyances to his daily routine.

Less than a minute after entering the brain shack, they were back in the corridor and hurrying to the front gate. They stepped into the scanner at the gate, which logged each piece of equipment they carried and compared that with their authorization to leave the battalion area with said equipment—notably, their M99's—and a moment later, they were back out in the corridor.

"You've got to be kidding me," Staff Sergeant York said from where he was sitting on a bench along the other side of the corridor. "You two are already locked and loaded while I'm still cooling my jets out here?"

"Sorry, Staff Sergeant, but we're on the alert platoon." Sergeant Orinda said. "I told them you needed to get your situation unfucked," she added as they jogged down the passage

Once in the main corridor, it wasn't hard to navigate. They could query their AIs, but that was considered less than grunt-worthy. Not that they needed them. Signs were everywhere, and they quickly found the A Terminal.

It felt weird to Esther to be walking out among civilians with an assault pack and carrying a weapon, but no one gave the two Marines a second glance.

They eschewed the moving walkway down the terminal's main corridor, but it had to be close to a klick to hump out the terminal's length. At A10, they could see the *UFS Gallipoli* on the screen. Unlike at any commercial terminal that Esther had ever seen, there was no one at the gate counter. Sergeant Orinda approached the door, then looked into yet one more scanner. The light turned green, and the door opened.

"You waiting for an invitation, boot?" she asked.

"No, Sergeant!"

Esther scanned herself, then stepped into the snake, the flexible tunnel that connected the terminal to the ship's hatch. The two hurried down the length, reaching the end where an armed sailor waited just inside the ship's quarterdeck.

"Sergeant Tikka Orinda, UFMC, requesting permission to come aboard!"

The sailor pointed to another scanner, into which the sergeant leaned. Once again, as it had the last dozen times she'd been scanned, the light turned green.

Esther requested permission to come aboard, and then got scanned as well.

"New meat," the sailor said. "Your staff sergeant's waiting for you in the ready room."

Since they had no idea where this ship's ready room was, the sergeant broke down and queried her AI. The ship wasn't large, but Esther was glad they weren't wandering blind. As it was, she wasn't sure she could find her way back to the quarterdeck unaided.

A few minutes later, the two entered an open hatch. Marines filled the ready room, and all eyes rose to look at them. For a moment, Esther felt nervous and more than a little tentative.

"Sergeant Orinda, PFC Lysander, you just made it in time," a staff sergeant told them. "Grab a seat and strap in. We're at One-Alpha, just waiting for final clearance. Welcome to the Thundering Third, and get ready for some action!"

Chapter 15

Noah

Noah was almost trembling with excitement. There, standing in front of him, was his PICS. The civilian tech still had to input some last-minute adjustments, but in a few moments, he'd be slipping inside of it. This was every gameboy's dream. No matter how good the sim, it couldn't match the real thing.

He'd been in a PICS before, at IUT. But that had been an off-the-shelf, one-size-fits-most model worn by at least a dozen trainees that day. Sure, it had been fun to stomp around and fire the main weapons systems, but like having a wrinkled sock in your boots or a helmet that kept slipping down, it could be a little annoying and didn't feel like the melding of human and technology he'd expected. This, would be different. This was his PICS, one fitted to him.

It had been a fairly long day, from landing on the station to waiting for that ridiculously short ride to the battalion to getting all his check-in blocks marked off. But he was happy that he hadn't had to wait another day for the PICS fitting. Or another three days, as it were. The civilian techs worked different hours, and if the four Marines going into PICS units hadn't been fitted today, they'd have had to wait until Friday, the next time the tech would be available.

All four Marines had gotten into their long johns, the tight undersuit fitted with the various sensors and node-lines that created the interface between combat suit and Marine. The suits automatically adjusted over a standard deviation, so they were "tech-free." Not so the PICS themselves.

Each Marine stood inside a body scanner while the coil rotated around him or her from a dozen different aspects. With their current body specs, to include skin induction rates and other esoteric measurements, in the system, it was time for fitting.

When his father was a PICS Marine, the combat suits were not as sophisticated, of course, and one difference was that the PICS interiors had limited individual fitting options then. The interiors could be adjusted much in the same way a hover seat could be adjusted, mostly along the three major axes. Straps could tighten and loosen, but that was about the limit of personalizing each unit. Now, with the Model Js, the interiors were fitted with nanogel, which served to make as tight a fit as possible, taking into account all the variations in the human body.

It would still be possible for a Marine to use a PICS not specifically fitted to him as long as the interior structure was within his or her body's parameters, but test after test proved the efficacy of the newer, more encompassing fitting. Marines just performed better with a personally-fitted PICS.

Lance Corporal Omaru stepped out from behind her PICS, stretching before stepping off the fitting cradle. She'd been in a PICS platoon at her former battalion and had arrived with her existing long johns. The long johns left nothing on a human body to the imagination, and as a slim, fit woman, Noah might have noted her physique as she stretched, but he barely noticed her, he was so amped. The lifting arm picked up her PICS and sent it back into the pool, while a second arm lifted Noah's PICS, slipping it into the cradle. The tech did his thing for about a minute before directing Noah to get into it.

One thing that hadn't changed since well before his father's time was the gymnastics required to slip inside a combat suit. He'd only performed the spine-breaking task twice, and mindful of Lance Corporal Omaru, who hadn't left the fitting room yet, and the tech, he hoped he wouldn't look like an uncoordinated dweeb donning the unit. He casually walked to the back of the suit, faced away, then slid his head and torso into the body cavity until with crossed arms, he could reach the donning handles. With that support, he pulled up his legs, knees almost to his chest, before pulling and completing the "flip" while forcing his legs down at the same time.

It wasn't pretty, it wasn't smooth, but at least he hadn't had to stop and start over again. He settled into the inner frame, wiggling slightly as if to seat himself. Everything felt right. He could see out the display, the finger controls were at the right spot, and his feet were solid in the bootplates.

"Don't move, Private," the tech said over the PICS' comms. "OK, initiating body-forming."

Noah didn't feel much. It was more like a gentle hug from his mother tucking him in when he was a child. The PICS got a little snugger, if anything.

"Move your right hand and arm," the tech said.

Noah complied, marveling at how easily the PICS translated his arm movements into the combat suit's movements.

"Wait one," the tech said.

Noah thought he felt the slightest pressure change, then the tech said, "Right hand and arm again, please."

Once again, if there was any difference, it was too slight for Noah to notice. The tech evidently was satisfied because he moved onto the left arm, followed by all the major movements. Twice, he had Noah repeat a movement after additional adjustments. Five minutes later, the fitting was complete.

"That's all, Private. Molt now," the tech told him.

Molting, or getting out of the PICS was more difficult than getting in. The most difficult part was the legs. Noah didn't clear the knees on his first attempt, but he managed on the second. He was almost sad when he made it out. He'd have loved to put the PICS—*his* PICS—through a few paces.

Lance Corporal Omaru was still waiting for him, having gotten out of her long johns and back into her utilities while Noah was being fitted.

"Make some time, Boot," she told him. "Chow ends in 20."

He hurried off the platform and down to where his utilities were hanging on a hook. He quickly stripped off his long johns, putting them into his pack, and put on his uniform.

It had been a hectic day, but getting his own PICS was a huge step forward. He couldn't wait until he'd be able to train in it.

For the first time in a few hours, he thought about Esther as he followed Omaru out of the PICS pool.

Whatever she was doing couldn't top his afternoon!

FS GALLIPOLI

Chapter 16

Esther

After the big rush to join the platoon, Esther had sat in her seat for three hours. No one knew what was happening. Even the lieutenant seemed out of the loop, stretched out on a reclined chair, cover on his/her face and napping.

Esther hadn't heard Lieutenant Uluiviva say a word—the lieutenant had barely moved since she'd arrived. A big, somewhat shapeless person, Esther wasn't even sure of the lieutenant's gender.

Staff Sergeant Ski was more energetic, constantly making the rounds of the Marines and the two Navy corpsmen in the platoon (there should have been three corpsmen, Esther noted, one for each squad). He'd spent ten minutes with the two new joins, telling Sergeant Orinda that she was the new First Squad leader and assigning Esther to the squad as well. He gave them a basic lowdown of the platoon before moving off—but not before making sure the two were given some combat rats. Esther was not fond of the rats, which had all the calories and nutrients a Marine needed to fight even if they were not strong on taste, but she was happy to quiet her growling stomach.

Sergeant Orinda immediately got together with her three corporal team leaders, trying to get a feel for her squad. None of this made sense to Esther. If they were potentially going into action, why would they put a sergeant in charge of a squad that she'd never even seen before? And why was Esther sitting there marking time without any sort of briefing. She knew the philosophy that any Marine could step into any billet, but this seemed to be taking it too far.

The long day was beginning to tell on her, and her eyes started drooping when one of the ship's officers stuck his head in the hatch and called for the lieutenant.

All of the Marines turned as one as the lieutenant opened her eyes and slowly pulled herself out of her chair—Esther still wasn't positive, but she thought the lieutenant was female, which would make her one of the first women to get commissioned since the Corps was opened back up to them. The platoon commander calmly strode out the hatch and disappeared from sight. It took a moment for the Marines to break out into a babble of questions, opinions, and wagers on what was going on.

"You hanging in there, Boot?" Sergeant Orinda asked.

"Uh, sure, Sergeant. Just wondering what's going on."

"As we all are. Look, sorry I haven't really welcomed you to the squad, but I'm just as new, and I was getting myself up-to-date. I'm putting you in Second Fire Team," she told her before turning and saying, "Corporal Kinder, come sweep up your new PFC. You might want to get her locked on if we've got a mission coming."

The corporal nodded, then came over, hand out to shake.

"PFC, huh? Just starting out or coming back down?' he asked.

Esther knew he was questioning her rank, if she was a newbie or possibly someone who'd been in grade for a tour or even busted down from lance corporal.

"Just got out of IUT, Corporal."

"Meritorious?"

"Series honor grad," she said, not without a degree of pride.

It isn't boasting if he asks.

"That don't mean jack out here in the fleet, but it don't hurt none neither. Welcome."

For the first time, he looked at her nametag embedded in her utilities breast.

"Lys—," he started as realization came over him—it wasn't as if her enlistment had been kept quiet. He switched his comment to, "What do they call you?"

"Just Esther, Corporal."

"Well, 'Just Esther,' that's a little wordy, dontcha think? Give us a day or two, and I'm sure someone will come up with something a little better."

Esther didn't want anything "better." However, the Corps loved nicknames, and she realized that some, if not most, of the other Marines might not want to keep calling her Lysander.

"I'm going to talk with the staff sergeant," Sergeant Orinda told the corporal. "You lock her on the best you can."

Corporal Kinder called over the other two Marines in the fire team. Lance Corporal Eason was obviously a heavy-worlder: short, with broad shoulders and no neck. His voice was surprisingly high-pitched for such a bulky and powerful body. PFC Woutou was his polar opposite: tall, thin, and yes, with a deep, resonating voice.

"The boot here got her stripe meritoriously," the corporal started.

"Just like Woowoo," the lance corporal said with a laugh. "Got it straight from the CO along with half pay for three months."

It took Esther a moment to decipher what the heavy-worlder meant, and when it did, she was shocked. The other PFC had been reduced in rank by the battalion CO. Esther knew that Marines could get office hours or even courts martial, but in her father's rarefied atmosphere, she didn't think she'd ever met anyone who'd received either.

"You got NJP?" she blurted out before remembering that he might be sensitive about that.

"Twice. I'm going for a triple before I'm done here," Woowoo said.

Esther didn't know what to make of that. First, that he'd had two NJPs, second, that he seemed proud of the fact. If, God forbid, she was ever on the receiving end of any kind of punishment, she sure the hell wouldn't be bragging about it.

"Esther, you any good with the dunker?" Corporal Kinder asked.

The "dunker," nicknamed for the sound it made when firing a grenade, was a grenade/rocket launcher that could be attached underneath the M99 barrel. Depending on its configuration, it could fire either a 30mm grenade or a short, stubby, anti-armor rocket.

"Passably good," she admitted.

"OK, normally, as the boot, you'd be the team's rifleman, but since you haven't been with us, I'm keeping Woowoo there. You've got the dunker. If anything goes down, you just get ready to engage what I tell you. Capisce?"

"Roger that," she said, keeping what she wanted to say in check.

His lack of confidence in her abilities was more than annoying. She made meritorious PFC, and she felt that was proof enough of what she could do. The fact that the grenadier was usually the second highest-ranking Marine in the team was irrelevant. She got the position because he didn't trust her yet.

"Where do I get the M333?" she asked. "I don't have to go back to the armory, do I?"

"Sergeant Quiero has them—he's Third Squad's leader, and he's acting as the police sergeant. If we're getting into the shit here, he'll hook you up."

"Don't worry about it, Boot. Nine times out of ten, these heightened alerts never come to anything" Lance Corporal Eason said.

"Give me three to one odds on that," Woowoo said. "I'm feeling a fight in my bones."

"Five credits," the lance corporal said.

"Done!"

"Not too smart, Woowoo," Corporal Kinder said. "We haven't had a mission in three months."

"All the more reason. We're due, and I feel it in my bones."

"Yeah, in your bone," Lance Corporal Eason said, aiming a hard shot at Woowoo's crotch which the PFC deftly avoided.

Almost as if on cue, the hatch opened, and the lieutenant barged into the space.

"Squad leaders up!" she shouted. "Now!"

"We've got a mission, boys and girls," she told them, but with the space being so small, every Marine was listening in. "It's a pirate hunt. The *Rio Tinto Excavator King* has been jacked. The crew were all put into lifeboats and scattered, with evidently no loss of life, so this is not a kill mission. The good folks at Rio Tinto just want their barge back in one piece and with her cargo intact.

"We've got four hours to get a plan together, so let's get cracking."

A few moments ago, Esther was complaining to herself that her team leader was keeping her back, not trusting her to handle the rifleman position. Now, that she was actually facing potential combat, she wondered if he was right. She'd just reported aboard three hours ago, and now she was being shoved into the breach.

She'd wanted action, and now she had it, ready or not.

WAYFARER STATION

Chapter 17

Noah

"First pitcher's on you, Boot, so better go get it. And not any of that Presidential piss, either," Lance Corporal Thaddeus Morton said.

"Tad" was in Noah's fire team, and as soon as chow was over, he'd grabbed Noah, and like a huge wet-water tanker sweeping up a small sailboat, he'd pretty much dragged Noah out in the ville. Noah would rather have crashed early, but he knew first impressions were hard to break, and he didn't want to come across as stand-offish. He had enough problems socializing that he didn't need to shoot himself in the foot starting off.

Noah wasn't completely oblivious to the fact that Tad was more than happy to both have a willing—well, captive—ear and for someone else to buy the beer. Still, he didn't mind, even if he couldn't simply buy the economical (that was the politest way to put it) Presidential Ale.

"Turtle, you bastard, they let you out of the brig?" Tad asked a stocky, ebony-skinned Marine in civilian clothes—in uniform or in civvies, anyone could always identify the Marines.

Noah's eyes rose as Tad flowed into one of the ratty, faux-leather chairs that surrounded an equally decrepit table.

Brig?

"I broke out of max tonight, Tad-my-boy, so I can show you how a real man drinks!"

"Real man? Who're you talking about? In case you haven't noticed, I'm 100% female, and I'll out-drink you all," a stocky, shaved-headed Marine said.

"She's got you there, Turtle. Remember last Saturday?"

"Hey, that's because you guys were late, and I already finished off a pitcher on my own."

"Fucking excuses, Turtle. Just man up and admit you puked all over that sergeant from Alpha."

"It was pretty fucking funny," the female Marine said, lifting a glass to clink with Turtle. "And who'd you drag with you?" she asked Tad.

"This here boot's Noah. Just reported aboard today. I thought I'd show him the ropes."

"And buy the beer?" she asked with a short laugh.

"Ah, you know me so well. We should be married, me and you."

"In your dreams. You ain't man enough for the likes of Princess Mayhem."

"Noah, that's Dora Hwang. 'Princess Mayhem.' As much as I hate to admit it, she's a passably decent PICS jockey."

"Passably? My ass I'm passably. Best cap scores in the battalion and tons better than you!"

"And very modest," the Marine Tad called Turtle told Noah as he held out a hand over the table. "I'm Gregori de Matta, 'Turtle' to my friends."

"Where're the rest?" Tad asked.

"Rory's got the duty, but I guess anyone's who's coming will be coming," Dora said. "But why's your new boot just standing there? I thought you said he's buying the beer, and my glass is about empty."

"Shit, I wouldn't keep the princess' glass empty if I were you, Noah," Turtle said. "You don't want to see her when's she's in a mood."

"Is that some sort of 'woman's time' comment?" she asked as she leveled a wicked punch on Turtle's shoulder. Noah didn't need to see Turtle's expression to know she'd hit hard; the sound alone made Noah wince.

"Never ma'am, never!" Turtle protested as Tad laughed. "It's just that you can be a mean-ass drunk."

"And don't you forget it!" she said, giving him another, lighter punch.

"So what're you doing standing there gawking? Hup to it, Boot," she said.

Noah turned to do his duty. He wasn't used to this kind of recreation. He was a gamer, and even at the few local game conventions he'd attended, the vibe was totally different. This was almost a Hollybolly trope, and frankly, it fascinated him. He was out of his element, but he wanted to try and fit in.

"And none of the Presidential shit, either!" Dora shouted out as his retreating back.

Noah waved an acknowledgment over his shoulder. He seemed to be being accepted by the others, which was not always the case with him. Esther was the social one. Hell, she'd probably end up making Princess Mayhem buy the first pitcher. But now, he was getting a head start on his sister by being introduced to the station's bar district while she was sitting on her butt with the alert platoon, probably bored out of her mind. For once, he was getting the adventure while she did nothing.

FS GALLIPOLI

Chapter 18

Esther

"Just concentrate on your training, Esther. You'll be fine," Corporal Kinder said over the EVA suit's P2P.

"I know. Don't worry about me, Corporal," Esther said with a tone of conviction she didn't quite feel in her heart.

Esther had trained in EVA missions, of course, both at boot camp and IUT. She'd been on four exercises, but she was discovering that there was a huge difference between training and a hot mission. She was nervous, no getting around it.

She didn't think she was afraid in the conventional sense. Yes, she was going into harm's way for the first time, but they only faced half-a-dozen or so pirates with an entire Marine rifle platoon and a Federation Navy schooner. This was not a high-risk mission.

What she feared was making a mistake, making a fool of herself. She had to excel at combat, and all she could think of was screwing up.

Esther was not a person given to self-doubt. Whatever task she undertook, she excelled at it. That was just the way it was. To feel the unease that permeated her thoughts was a new experience.

She nervously shook her shoulders to seat the clavicular strapping. Unlike a PICS, the EVAs came in four basic sizes; individual fitting was done by the smart lining and adjustable harness. Her EVA was fairly new, unlike the ones she'd worn during training, EVAs that hundreds of other recruits had worn and filled with their sweat and who knows what else. But unlike the school EVAs, this was a full combat suit, complete with MR armor.

Magnetorheological armor was heavier than the STF[8] armor of the Marine's "bones," the inserts used in their "skins," or field uniform, and it was slightly bulkier. In an already bulky EVA, used mostly in Null G, that didn't make much difference, but this was Esther's first time in a combat EVA, and she felt as if she'd been wrapped up in bubble wrap. In the *Gallipoli's* artificial gravity, even at .75 G, the EVA felt heavy to her.

Whereas the STF of a Marine's "bones" hardened instantly with the shock wave of an impact, the MR armor used magnetic fields to align the ferrous particles in the suspension fluid. The advantage of that was that it could be hit in the same spot repeatedly without compromise. With the STF armor, repeated hits at the same spot could defeat the it.

The MR armor for EVAs was a fairly new development. In her father's day, the EVAs were pretty much naked to projectile weapons. Esther might not like the way her EVA felt on her, but she welcomed the extra protection. As the lieutenant had pointed out, not one battalion Marine had been killed in an EVA op in the almost year-and-a-half she'd been with them.

Esther still thought that any risk in this case was stupid. Their mission was to retake the ore carrier. Up to half-a-dozen pirates had taken her, jettisoning the four-man crew in separate lifeboats. To her surprise, the ship's captain had ignored the crew, saying they could be picked up after the *Rio Tinto Excavator King* was recovered. Esther didn't really care for closed-in spaces, and the thought of floating around in the Black for a dozen hours, not knowing for sure that rescue was imminent, was rather disturbing.

Still, if they had to recover the ore carrier, why not just stand off with the *Gallipoli* and fire on the bridge? Most of the carrier was a huge, 500-meter expanse of framing that used force grapples to hold the ore in place. The brain of the carrier was the relatively small bridge and crew quarters linked to the power train. One round from any of the *Gallipoli's* weapons systems, and all they'd have to do was eject the pirates' remains into the Black and wash out the mess.

---

[8] STF: Shear-Thickening Fluid, a liquid-based armor that thickened to a solid when subjected to a shock.

"You are such a naive boot," Sergeant Orinda had said with a wry smile when Esther had asked why the Navy just didn't shoot up the pirates. "Rio Tinto doesn't want their carrier damaged, and they want their ore at the processing station now. If they have to replace the bridge unit, that could take weeks, and then their processing station goes idle."

So we put Marines in danger so Rio Tinto can save a few credits, she thought sourly.

Her father had been wary of the power the huge corporations wielded and how the Marines were seemingly often at their bidding. Esther had never really considered the issue, but now, when it was her platoon's ass on the line simply to save Rio Tinto a miniscule fraction of its yearly revenues, she was beginning to see his point.

"Three minutes," Staff Sergeant Ski passed on the platoon net.

Esther shrugged again, trying to seat the clavicular strapping. It didn't feel like it was smooth against her shoulders, and that was annoying more than anything else.

Forget it! Get your mind back on the mission!

She turned over her M99 and checked the M333 attached to it. The launcher looked pretty fierce, she had to acknowledge, and she felt powerful with it in her hands. While she still resented being shifted from rifleman, being the grenadier did have its benefits. She was locked and loaded with the "shotgun" grenade—75 pellets encased in a polyglycolide smart-jacket. Firing it was pretty foolproof. All she had to do was aim her weapon in the general direction of a pirate, and the tiny sensor would do the rest, releasing the pellets at the proper distance and pattern to turn a human body into just so much hamburger. And if a breach was needed, a simple press of the selector lever rotated the chamber so that she could fire the Airy rocket.

She really should have personally zeroed-in her M99 itself before going hot on a mission, but at close-range, both the standard set and the automatic zeroing done by the weapon reading her eye placement was probably good enough. For the dunker, zeroing wasn't necessary.

"Two minutes," the platoon sergeant passed. "Second Squad, get ready."

That last command was probably unneeded. The entire platoon had been ready for the last ten minutes, waiting in the cramped hangar bay for the ship's bosun to release them. The *Excavator King* was unarmed, and the Gallipoli's scanners could not detect any weapons capable of doing her harm, so it was matching speed 300 meters off the carrier. At that distance, the rekkis wouldn't be used. The Marines would fly themselves across the intervening distance—the carrier was too ungainly to change direction before the Marines reached her.

Due to the cramped space in the hangar, Esther's First Squad was standing in the top rekki. All three of the space sleds were stacked one on top of the other. With the lone ship's shuttle in the hangar as well, that left very little room for the Marines.

"One minute!"

The ship's hangar doors began to open. The electrostatic gate was still in place, so the ship's air was intact, but Esther felt a thrill as she looked into open space. As much as she didn't like cramped spaces, she'd loved her EVA training. Some others had problems staring into the Black, and a few recruits had been dropped due to their inability to function while on an EVA. Esther found the void compelling.

The bosun spun around, whirling one arm to point out past the gate just as Staff Sergeant Ski shouted "Second, go!"

As one, the 12 Marines and one corpsman stepped through the gate, a small flare haloing each one. The lieutenant was right on their tails, and almost immediately, Third Squad followed. Esther's First Squad was already climbing down off the rekkis, and with Staff Sergeant Ski urging them on, they stepped into the Black.

After the initial flare of the gate against her EVA, suddenly, she could see forever. This section of space was closer to the galactic center, so the "Black" was not as appropriate a term. Thousands of stars spread out around her. Esther's face shield barely had to magnify the starlight.

"On my ass, Lysander," Corporal Kinder said, snapping her attention back.

Esther quickly hit her jets to pull within five meters of her team leader as the squad circled around the *Gallipoli* to face the ore carrier. Even a hand-held weapon could fire through a hangar gate, so the ship had rotated the hangar doors away from the carrier.

The *Excavator King* was huge! Esther had taken in the dimensions during the brief, but to see the carrier, full of ore, stretch out before her made it hit home. Second Squad was already halfway to the ship, which showed no signs of evasion, not that it would do much good. The pirates had been betting on getting away before the Navy could reach them. They had released the crew and scattered them, obviously hoping that the first ship to respond would spend time rounding the crew members up. Somewhere up ahead would be their compatriots, ready to divvy up the ore for basic pirate operations, or for the more advanced crews, cloaking teams that would make the carrier disappear from detection.

"Keep your dispersion," Sergeant Orinda passed on the squad circuit.

"Se. . .ight. . .et rea. . ." the lieutenant's voice sputtered over the platoon circuit. ". . .it!"

"The lieutenant's got comm problems," Staff Sergeant Ski passed a few seconds later. "But we know the plan, so nothing's changed."

Comms were often ineffective, usually due to enemy jamming. To have it just go out like that wasn't that rare of an occurrence, but for it to be the platoon commander's comms was just bad luck.

Right about now, the *Gallipoli* would be aiming a tight beam to the *Excavator King,* using the carrier's skin as a speaker membrane to demand the pirate's surrender. The beam was supposedly harmless to humans, but Esther kept expecting to feel it pass through her.

If the *Gallipoli* passed the surrender demand, evidently the pirates refused, because 150 meters away, the entry hatch of the *Excavator King opened,* overridden by the Navy ship. Second Squad disappeared inside the carrier.

First Squad closed the distance as Third followed Second inside the ship. Esther tried to see something, anything, to let her know what was happening. All was silent, broken only the sound of her breathing.

She reversed her jets, slowing down to enter the ship as all hell suddenly broke loose, first on the net, then as she passed the hatch and entered the ship's atmosphere, as normal sound. First Squad broke immediately to the right to secure the propulsion train. None of the Marines had ever been aboard this class of carrier, but the ship's plans had been extremely accurate, and everyone knew just where to go.

The heavy sound of firing reached them, and Esther's instincts were to rush to help the Marines in contact, but the squad's mission was not the bridge. It was harder to ignore the rounds that reached them, especially when Woowoo shouted "Shit! The fuckers hit me!"

Esther's heart raced, but Woowoo's MR armor did its job. He stumbled a step as the ferrous particles aligned and turned his lower back and legs into a solid piece of armor for a fraction of a second before shifting back to normal.

At the rear of the squad, and the closest to the firing reaching out from the bridge, Esther instinctively turned, her M99 and attached dunker at the ready. Second Squad was in heavy contact, the Marines hugging the corridor bulkheads and the deck as they bounded forward, one team moving while two teams provided cover. She could just make out a barricade inside the bridge itself, extending from the deck to the overhead, from where the pirate fire was coming. She was tempted to try and get a clear shot when one of the Second Squad Marines fired his dunker. Esther couldn't see if he had effect on target, but she knew he had a much better line of sight to the bad guys than she had.

The propulsion train was located down a circular deck hatch. It was big enough for only one Marine at a time, and the squad was bunching up at the hatch.

"Kinder, cover our six," Sergeant Orinda ordered as she started down. "There's not enough room down here for all of us, and it looks clear."

"You heard her," the corporal said as the four turned back towards the passage to the bridge.

"Crew quarters clear," Sergeant Quiero passed on the platoon net from Third Squad's objective.

It looked like all the pirates were on the bridge, and from the sound of it, they were putting up a fierce resistance. Esther wished she could listen in to Second Squad to know what was happening, but she was not on their net.

"Propulsion clear!" Sergeant Orinda passed.

"Should we, you know, move forward?" Eason asked Kinder though his external speaker.

The corporal looked back at the hatch leading down to propulsion for a moment before saying, "We can still keep security from up ahead. Move up to the main passage."

At the bridge, the sheer number of weapons being discharged was amazing, and Esther was astounded that anyone could still be alive, pirate or Marine. The bridge was less than 20 meters across and maybe 10 meters deep, and while it was the largest space in the manned area of the ship, it seemed way too small for a firefight of this magnitude.

Corporal Kinder waved Woowoo and Eason across the passage where they hugged the bulkhead. Three Marines were prone where the passage entered the bridge. The rest of the squad was inside the bridge, taking cover the best they could while still firing on the barricade, which looked to be welded plates between the captain's chair and the control pillar. Whoever had constructed it had a sound tactical mind, Esther realized.

". . . ere now . . ." the lieutenant tried to pass.

Up ahead, one of the prone Marines turned around, and to Esther's surprised, popped his face shield. Only it wasn't a "him"—it was the lieutenant.

"Get Third Squad and Ski up here now!" she shouted back down the passage.

"Woowoo, go!" Corporal Kinder ordered as the PFC immediately took off towards the crew quarters.

The lieutenant started to turn back, hand reaching to close her face shield when her head snapped back and she went limp. One of the Marines darted to her side and rolled her over.

"The lieutenant's down!" someone shouted over the platoon net. "Staff Sergeant Ski, the lieutenant's down."

"I'm on my way," the platoon sergeant passed, his voice calm and steady.

Esther was shocked. This was supposed to be a cakewalk! And now they got the lieutenant!

"Kinder, what's going on?" Sergeant Orinda asked over the squad circuit.

"The lieutenant's down hard, Sergeant. Second's in the shit."

A string of darts impacted along the bulkhead beside Esther, making her jump.

"I'm coming up," the sergeant said.

Esther fingered her M99, trying not to stare at what was now two Marines dragging the inert body of the lieutenant out of the way. The EVAs had only limited med capabilities. They would be injecting nano activators into her body, trying to keep her functions working until she could be put in stasis.

One of the Marines with the lieutenant went down, and Esther's heart jumped, but a moment later, he was back up. The shock at seeing the lieutenant hit was being replaced by a growing anger, anger that they hadn't let the Navy take care of the situation, anger that pirates had thought they could just steal the ship, anger that the lieutenant—her lieutenant—had been hit. She wanted to hit them back. She barely noticed Staff Sergeant Ski arriving, accompanied by two teams from Third Squad.

"What's the situation?" he asked Corporal Kinder.

"I don't know everything, Staff Sergeant, but Second Squad's pinned down, and the lieutenant's been hit."

"With what? What weapons do they have?"

"She opened her face shield to tell us to get you, you know, 'cause her comms are out. It was still open when she took a round in the face."

"So all they've got is small arms? Holy shit, what the fuck are we waiting for? You three, you're with me," she said, pointing to Kinder, Eason and Esther. "Sergeant Quiero, let's do this."

"Do what?"

"Hell, they've only got small arms. We bull rush them!"

"What if that barrier's booby-trapped?" Sergeant Orinda, who'd just arrived, asked.

"Well, we'll find out now, won't we?" he said before passing on the net, "Second, clear a way in the middle and lay down some cover. But watch out for us, especially you grenadiers. I don't need an Airy up my ass."

"On three . . . one . . . two . . . three!"

Esther was already in the passage, so as the staff sergeant surged forward, she rode him like a dolphin on a bow wave, using his bulk to propel her forward. She screamed a wordless expression of anger as she ran, vaulting over a prone Marine to bound up to the barricade. The pirates had been firing out of small slits, just large enough for their rounds to pass through. Esther figured that some of the M99 hypervelocity darts must have made it through the slits based purely on the number of darts fired. As Marines rushed up on either side of her, she put the muzzle of her dunker right up against the slit and triggered the grenade. The blast knocked her on her ass as pellets ricocheted back, at least a couple hitting her. At 30 mm, the dunker was wider than the slit, but while some of the pellets hit the edge of the slit, some had to have gotten through. She thought— she hoped—she heard the cries of anguish coming from the other side.

She started to scramble up, but Marines had swarmed the barricade, pushing their M99 muzzles into the four slits and emptying hundreds of darts into the openings. There wasn't room for Esther to worm her way in.

"Stand by for a breaching charge!" Staff Sergeant Ski yelled out as he slapped a 10 x 10 square charge at the base of the barricade.

Esther looked up in surprise, and Sergeant Quiero said, "But we weren't allowed Cat-2 explosives!"

To limit damage to the *Excavator King,* the platoon had been restricted to their small arms. Esther had been surprised that the grenadiers had been allowed their Airies, but she figured that was a case of do first and ask permission later, especially if the rockets hadn't been expressly forbidden.

"I really don't give a shit now. Do you?"

"Uh, no Staff Sergeant."

"OK, now. I'm arming this for ten seconds, so you all better get back. Fire in the hole!"

Esther joined the rush back. Three of the firing slits were quiet, and only from one did rounds continue to chase them. Even those rounds faltered as Staff Sergeant Ski, who was counting down, reached "four."

"Stop! We surrender!" a voice called out.

"Too fucking late," another Marine muttered as a blast filled the bridge, sending a cloud of smoke outwards for an instant before the cloud was sucked back into the gaping hole. Immediately, the ship's alarms went off as the air rushed out.

"Seal the lieutenant's face shield!" the platoon sergeant shouted.

A pirate, no more than a teenager, stumbled half out of the breach before falling, gasping for breath as he fought the rush of air evacuating the ship. His face was bloody, but it was obvious that the lack of oxygen was his biggest problem. Esther stared at the pirate, fascinated as he fought for life. She wondered how long it would take him to die. The ship might be small, but there was still a lot of air in her, and it would take a while to completely blow out.

"Quiero, take a team and check it out."

Sergeant Quiero, along with four Marines, rushed forward. One of the Marines kicked the contorting pirate aside. The Marine carefully stepped through the hole in the barricade—the MR armor was great against projectiles, but not so great against a slow, steady tear, and he didn't want to snag his EVA on the shredded metal.

Without much air left, the externals were worthless, so Sergeant Quiero passed on the net, "Five pirates. Three KIA. The breaching charge went all the way through the ship's skin."

"Doc, check on the lieutenant. You two," he said, pointing at Esther and Eason, "slap some emergency hoods on that guy and the other WIA."

Esther ran to the bulkhead and pulled off two emergency hoods from the bright orange canister while the staff sergeant started his report back to the ship. Giving one hood to Eason, she bypassed the barely moving pirate still lying in the breach and stepped behind the barricade. Sergeant Quiero pointed at one of the pirates, a middle-aged man who looked like he could be the local librarian. One of his legs was a bloody mess, and he was motionless. Alive or dead, she'd been told to put a hood on him, so that is what she did. She checked the O2 flow, then stood up and looked around. The space behind the barricade was only about two meters deep. Across from the breach, above a data readout desk, a 15 cm-wide hole reached to open space. This wasn't a man-o-war, of course, so it didn't need a heavy skin, but still, there was plenty of debris in space, and radiation could be a problem near any star, so she was surprised a mere breaching charge could penetrate the hull, especially after blowing through the barricade first.

Her eyes dropped to the three bodies at her feet. She thought she'd have felt something more significant upon seeing a casualty of war. But she didn't feel much one way or the other.

"Hey, Boot. That was you firing your dunker through the firing port, right?" one of the Marines, a corporal, asked over the P2P.

Remembering falling back on her butt, she was tempted to say no, but the truth would out anyway, so she admitted it.

"Well, you zeroed this poor sucker," the corporal said, nudging one of the bodies with his foot.

"How do you know it was me?"

"Look," he said, using his foot to turn the body over.

Most of the pirate's chest was gone, from the collar to the bottom of the sternum. A few bright pieces of white bone showed through the red mess.

"That's not darts there. That there's dunker pellets."

"Really?" she asked, stepping forward for a closer look.

She knelt putting her face shield close to the mangled body.

He's right. Those are pellet hits. I killed this guy!

Where she had been complacent before, now a surge of excitement threatened to make her scream out in victory. Only moments before, the dead pirates were just so many hunks of meat. But now, she had a connection with one. She'd taken his life. It was personal. Some people probably thought she should be somber, reflecting some deep philosophical insights on the fragility of life.

She didn't give a flying fuck on that. She was pumped, pure and simple.

Her father had been a student of history, and one of his favorite quotes had been from a 21st Century, Old Reckoning, US Marine general.

The first time you blow someone away is not an insignificant event. That said, there are some assholes in the world who just need to be shot.

Esther had always thought the quote to be somewhat intriguing, but she'd never really put that much significance to it— until this moment. She was a blooded warrior now, she'd taken a life. This was a significant event, a rite of passage. Whatever self-doubts she'd had back on the *Gallipoli* had vanished in a puff of smoke. She was a combat Marine now.

She reached a gauntleted hand out and touched the bloody mess of what had been his chest. Bringing her finger to her EVA helmet, she touched her forehead, leaving a small red dot. "Blooding" like that was a trope in just about every military flick and novel ever made, but somehow, it felt right.

DX-4

Chapter 19

Noah

"Keep your alignment!" Staff Sergeant Primavera passed over the platoon net.

Noah's PICS subdued the platoon sergeant's voice to a normal level, but from the inflection, he could tell that the staff sergeant was screaming into his mic. Noah looked to his right and left. He was pretty much on line with the Marines on either side of him, so he didn't think the staff sergeant was singling him out. Still, he cut back a tiny bit, shortening his stride.

He was just happy to be in his PICS and actually maneuvering. Wayfarer Station was not really set up for PICS training. A Marine in a PICS was just too big for a good proportion of the station's passages. Up until now, the only training Noah had received in his PICS was in the mobile RCET. Unlike the huge RCET at Camp Charles, there was no actual maneuver taking place. The chamber was barely four meters square, so when Noah "walked" his PICS, it was over a sliding platform. From inside his PICS, it seemed like he was moving forward—that was the party line, at least. In reality, it felt like he was stuck on a slippery pillow. The high-end imaging was fine, but Noah had played in more than a few immersion games where movement seemed more realistic.

This, though, this was grubbing wicked. It was better than he'd imagined. He felt invincible as he trotted at 50 KPH along with the rest of the platoon in the movement to contact. Ten klicks up ahead, a squad from Alpha was waiting for them, and Noah uncharacteristically wanted nothing more than to kick their sorry asses.

DX-4, or "Dixie," was rapidly becoming Noah's favorite planet in the Federation. Sure, it was only in Phase 3 of terraforming. Sure, it only had a 10.4% O2 level in the atmosphere. But the wide-open spaces and lack of much of a population made it a playground for not only the battalion, but for all Marine units in this sector of space. With fewer than 3,000 terraforming techs on the planet and probably fewer than 100 buildings, that left a lot of room for Marines to train as they would.

It wasn't an easy slog for the foot infantry. The O2 level was the same as a simulated 5500 meters on Earth, which made it difficult to train, but not impossible. But for Marines in PICS or armor, that didn't make any difference.

The O2 projectors scattered around the planet were completely off-limits as were various forests and newly established grasslands, but that still left millions of square kilometers where they could maneuver, fire their weapons, or do just about anything they wanted. The Marines had two expeditionary camps on the planet, and both were usually occupied with units training.

Some Marines new to PICS had problems with coordinating their displays with jockeying their PICS; that wasn't a problem for Noah. Too much time gaming had at least prepared him for something worthwhile. He felt as if he'd been in a PICS all his life rather than his logged 10 hours actual, 14 simulated.

Thirty-nine PICS thundered over the rocky lowlands, a fighting force with more firepower than an Old Earth regiment. Noah was outfitted with the Combat Pack 1, which packed the least amount of punch, but "least" was relative. Pop him back in time to the Water Wars on Earth, and he could probably take on a tank company by himself.

On his display, he could see that Turtle and Tad were falling back, and sure enough, a moment later, the staff sergeant was on the comms again, yelping for them to catch back up. This far from the objective, it probably didn't make much of a difference, but they were there for training, and it was good to eliminate bad habits. If a Marine fell back, then he or she would have more limited fields of fire due to the Marines in front of him or her. It took a lot to knock out a PICS, but getting a friendly fire rocket up the ass by another Marine in the team could pretty much do it.

At Phase Line Pork Chop, First Squad, along with the staff sergeant, pivoted on its axis, switched to a squad V, and headed off towards the gully to the left. They were the enveloping force, ready to sweep down whatever defense the Alpha Company Marines had set. Second and Third Squads were to conduct a frontal assault. If they could sweep over the Alpha Marines, all the better. But if not, they were to pin down the aggressors until First Squad could crush them.

This was a full force-on-force. The weapons they fired were under-powered, but they functioned as if they were in full combat mode. The individual AIs would shut down a PICS if it determined it had taken enough simulated damage that it would have been knocked out in real-life situation. That wasn't going to happen to Noah, he vowed. He wasn't quite comfortable with the frontal assault—it seemed too much like the infantry battles of the 19th Century wars in Europe. But as they got within range of the aggressor force's weapons, they would begin team fire-and-maneuver, finally breaking down into individual fire-and-maneuver at about 500 meters out.

With First out of the line, the remaining two squads slowly spread out to keep the same frontage. They managed to shift surprisingly well, even without the staff sergeant haranguing them. Quickly, the range closed. At 6,000 meters, the Marines were within range of the opposing PICS armed with Combat Pack 2s, which had a HGL, firing a 20mm grenade instead of the Combat Pack 1's M901 Hypervelocity Rifle. With one CP2 per fire team, there should be three of them facing the platoon. The lieutenant, however, had chosen an avenue of approach that wound its way through a wash. They were effectively in defilade to the objective and should be until they reached 1,500 meters out.

Noah felt a rise of excitement as they closed the distance. They were like a tsunami, unstoppable in their righteous quest. They would roll over the Alpha Marines like so many plastiboard cutouts. He could taste the victory!

And then an explosion sounded just off to Noah's right. Immediately, the avatar for Turtle's PICS grayed out. He was KIA.

Shocked, Noah glanced over to his friend who'd evidently just triggered a mine of some sort. Turtle's PICS had come to the ready position and then stopped. He'd be stuck like that until after the battle when all the KIA Marines would be resurrected.

Without slowing down, Noah tried to scan the ground, but nothing was showing up. He hoped for a moment that the mine had been a one-off, but that hope was quashed when another explosion sounded to his left, and Sergeant Lewskorski was grayed out.

"Shift to Rose," the lieutenant passed.

Evidently, their approach had been too predictable, and the Alpha Company squad had mined it. The lieutenant switched them to a different avenue of approach, out on the higher ground. The problem with that was that at 4,200 meters out, they were well within range of the aggressor's weapons—but the aggressors were within range of their weapons, too.

The fire team on the far right climbed out of the wash, immediately went prone, and laid down covering fire for the rest of Second Squad as they rushed out. A PICS was not particularly suited to be prone—it was designed for closing with and destroying the enemy, and to go prone, the servo-gyro had to be cut-off. This was one area in which Noah hadn't quite got down yet. Timing had to be perfect, both for going prone and rising back up. If the servo-gyro was cut too late, the "dive" to the prone would be more of a stumble and loss of momentum, and that could be lethal on the battlefield. Cutting it off too early left the Marine vulnerable to being knocked off his or her feet.

The wash was almost five meters deep. As Noah approached it, he flexed and jumped, hitting the assist. Once again, this required timing and finesse. Noah just wanted to clear the edge of the wash. Jumping too high made him a target. To his relief, he barely cleared the edge and was immediately running with the other three—no, two now with Turtle down—to get past Second Squad and turn back towards the objective.

His display was alight with weapons trails. The aggressors had them under fire, and they were firing back. His PICS AI gave him the near miss alarm, and Noah felt his heart jump, but the AI kept him in the fight.

Each PICS was in "LSD-mode." It was almost impossible to hide a PICS from observation. But the fractured-array made it difficult to focus on an individual PICS, whether from eyesight or sensors. In his father's day, a fractured-array merely "bent" the lights waves. Now, not only were the waves distorted, but 50 times a second, the array shifted, which sent spoofing images randomly up to five meters to either side. The enemy's AIs were in a continual battle to anticipate where the PICS actually were as the Marines assaulted. Energy weapons could envelope the entire area, of course, but at this distance, even in the light atmosphere of DX-4, the beams would be too dissipated to damage a PICS. At this range, a PICS needed to be hit with a kinetic weapon to be taken out.

"Down in three. . .two. . .one!" Corporal Viejas passed.

Noah blinked his gyro release just as he launched himself forward. He hit the dirt hard and bounced once, almost turning over. Thrusting out an arm, he managed to keep himself belly down. Immediately, he brought up his M901, looking for a target. He caught an energy bloom of a rocket being fired from a shoulder launcher, so he returned fire at the spot. Whether he hit anyone or not, he wouldn't know until the debrief, but he at least hoped he was keeping someone's head down.

He fired twice more before the corporal passed, "Up in three. . .two. . .one!"

Noah brought his knees up under him and with the little hitch-jump he'd been taught, pushed forward, blinking the servo-gyro just as he extended his legs. If he pushed up too low, the gyro would fail to catch, and he'd be out of control for a few moments. This was the first time he'd tried it while under pressure, and for a moment, he thought he screwed up, but with an almost palpable groaning, the servo-gyro managed to right him, and only a step behind the others, he was running forward again.

One after another, four fellow Marines were knocked out, which was more than Noah would have imagined. Twice more, Noah's team went prone to give covering fire, and each time, Noah was smoother in both going down and getting back up. The distance was closing, and Noah's AI was finally beginning to detect the enemy. At least two were KIA, and probably more. Any moment, Noah expected to see First Squad sweep in from the right, rolling through the aggressor position.

"Prepare for individual rushes," the lieutenant passed.

Noah was in the middle of this team, so when they bounded forward, he didn't have to worry as much as to where other Marines were. Now, about to shift to individual rushes, he had to be more cognizant of where he was with relationship to others. Each Marine's AI should keep them from friendly fire, but that had been known to fail, and even without getting hit by one of his platoon, he could mask one and keep him or her from firing by being out of position.

Suddenly, within five seconds, three Marines were KIA, including the lieutenant. Noah's AI screamed an alarm, one that took Noah a few moments to recognize. He spun in the direction indicated by the big yellow avatars, and there, rushing out of a bunch of razor grass, were the battalion's three Mambas.

That's not fair! Noah thought just before his world flashed bright, and his AI shut him down.

Grubbing hell! I can't believe it.

His PICS slowly came to the ready position. Noah tentatively tried to kick out a leg, but nothing doing. He was a prisoner in his own combat unit.

At least he had a good view of the remainder of the battle. The assault tanks, sleek sharks, tore up the battle space as the two squads scattered. One of the tanks sped past Noah, only five meters in front of him, its big gun flashing. He knew the tank's AI would keep it from running over any Marines, but still, he flinched. He had to acknowledge, though, that the Mamba looked wicked fierce.

Within two minutes, the tanks, combined with the remainder of the aggressor squad, wiped up the First Platoon squads. They wheeled and roared off to engage Third Squad. Noah couldn't turn to watch, but he could follow the battle on his display. To his surprise, Third Squad managed to take out one Mamba, but with the aggressor squad leaving their positions to join the tanks, the battle was a foregone conclusion. Twenty-two minutes after Noah was KIA, the battle was over. Third Platoon had lost.

Noah's PICS came back to life, and all Marines were directed to the objective for an initial debrief. Third Platoon had to endure some catcalls from the lone Alpha Company Squad as they marched up, but Noah ignored them. His eyes were on the three tanks that swept up, each pulling a half donut to form a line facing the PICS Marines. A moment later, the hatches opened, one after the other, and the grinning faces of the tank commanders popped up.

While growing up, Noah had attended more than a few birthday pageants and Patron Day celebrations, and he'd always taken an interest in the tanks and aircraft, which to a small boy and then young man were infinitely more interesting that massed Marines in formation. He'd never imagined enlisting the Corps, though, and have to deal with them. At the moment, Noah was royally pissed that he'd been killed, but he had to admit, the Mambas were grubbing cool.

WAYFARER STATION

Chapter 20

Esther

"Congratulations, Ess," Noah said, coming up to shake Esther's hand.

"I've told you, no one calls me that anymore," she said, more than a little annoyed.

"Well, I'm not calling you 'Lysander,'" he said. "I wouldn't know which one of us I was talking to. Anyway, it looks good. Dad would be proud."

Esther felt a warm glow rush through her chest. Noah still raised uncomfortable feelings within her that she still couldn't figure out, but he knew how to get to her. She looked down at the Battle Commendation 3 on her chest. It wasn't much of an award, being the lowest combat medal. The Navy and Marine Corps Achievement Medal was the only lower personal award, and that was given for meritorious non-combat related service. With two Federation Novas, their father sported a far more prestigious chest. Still, she hoped Noah was right. She'd like to think her father would be proud of her.

Three Marines had received an award for the retaking of the *Excavator King*. Lieutenant Uluiviva had been awarded a BC2, posthumously, and Lance Corporal Greg O'Brien-Tasker had been awarded a BC3. When Esther had found out she was being awarded the BC3, too, she'd been dumbfounded. All she had done was stick her M333 up against a firing slit and blasted off a round. In the back of her mind, she wondered if politics had anything to do with it, her father being who he was. The Marines were supposed to be above politics, but being a Lysander, she'd seen enough to realize that wasn't exactly the case.

The recovery of the *Excavator King* had not been a major operation. It probably hadn't made much of a mention back on Earth or even Tarawa. But there had been three reporters and a camcorderman at the ceremony, one from the Australian News Agency, so the Corps could get some press. The Lysander name was still newsworthy.

For the battalion, the operation had a much greater impact. With the lieutenant KIA, two Marines WIA and CASEVAC'd to Malika for regen, and two more walking wounded WIA who stayed on station, the recovery mission had resulted in its highest casualty rate during a mission in almost three years. The scuttlebutt was that the CO and the Navy Squadron CO had some very pointed discussions on when the Marines needed to be deployed and when the Navy could simply stand off and take care of a situation.

"Well, thanks, Noah. I'd like to think he'd be proud, too."

"Hey, Lysander, looking good!" Woowoo said, making his way around the civilian mess attendants who were trying to turn the messhall back from a battalion formation to a serving space for the rest of the festivities.

Of course, "battalion formation" was an overstatement. Wayfarer Station did not boast an area large enough for the entire battalion to stand in formation, except for maybe the commercial maintenance hangar, and the management would not be too conducive to emptying that out of ships just so the Marines could stand tall. The awards ceremony was conducted in the messhall, with only the company and the headquarters staff standing in the cleared area. The rest of the battalion watched from their quarters. And now, with the Patron Day activities still to conduct, the mess attendants were rushing to get the meal ready.

"Thanks, Woowoo. It's just a BC 3, though." She looked up at her brother, who was slowly backing up, his face an expressionless mask. 'Uh, Woowoo, do you know my brother?"

"Sure, I know who he is. Noah, right?" Woowoo said, holding out a hand.

"That's right. You're PFC Woutou. I've heard about you," Noah said.

"It's all a lie, I promise you!" Woowoo said with a laugh. "I never even kissed that girl!"

Noah looked confused, so Esther said, "He's joking, Noah. Just joking."

"Oh, OK. Well, uh, I've got to get back to my company. We've got the parade in a few," Noah said as he backed up farther. "Nice meeting you," he said to Woowoo.

"I bet he's fun at a party," Woowoo said as Noah made his way out of the messhall.

Esther understood that Noah could seem like a stick-in-the-mud, but she suddenly felt defensive.

"Oh, he's OK. It just takes a bit of time to get to know him."

"That's not what I'm hearing from some of the others. He's a little full of himself, at least that's the skinny."

Full of himself? Noah? No way.

She wondered how Noah could give anyone that impression. If there was anyone who wasn't full of himself, it was her brother.

The rest of the platoon crowded around her, offering their congrats, and she quickly pushed Noah out of her mind. She happily accepted her due from the others. She regretted the lieutenant's death, and she felt for the two Marines going through regen. However, the operation had done her well. She'd immediately lost the "boot" label after the fight and been accepted as a competent, capable Marine. And now with the BC3, she had that affirmation. Still, she kept telling the other Marines that it was nothing, that she didn't deserve it.

I guess we are all politicians when it gets down to it, she thought wryly.

She might tell the others it was nothing, but she was damned proud of it all the same. She posed with Greg O'Brien-Tasker, she posed with the company commander. When the battalion XO escorted the ANA newsies to meet her, she ended up posing with the battalion CO and sergeant major. The ANA team was on hand to cover the Patron Day celebrations, but they were more than willing to record General Lysander's daughter making good.

"PFC Lysander, if you can tell all the Aussies back on the homeworld and scattered through human space, do you think your father would be proud of you?" the reporter, whose name she'd never caught, asked.

"I hope he would be proud of me for being a Marine," she told him. "Yes, today, I was honored to receive this Battle Commendation 3, but I was simply doing my duty. I accepted it today only as a representative of my platoon, each of whom could just as easily been awarded it. All of my fellow Marines showed exceptional courage, and one, our leader, Lieutenant Uluiviva, paid the ultimate sacrifice."

I hope I didn't lay it on too thick.

"This is a memorable day for the Roos," the reporter said, facing his camcorderman. "Making the Aussie universe proud. And I'm personally proud to be here with PFC Esther Lysander, daughter of the late General and Chairman Ryck Lysander. She's been serving for only a very short time, and already she's distinguished herself in combat. Her father, of course, was only one of two two-time recipients of the Federation Nova, and before he was the Chairman of the Federation Council, he was the Commandant of the Marine Corps. Who knows? Maybe like father, like daughter?"

Esther, ever aware that the camcorderman was still recording, kept her face still. This was the first time she'd heard anyone else voice the goal she'd set for herself after her parents were murdered.

General Esther Lysander, Commandant of the Marine Corps, had such a nice ring to it.

Chapter 21

Noah

Noah slowly backed away from his sister as her platoon-mates came up to congratulate her. He felt a growing certainty that something had come between them, something he couldn't quite understand. It had started at Camp Charles, and while he'd hoped things would get back to normal at Wayfarer, her "no one calls me Ess" comment seemed to be an attempt by her to cut off her past.

What does she expect me to call her? She's been "Ess" ever since we both could speak.

He'd been only half-joking when he'd told her he wasn't going to call her "Lysander," as it seemed the rest of the Marines had adopted. Not "Esther," not another nickname, but as if she'd inherited the family legacy, simply "Lysander."

Noah, on the other hand, was simply "Noah." A few, mostly more senior Marines had approached him to mention serving with his father, but for the most part, his peers either didn't know or ignored that aspect of his background. For the most part, that was fine with him; however, a small piece of him was jealous that his sister was considered the heir to the Lysander name while he was seemingly cut off.

He turned and left the messhall. He hadn't been lying when he'd told Esther he had to get ready. He'd been given permission to attend her awards ceremony in person, but the company would now be getting ready for the parade, and First Platoon was going mounted. The Marines couldn't very well run their vehicles through the station, so the PICS would serve to represent the power of a Marine infantry battalion.

With the Marines and the rest of the station living in such close quarters, the Patron Day celebration, along with the Marine Corps-wide birthday pageant and ball and the Remembrance Day ceremonies, was a time for public relations, to share with the civilians and Navy what it meant to be a Marine. But there was also a warning in there. Some of the civilians at the station at any given time were criminals, pure and simple. Some could be plotting against Federation worlds or installations. It was also a good idea to remind all of the people at the station of the Marines' fighting capabilities, capabilities that could be unleashed should the call come up.

"'Bout time you got here," Tad said as Noah rushed into the four-man berthing space.

"I needed to wait until you guys were already in your long johns before I got here. I don't need your fat ass in my face while I'm dressing."

"You'd better hurry. We're the last squad to get suited up."

Noah was only a little disappointed that his jibe was evidently considered too weak for a response. He'd thought it was a good one when he'd come up with it the week before and was only waiting for a time to unleash it. Their small compartment was narrow, with barely enough room for all four of them to stand and do anything at the same time, so it had only been a matter of time when the situation would come up.

His three roommates left, leaving Noah to strip and change. A few minutes later, he was hurrying to the PICS closet. He needn't have worried. Not only was the squad lined up outside, Second Squad hadn't even entered. Noah joined the end of the queue and waited. Up ahead of him, Mayhem was huddled with Lance Corporal Omaru, the same Omaru who'd come aboard the with Noah and with whom he'd gotten fitted with his PICS. Mayhem was, well Princess Mayhem, one of the guys. Omaru, though, was in Second Squad, and the long johns left absolutely nothing to the imagination. And with nobody talking to him, his own imagination took flight. Noah was not a complete negat—he'd had a few girlfriends before, one from school and the other two fellow gamers. That didn't mean he was some sort of Don Juan, though, and he knew Omaru was out of his league. Still, it was hard not to let certain thoughts enter his mind as he took in her figure.

"You here with us, Noah?" Turtle asked.

"Uh, what?" he stammered out, suddenly embarrassed at the direction of this thoughts.

"I asked you if you're coming with us to the Alibi after the ceremony and chow, but you're off in lala land."

"What? The Alibi? OK, yeah," he answered, sure his face was turning red.

He kept his eyes averted as the line moved up, and ten minutes later, he was in the rack, sliding into his PICS. He was getting to be a pro at it. Within 15 seconds, quicker than even some of the smaller guys and gals, he was inside and initiating his boot-up. Thirty more seconds, he was stepping off the platform and stepping out of the closet, following handwritten signs to the receiving dock where most of the 78 PICS Marines were waiting for the signal to move out.

The parade had been a tradition since before the Evolution. It wasn't long—most of the station's corridors and passages were simply too small to accommodate a battalion of straight-leg Marines, much less two platoons in PICS, as they marched through. So the route left the battalion area, entered Alamagordy Boulevard (the station's main passage), around the restaurant district, then up and back each of the station's four main terminals. All told, the parade route was about five klicks long.

At 1500, the color guard led off the parade—not that Noah or any of the other PICS Marines could see. They waited in the loading bay, watching the progress on one of the monitors.

Headquarters Company, with the battalion staff, followed, then Alpha—minus their PICS platoon, came up next. Bravo was next in line, and Noah zoomed his view to see if he could spot Esther. But either he missed her or the monitor just didn't have the resolution for him to spot her.

As Charlie Company started out, Alpha's Second Platoon left the PICS assembly area. The route from the loading bay into the main passage was slightly convoluted, so they were moving before Weapons Company and the arty, tank, and air detachments began to move. And right on Second Platoon's asses, Noah's own platoon started moving out.

Noah resisted ducking as he left the loading bay and entered the first passage. He knew the top of his PICS was just under the overhead, and he had to shuffle along, almost scraping his feet along the deck as he moved forward. After a couple of twists and turns, he passed through the final hatch out onto Alamagordy. Second Platoon was just stepping off as Noah rushed into position. They'd be marching four abreast through the course of the parade.

Noah was focusing on taking his position of the right side of his rank of four. It wasn't until they actually stepped forward into the parade that he realized the route was packed with people. They were lined five or six deep, and all cheering. Some were waving Federation flags; some were even waving Australian flags.

"Yepper! They love us now!" Tad passed on the team circuit. "Think I can score tonight with some lovely honeywa?"

"Keep off the circuit, Tad," Corporal Inca Saint Fyodor, Noah's team leader passed from her position on the left side of their rank. "You never know who's listening in."

He's right, though. They do love us! Noah thought, surprised at the turnout.

Someone slapped him on the arm as he marched, which did nothing to impede his progress, but still surprised him. Noah turned to look where a burly man, his face red with the effects of too much alcohol, gave him a thumbs up with one hand while sloshing a cup of beer with the other.

All of the Marines' parades, save one, that Noah had seen before had been formal affairs, out on a parade deck while spectators sat in bleachers. The one more "normal" parade had been at a Founder's Day celebration where the Marines had joined others to march down the middle of a city street. Nowhere had he seen the, well, jubilation, it seemed to him, that he saw now.

The common perception among the Marines in the battalion was that the civilians on the station were ambivalent to the Marines at best, hostile at worst. More often than should be, Marines and civvies knocked heads together at the station's night spots. What he was seeing now belied that.

Some of the Marines in front of him were waving, at the crowds. It probably wasn't proper—they were in a formation after all, but Noah tentatively waved once, then again. Pretty soon, he was in full beauty queen mode.

"This is grubbing cool as all git-out," he told Turtle on the P2P.

"This is only me second Patron Day here, and yeah, it gets good. We might not even have to pay for a single drink tonight."

"Is that why you picked the Alibi?"

The Alibi was a large, mostly civilian bar, not one Marines usually hung out in.

"Damned right it is. Can't get free drinks if there're only a bunch of jarheads there now, right?"

"Good thinking. That's why this poor boot bows to your experience," Noah said, only half-joking.

"You'll learn Boot, you'll learn."

Technically, Noah wasn't even the platoon boot anymore. Private Padam Bhandry, "Pad-Man," had only joined the platoon three weeks before (and already had a nickname). Noah was even due to be promoted to PFC on the first. But Turtle was the closest he had to a friend, and Noah knew he wasn't serious.

They reached the far side of Alamagordy and looped through the restaurant district. If it was possible, even more of the spectators looked deep into their cups. All were excited, though, all cheering. One little boy, no more than five years old, rushed out, and Noah had to stop to keep from crushing the little guy. The boy slapped his leg as Kyle Montree almost crashed into him from behind.

"Hi!" he said, hands clasped together as he looked up at Noah.

"Hi," Noah replied, first over the platoon circuit before realizing his mistake, and repeating it after turning on his exterior speakers.

He slowly lowered his huge gauntlet fist, which the boy happily fist-bumped before running back to his parents at the side of the route.

"Get going, Noah," Kyle passed on the P2P.

Kyle and Second Team were the second to last rank, with Third Team bringing up the rear of the battalion. Noah hurried a few steps to catch up, but he wasn't too concerned with interrupting the entire parade. He wasn't going to risk stomping on a little kid, after all.

The rest of the parade was more of the same. There were fewer people along the terminals, but still, there seemed to be more spectators than total residents of the station. At each terminal, as the platoon marched out to the end, Noah could see the front of the battalion as it doubled back, and twice he spotted Esther. He waved each time, but she probably couldn't tell him from any of the other PICS Marines.

Forty minutes after starting out, Noah was filing back to the loading bay with the other Marines. He was frankly exhilarated. He hadn't thought much about the parade, but it had exceeded any expectations he might have had. Their boisterous reception had been better than anything he'd seen before.

Along with the rest of the platoon, he had to wait in the loading bay for quite a while as Second Platoon molted, which was only fair as they'd had to stand around and wait while his platoon had suited up. Noah normally felt a small pang of regret when he molted, but this time, he didn't give it a second thought as he slid out and the arms took his PICS back into storage.

He gave Turtle a high-five and listened to Tad explain to anyone who would pay attention to him on how many women along the route had caught his eye, propositioning him. They still had the speeches and the dinner, and there would be the beating, at which the battalions with Anglo patrons made extreme efforts to excel, but Charlie Company was in the second seating, listening to the speeches and watching the beating over the monitors.

Beatings were pretty copacetic, Noah knew, what with the pounding of the drums, and some battalion drum corps put on some amazing shows. Listening to the bigwigs ramble on, however, was probably better endured in their berthing spaces. What excited Noah now was after all the official ceremonies, getting out into town. If today's reception to their parade were any indication, then maybe tonight would be even better.

He wanted to see if Turtle was right. He didn't drink much as a habit, but whatever he did drink would be so much better if some friendly civilian was buying!

Chapter 22

Esther

"Lysander," the first sergeant needs to see you," Sergeant Orinda said, poking her head into their berthing space.

"Do you know what for?" she asked, looking up from where she was cleaning her M99.

"Not a clue. Go ahead and stow your weapon, though. I got the impression from him that you might be awhile."

She looked down at her skivvy shirt. Weapons cleaning could be a little messy, and her shirt was blotched with polyblack.

"Yeah, better change that first," the sergeant said before ducking back out.

"Brown-nose," Vixen half-coughed, half-said.

"Fuck you, too," Esther replied without any real rancor.

She wondered why the first sergeant wanted to see her. She'd barely had four words with the man and never one-on-one. She whipped off her skivvy shirt, rolling it into a ball, and throwing it in her laundry bag. Pulling out a new one, she slipped it on, then put on her utility blouse. After a quick check in the mirror, she smoothed her short hair, grabbed her rifle, and opened the hatch.

"Say hello to the first sergeant from me," Vixen said.

Esther lifted her hand behind her, middle finger extended, as the hatch closed. Two minutes later, she was turning in her weapon, although she had to convince the armorer to take it, promising to come back and finish her cleaning.

Another four minutes, and she was standing tall outside the first sergeant's office. She knocked at the hatch, and a deep, gravelly voice shouted out "Enter!"

First Sergeant Parker was a whippet-thin Marine, supposedly able to run for hours, not that he had much chance to show that off on the station. Esther thought he looked almost like a rat, with a long-drawn-out face. His chest, when he wore his Charlies or Alphas, spoke of a very busy, very notable career, with two Silver Stars and a host of lesser awards. Now, in his utility trou and skivvy shirt, he didn't look the part.

"Take a seat, Lysander. I'll be wit you in a sec."

The first sergeant had a clipped way of speaking, the "wit you" just one example. Esther would have thought a first sergeant would have a better command of the language, but then she remembered his two Silver Stars. She had a feeling that many people over the years might have underestimated him, and they probably regretted it.

He was staring at his screen, so Esther looked around the office. He had a pretty impressive I Love Me wall, with plaques and pics. One caught her eye, and she leaned forward to get a better look.

"Aye-ah. That be your pa, after Yakima 4."

Esther stood up and moved closer. It was her father, then a colonel. Yakima 4 was where he'd stopped the Klethos, and a young Sergeant Parker was standing tall while her father pinned a Bronze Star on his chest.

"Good man, your pa."

She sat back down, wishing she could ask what he'd done to earn the Bronze Star, and had her father merely pinned it on him, or had he been more involved with the specific action. She knew a lot about her father, of course. There had to be a dozen books written about him, and there were the three Hollybolly flicks. He had told the three of them—Ben, Noah and her—stories, too. But Esther had not heard too much about him from his fellow Marines, what they thought of him as a peer or as a commander. And she yearned to know. He was her father, her hero, able to do nothing wrong. Was that even close to an accurate picture of him?

She straightened up in her seat, hands on her knees. To her disgust, she could feel a lump in her throat, and her eyes started to moisten.

Get it together, Esther!

She barely heard the muffled voice coming from the first sergeant's PA, but he responded, "I got her here now. We'll be down in a tic.

"Lysander, we're going to da CP now. The skipper's dere wit da CO."

"Uh, what for, First Sergeant? Did I do anything wrong?" she blurted out.

"No, nothin' wrong. The CO, he, well, I'll let him say."

He seemed to contemplate her, wondering if he should say something more. Esther looked at him expectantly as he opened his mouth, closed it, then opened it again.

"Look, PFC Lysander, you're OK. You got what it takes. But you ain't dere yet."

"Pardon me, First Sergeant?" Esther asked, confused.

"Sergeant Orinda an' Staff Sergeant Czyżewski," he said, using the Staff Sergeant Ski's full name. "Dey say you're doin' good, dat you got a future in da Corps. But you got a ways to go, Marine. You need to be tempered still."

Of course, I need to be "tempered," she thought. That's what I'm doing now, aren't I?

"If da high 'n mighty are noticing you, that might be intriguing, if you know what I mean. And for someone like you wit big plans, it might seem like a shortcut."

Am I that obvious? she wondered.

As slow as the first sergeant might seem with his speaking style, Esther realized that not much got past him. His awards spoke volumes as to his skill and courage, but Esther thought there was also a very sharp mind hidden behind his rat face.

"Just remember, you need more time in da trenches."

"What's this about, First Sergeant, if I can ask?"

"Not up to me to say," he said as he put on his blouse. "Let's go."

All of the company and battalion offices were in "Command Alley," so it took less than a minute to reach the sergeant major's office. First Sergeant Parker didn't knock and just entered. Esther had flashbacks to Camp Charles and being called in with Noah before seeing the battalion commander, and she felt the first tendrils of nervousness snake their way into her psyche. She still didn't know what was going on, and the first sergeant's little speech had her on edge.

"PFC Lysander, thanks for coming," the sergeant major said.

As if I had a choice.

"The CO wants to talk to you," he said, offering nothing else.

About what? About what?

"Sir, I've got PFC Lysander here. Are you ready?" he spoke aloud.

"Thanks, Sergeant Major. Please, send her in," the CO's voice filled the room.

The sergeant major started out, motioning Esther to follow. When the first sergeant started to follow as well, the sergeant major waved him back.

The commanding officer's office was next to the sergeant major's, so Esther barely had time to compose herself before the sergeant major was knocking on the jamb of the hatch, announcing, "Sir, PFC Lysander," then telling her, "Report to the CO."

Esther drew herself up into a position of attention, then marched in, centering herself on the CO's desk, saying, "Private First Class Lysander, reporting as ordered, sir!"

Esther had lived her life around colonels and generals. She was on a first-name basis with more than a few flag ranks. Before she enlisted, she would barely have noticed a lieutenant colonel.

How things had changed.

Lieutenant Colonel Oscar de Hugh was not a particularly menacing individual, and his reputation was not that of a hard-ass, yet Esther couldn't control the trembling in her legs. This was her commanding officer, and he literally had life-and-death power over her. He might as well have been a god.

"Stand at ease," he said in a pleasant voice, which did nothing to calm her trembling.

"PFC Lysander, I've been talking with Captain Mikhailov."

It was only then that Esther noticed her company commander sitting there, along with the battalion XO.

"You've performed quite well in the battalion, quite well. Your BC3 attests to your combat instincts, but beyond that, you've exhibited leadership abilities, yes, leadership, that go beyond your rank. That probably can be expected, given your pedigree. Expected."

Where is all of this going? Esther wondered, more than a little confused.

"You've already earned a degree, from an old Earth university, none-the-less." He looked over at Captain Mikhailov and added, "I only received mine from Sunset."

Sunset University was one of mankind's largest off-campus schools, very popular in the military as sailors and Marines could enroll and take classes no matter where they were stationed.

"We, that is Captain Mikhailov, Major Westmoreland, and I are making an assumption, an assumption that you have aspirations, given your pedigree. Are we correct?"

Esther stared at the CO. This was not what she'd been expecting, and she wasn't sure what she should say. Of course, she had "aspirations." Who wouldn't? But she didn't want to come across as arrogant, or worse, as someone riding her father's reputation. That last "give your pedigree" could be a loaded statement. But, she couldn't deny her ambition, so she decided truth was best.

"Yes, sir. I have certain aspirations for my career."

He beamed at her and said, "Of course, of course. And that includes getting commissioned."

The CO wasn't specifically asking her a question, so she remained silent.

"And that's why I've called you here. You've proven yourself in combat. You've shown leadership tendencies. You've already earned your degree. I—we—think you're ready. I'd like to bring you to H&S. You'll be one of my clerks, and I want you to observe how the command structure works. The command staff is a well-oiled, a well-oiled machine, something those in the rifle squads don't realize. If you're going to be a success as an officer, you need to understand the intricacies of the process.

"You'll serve with me here, as an intern, so-to-speak, until. . .Major Westmorland, what class would it be?"

"83-3, sir."

"Yes, 83-3, 83-3, which forms up in February. That gives us time to get in the paperwork, and you can start the next phase of your career. And next June, you'll be commissioned as a second lieutenant.

The CO stood in front of her, a huge smile on his face, as he waited for her to respond.

Esther felt a rush of excitement. Of course, she wanted to be commissioned—she just thought it would take more time in the trenches. And to have it offered to her on a platter like this was more than surprising; it was simply astounding. She really didn't think she was qualified yet, that she had paid her dues.

She wasn't qualified, though, she quickly realized. Sure, she'd been in combat, but she had hardly "proven herself." All she had proved was that she didn't run away in fear and that she could trigger an M333. Despite her BC3, that was all she'd proven. And as far as leadership, that was pure BS. She was still a PFC, soon to be a lance corporal, but far from being an NCO. She had no real leadership experience—choosing what flick she and her friends were going to watch on a Sunday afternoon did not qualify.

Esther knew she had it in her. She knew in her heart that she would make a great NCO. But knowing she had the capacity and learning how to be a leader and acting as one were not the same thing.

She yearned to agree with the CO. He was standing there, waiting for a response. He looked positively eager. But why? Did he think that recommending the daughter of Ryck Lysander would reflect on him?

She blinked several times as if she could erase that thought from her mind. She was being unfair. Politics were undoubtedly part of the equation. He wasn't offering this to Vixen, after all, who had seven more months in the battalion than she had. But he had to think she was qualified. Sending her to NSA Annapolis only to wash out wouldn't reflect well on his judgment, and, yes, given her "pedigree," some might blame him for "wasting" her potential.

Esther wanted to say yes. It would be so easy just to say yes and bypass years of experience.

I could learn leadership as a lieutenant, after all, she thought, trying to convince herself that the shortcut would be feasible.

Shortcut!

The first sergeant had warned her about taking a shortcut. He had known what was going to be offered, and without overtly coming out against what the CO was offering, he'd let her know his opinion.

And he was right, Esther realized. She wasn't ready. The most beautiful blade made by master swordsmiths would shatter like glass if swung too early, before the process was finished. It had to be tempered, just as the first sergeant had said. Esther knew she was the blade, made from the finest steels and full of potential. But she also knew she wasn't ready. In order to realize that potential, she needed more time and experience.

She took a deep breath and said, "Sir, I am humbly honored by your confidence in me, but I have to respectfully decline."

His eyes clouded over, and she hurriedly added, "It's not that I don't want a commission. You are right, sir, I do want one. But I think I need more time. I'm not even an NCO, and if I want to be the best I can be, to best serve the Corps and Federation, I need that experience from which to draw.

"After all, sir, my father was a sergeant before he was commissioned, and it seemed to work out pretty well for him."

That last was a cheap shot, she knew. But he'd used her "pedigree" on her, and she thought it fair to throw it back. She waited for his response. He was her CO, after all, and she couldn't afford to have him as an enemy. That could forever destroy her future in the Corps.

The CO stood there, eyes furrowed, and when his eyebrows relaxed, Esther let out the breath she'd been holding.

"I think you are ready, PFC, and your reasoning for not accepting only goes to prove I'm correct. Your maturity far surpasses your age and current rank. Far surpasses. But I will honor your decision. Let's revisit this in a year or so, after you gain the experiences you think you require. So, I am not taking your response as a refusal, but merely a request to postpone a decision. Does that meet with your approval?"

Relief swept through her. She'd managed to tiptoe through a potential minefield and come out relatively unscathed.

"Yes, sir. Thank you, sir."

"Well, then, PFC Lysander. I'll release you back to Bravo where you can gain experience. I'll keep my eyes on you, though. Dismissed."

"Thank you, sir," Esther said, coming to attention before performing an about face and marching out of the office.

Did I make the right decision? I could have gotten commissioned, but if I fuck up now somehow, that chance could be gone forever.

First Sergeant Parker was waiting in the passage. He looked up as the sergeant major merely said, "Back to Bravo."

"Let's go, Lysander," he said, the beginnings of a smile ever-so-slightly creasing the corner of his mouth.

Chapter 23

Noah

The "skeeter wings"—the single chevron of his new rank's insignia—on Noah's collar felt heavy. He thought everyone had to be noticing them. He was inordinately proud of them, despite the fact that his promotion had been simply due to time-in-grade. There hadn't even been a real ceremony. The company had filled Classroom A, and after a short lecture on the status of the company and the upcoming month's general training schedule, several Marines were awarded their Good Conduct Medals, five were given hash marks, and Turtle, Noah, and two other Marines were promoted: Turtle and the other three to lance corporal, Noah to private first class. Now, with ten privates in the company, Noah finally outranked someone.

"No more 'boot,' eh Turtle?" Noah said after the officers and SNCO's shook their hands.

"You'll always be a boot to me, Boot." Turtle said. "I'm Old Corps, dontcha know."

"Yeah, real Old Corps," Noah said, reaching out with his hand. "Congrats, lance coolie."

"You, too, PFC. You owe us a pitcher at the E-club tonight."

"Hey, you do, too. And you've got the big E3 paycheck."

"I guess you're right. OK, you buy one, and I'll buy one."

"No way. You're my senior non-rate. You need to lead by example. You buy first, then I'll buy."

Turtle laughed, then said, "OK, OK. You win. See you tonight after chow. I've got to go call the wife now, show off my new bling."

Turtle was one of the few junior Marines in the company who was married. It wasn't technically against regs, but the Corps made it difficult. Until a Marine made sergeant, spouses were not allowed to accompany their Marines, nor did the Corps provide housing or a marriage allowance. Not that it mattered much on the station. Orders to 1/16 were always unaccompanied, even for the battalion CO. Some Marines brought their spouses to the Station, but that was on their own dime, and life on the station was not cheap.

Turtle was not only married, but he had a kid, a year-old son. Noah couldn't imagine being married and living apart from his wife. He'd seen first-hand how much it sucked. His mother was a strong woman, but with his father gone so often, things had been difficult, both for her and the kids.

Not that there was anything like that on Noah's horizon. He hadn't even been on a date since enlisting, and while a few fellow Marines had caught his eye, like Omaru, he probably wouldn't have the nerve to approach any of them even if someone had expressed any interest.

"OK, tell her 'hi' from me."

Noah had never met Turtle's wife, not even to chat over the comms, but it seemed like the thing to say.

Uh, well, I'm going to the exchange to get my chevrons. You want me to pick up yours?" he asked Turtle.

"Nah, no need. I'll pick them up later."

Noah left the front of the classroom, thanked a few other Marines who congratulated him, and headed out of the training wing, making his way down two decks, past the library and chapel, to the small base exchange. It really wasn't much of one as exchanges went. Noah had spent more than half of his life patronizing the huge main exchange on Tarawa, and while transiting to Earth, had twice visited the huge Navy exchange at Station 1, so large and wonderful that it was simply called "Nirvana" by everyone in the military or FCDC.

The small battalion exchange didn't even have a name; the sign at the hatch simply said "Exchange."

Inside, there was a limited selection of personal necessities as well and civilian clothing, electronics, and gift items. The selection was limited, but the prices were the same as back at Nirvana, kept that way by regulations. This meant that shaving cream and skivvies were cheaper than out in the station economy. A third of the exchange was taken up with military gear, though, both issue and non-issue. Noah went to the left side and up against the bulkhead where the medals and insignia were. His eyes barely lingered over the purple and gold BC3 medals—after Esther had been awarded hers, he had picked one up out of the rack, wondering what it would be like to wear one on his uniform. Now, he barely gave the medals a second thought. Instead, he went right to the insignia. He picked up three sets, then two sets of the larger shoulder chevrons. The gold chevron on the red background would go on both his Alphas and his Dress Blues, two uniforms he hadn't even worn yet. He'd wear the Blues at the Marine Corps Birthday in two months, but he doubted he'd wear the Alphas before he'd hopefully pick up lance corporal. He considered simply not buying the second set and skipping the Alphas, but better safe than sorry.

Noah made his way back to the cashier, a young civilian who was buried in her PA. She didn't seem to notice Noah until he plopped down his rank insignia.

Most stores at the station didn't even have cashiers anymore. Purchases were selected and carried out. The scanners would note the item and automatically deduct the payment from the purchaser's account. The Marine Corps, though, in keeping with Federal policy to increase employment, hired people to do some of these mundane tasks. Noah couldn't imagine sitting in back of a reader for however many hours a day, but if it paid the bills, he figured it was worth it.

The young lady picked up the insignia and passed them over the scanner, not looking up at Noah.

"I just got promoted," he said, just to break the silence."

"That's good," she replied, obviously not meaning it.

It was hard to tell as she was sitting down, but Noah didn't think she topped 150 cm. Her short strawberry blonde hair framed her round, freckled face, making it difficult for Noah to place her age. She looked up while Noah was staring at her, and he immediately dropped his gaze.

That was when he noticed her nametag, which read, M. Seek Grace.

"Are you a Torritite?" his asked, his surprise overcoming his normal shyness.

She looked up at him, her eyes guarded, as she said, "You're not allowed to ask about religion, sir. My performance is the only thing that matters here."

Shit! She thinks I'm prejudiced!

"No, I'm not meaning anything. It's just, I didn't think I'd find any Torritites way out here, and well, I know your name, it's, I mean, it might not be Torritite, but it could, you know. . .I mean if it was, that's. . ." he stumbled out as his face turned red.

"So why do you want to know?" she asked, her voice hard and cold as ice.

"It's nothing bad, I mean. . .I. . .I'm Torritite!"

She looked at his nametag, then frowned.

"That not be a Torritite name," she said, her voice slipping into an accent he knew well.

She is a Torritite!

"No, that's my dad's name. Lysander. Like in Ryck Lysander?"

She didn't bat an eye.

She doesn't know dad? Or mom? he wondered, surprised how anyone in human space couldn't put it together.

"Uh, my mother was Hannah Hope-of-Life. From Prophesy."

The dark suspicion faded from her eyes, and she said, "Oh, from Prophesy. I'm from Nova Esperança."

Nova Esperança? There aren't Torritites there.

She must have seen the confusion on his face, because she offered, "Not many of the followers in the favelas, not like on Prophesy or Uncle's End, but there's some."

"So you *are* a Torritite!"

A gunny put a selection of geedunk on the counter, and Noah stepped back. Miss Seek Grace scanned the gunny's items and placed them in a bag.

"So, how did you get here, all the way out on Wayfarer Station?" Noah asked when the gunny left.

Her eyes clouded over again, and she only said, "The Lord works in mysterious ways," in a flat perfunctory voice.

Noah wasn't completely attuned to social graces, but he knew he'd asked something raw.

"Uh, my name's Noah. That's what the 'N' is for," he said, pointing at his nametag. "Noah Lysander."

He held out his hand, and she took it with her right, and pointing to her own nametag with her left, said, "And I'm Miriam. That's what the 'M' stands for."

Her hand felt cool and soft in his, the lightest of butterfly touches, but at the same time, he could almost sense and underlying power, as if she could crush his hand if she wanted to. He held her hand a little longer than he should have, then released it suddenly as he realized that.

"I. . .I've got to go. But it was nice meeting you. I. . .I hope I'll see you again."

"I'm not going anywhere. Six days a week, four hours a day, right here."

"Well, like I said, I've got to get going," he said, wheeling about and hurrying out the hatch.

"Nice to meet you, too, Noah Lysander," she said to his retreating back, just loud enough for him to hear.

Chapter 24

Esther

"Hell, Leroy, are you blind?" Esther asked as she pulled open the door to the RCET.

A confused-looking Private Leroy Maltese turned to look back, saying, "I'm sorry, Lance Corporal. I didn't see you."

"So are you not going to 'see me' in a real battle? Are you going to shoot me in the back? Get your ass out of there, now!" she ordered, reaching in to grab the private by the collar and hauling him out.

Esther had been promoted to team leader two weeks ago, and she while she'd lose the team if a new corporal came aboard, she was bound and determined to make the team the best in the battalion in the meantime. That goal was becoming increasingly difficult given one Leroy Maltese. He might look the part of a Marine, but he had a brain the size of a sea slug.

They'd only been practicing a simply movement to contact, each Marine in the team in their own RCET cubical. As soon as a civilian child had appeared, Maltese had opened fire, missing the child, but hitting Esther in the back, rendering her KIA. Shit happens in war, and she should have let the other three Marines carry on, but she'd been so pissed off that she'd stopped the exercise. The civilian tech waited, a small look of disdain on her face, but Esther didn't care. She had to deal with Maltese, and she'd worry about getting the tech to reset the exercise afterward.

If she had her druthers, she'd shitcan the hulking Marine, making him someone else's problem. How he'd made it through boot and IUT was beyond her comprehension, and she had very little patience with incompetence.

I should have taken up the CO on his offer, she thought for the gazillionth time. *All of this crap would be behind me now.*

Turning the CO down had seemed like the right thing to do at the time, but it wasn't making things any easier for herself. She counted to five, taking deep breaths on each number, calming herself. Maltese was her cross to bear, and if she were even half as competent as she thought she was, she'd be able to handle him.

"So tell me, why the hell did you even fire? That was a civilian child!"

"I thought it was the enemy. You told me to be alert."

"You've got AI. You've got your eyes, for God's sake! You can see she was a child."

"I know. I'm sorry."

"And if you thought she was the enemy, why did you shoot me?"

"My gun went off."

"It just went off. And after Camp Charles, after IUT, you still call it a 'gun,' Maltese? Really?" How about using proper terminology?

"Look, we're going to get back in and try this again. Yes, stay alert, but for God's sake, make sure you identify your target. Got it?"

"Yes, Lance Corporal. Got it."

She opened up the comms to tell Yadry and Wells, "We're starting again. Stand by."

Esther looked up at the tech, who was watching her with heavy-lidded eyes. She told Maltese to get back in his cubicle, then walked over to the tech to tell her they were starting over, and God help her if the civilian gave Esther any guff.

SOROS REACH

Chapter 25

Nathan

"Look at that shit come down. Do they even have this much water on this fucking world?" Tad asked as he looked out the window.

"Evidently, yes," Turtle said. "We can see it right there."

"Fuck you, Turtle. You know what I mean."

Noah understood Tad's point. He'd never seen such torrential downpours in his life. The skies had to empty out of water at some point.

Pad-Man added, "Someone's really going to have to pay for all of this."

"Yeah, we know. That someone is FFW. It's their fuck-up," Princess said from where she was lying on the deck, feet propped on an old cushion, a skivvy shirt over her eyes.

"And not for the first time," Noah said. "How does that company keep getting contracts?"

"Low bidder," Princess said.

"Low bidder, but look at this! Look at us! Grubbing hell!" Noah groused.

"What do you care, Noah? Build yourself an ark," Tad said.

"Har, har, har, like I haven't heard that before," Noah groused.

The company had been on Soros Reach for five days now, trying to assist in the humanitarian operations, and if Noah never heard another "Noah's Ark" crack again, it would be none too soon.

He took another bite of gnocchi. He shouldn't even call it gnocchi. He could make better in his sleep with both hands tied behind his back. But the food pack was labeled gnocchi, and the soft potatoey globs might be a distant relative to the real thing. It was better than the Ghost Shit, but just barely. He still didn't understand why they couldn't just use the local fabricators. The food would be edible, and they were here to help out, after all. But the Corps has strict regulations on what could and could not be sourced out of the local economy.

When the mission had first come up, Noah had been excited. It wasn't combat, which was theoretically a good thing, but it still got him them off the station and out serving the citizens of the Federation. The reality of the situation hadn't been nearly as positive. For five days, they'd built retaining walls, set up sandbags and foam barriers. As a PICS platoon, much of the heavy lifting had fallen to them. A PICS wasn't designed with construction in mind, but it was still pretty effective at it.

As much as he liked being a PICS Marine, though, four days was a little long to be mounted. Ghost Shit, the high-energy gruel they ate while mounted, was excruciatingly bland, and the inability to get clean made Noah's skin itch. It had been a welcomed relief when Sergeant Natakarn had led them into a supply shed for eight hours of stand-down. After switching out cold packs and recharging the suits, the Marines had washed naked in the rain, eaten from food packs, and stretched out on the floor for real sleep.

Those eight hours had stretched out to twelve, and Sergeant Orinda and a few of the rest were still sleeping while eight of them, including Noah, were awake and doing what Marines have done best since Ramses III's Marines fought the Sea Peoples in the Battle of the Delta during 1175 BC—bitching.

The two line and Weapons Platoon had conducted actual evacuation operations, helping the civilians make it to the evac sites. First Platoon had been slave labor, trying to stem back the tide.

Not that they could. It was a commonly held maxim that planets had to be seduced into terraforming. They could not be forced. FFW had a reputation of under-bidding, and to reduce costs, they had a habit of forcing the process. Sometimes it worked, sometimes it didn't. This was the fourth FFW world that had serious problems to the point of evacuation. The FFW spokesman assured them that this was temporary, that the planet would recover. Maybe so, but over 150,000 people had to be evacuated, more than 90% being pioneers who'd invested their life and savings to make a start on a new world.

Outside, the rain continued to pour down, beating out a tattoo on the roof. It was wearing on Noah, and he'd be glad when the operation concluded. He'd get his first ribbon, the Humanitarian Action Ribbon, out of the mission, but that was little consolation. Noah wasn't very motivated by ribbons. He'd probably leave the battalion with two: the HAR and the Good Conduct. If he ever saw real combat, he would add the Combat Mission Medal. And that might even be all he had when his enlistment expired.

The Lieutenant's voice came over Sergeant Natakarn's PICS' externals, from where it stood against the wall, an empty cicada husk.

"Tallyho-Three, this is Tallyho-Six. Stand by for a mission."

All eyes swiveled as one to the squad leader's PICS.

A few moments later, the lieutenant passed, "Sergeant Natakarn, we've got a report of a stranded stakeholder and family at GU4487-7342. They were on the D-freq at 4700, but there is no connection now. You're the closest unit, so I want you to go see what you can do—if there is anything you can do. Sat photos show the area is pretty much being swept away, and there is no sign of the family.

"I don't want any of you to risk yourselves, but let's see if they're still alive."

"Roger, that, Tallyho-Six. We're on it."

Noah felt a rush of excitement. He'd been bitching only a moment before, but given and actual mission, one where they might be able to help someone, had the effect of recharging his batteries. He wasn't the only one. There was a palpable feeling of energy as Marines got up and started gathering their gear.

"You heard him!" Sergeant Natakarn shouted out. "Mount up!"

Most of the Marines had taken off their long johns and were either naked or in loose microfiber skivvies. Noah hated making sure all his parts were inserted into the various pockets that enabled Marines to piss and shit while in a PICS, so he had his long johns still on up to the waist with his torso bare. Still, it took him almost a minute to wriggle into the upper half of them. Sometimes he thought the long johns are more difficult that the PICS. He grabbed his gear, shoved them into the butt pack of his PICS, then did his Cirque de Soleil contortions to mount. The ingress hatch shut, and the familiar embrace of his lining closed in on him, connections seeking each other out until he was fully integrated. He performed his up-check, and all was green.

Sergeant Natakarn wasn't ready yet. He had detached the PA readout from his PICS and was furiously entering data. Finally, he slammed it home, and darted behind his PICS to mount. Immediately, Noah's display lit up with a map marked out to their objective.

Forty-three klicks? And we're the closest unit?

Third squad was the farthest east from the main population center, almost 30 klicks out. If this stakeholder and his family were another 43 klicks farther, they were in the veritable boonies. Soros Reach was only in Stage 4 terraforming, open to initial and limited settlers for not quite two years now. Most of the current settlers were within 25 klicks of the three population centers, and given the lack of infrastructure, seventy-three klicks might as well be a thousand for all intents and purposes.

Both of the battalion Storks were on the mission, and one of them would probably be better to check out the family, but Noah didn't know what else they might be doing. Forty-three klicks might not be that far in a PICS, but fighting the weather and poor footing, Noah figured it would probably take them two hours to cover the distance.

He was wrong. It took almost four hours. The lone trail was almost impassable, and deep water diverted them more than a few times. A PICS was a powerful war machine, and they could operate submerged for several hours if needed, but they were ungainly under water, and if there was a strong current, they could be swept away. Even chest deep, the displacement, coupled with a significant flow, could knock a PICS Marine off his feet.

Finally, they arrived at the location, which looked like any other piece of riverside forest on the planet. If the stakeholder family was in the area, they came from somewhere else. There wasn't any sign of habitation around. Sergeant Narakarn had tried to raise the family on the D-freq, but there had been no answer. Noah thought that didn't bode well for them.

Sergeant Natakarn split the fireteams up to search for the family. The river, swollen with water, was too deep and the current too fast for anyone to cross, so they could only search the near side. Noah's team was sent downriver. If the river had swept up the family, they'd be half-way to Fox Crossing by now, so Noah didn't have much hope they'd find anything.

So he was surprised when Turtle reported spotting someone. Noah hurried to him, and the "someone" was a corpse. The woman was lodged in a downed tree, her face and chest out of the water, her long brown hair flowing free in the current. Her skin was an extremely pale shade of white as if a vampire had drained her blood. Noah had never seen a dead person outside of a coffin before, and he couldn't tear away his eyes.

"Better get her," Corporal St. Fyodor said as he maneuvered from above to capture an image and pass it up the chain of command.

Noah started down the bank, slipping twice and grateful for his servo-gyros keeping him upright. The current caught at his legs as he waded knee-deep to the tree, breaking off several branches in the way so she could reach her.

"That's one of them," the team leader passed. "Battalion just confirmed it. She's the wife and mother. We've still got the husband and two kids missing."

Noah carefully reached out, and trying to be careful, closed his gauntlet around one of the woman's shoulders. He pulled, but the body resisted, stuck on something. He had the strength in his arms to tear the body apart, but that obviously was not an option. He pulled her shoulder away and saw it was her lower body that was stuck.

"Get her up here," Tad told him.

Noah wanted to tell him to shut up. He knew what he was supposed to do.

Kneeling, he felt along her body, trying to find out on what she was hung up. With more of his body in the water, it gushed up and out as it flowed past. He felt oddly obscene as he probed her unresisting body with his gauntlet; not sexually obscene, but the sacrilege of disturbing the dead. Kneeling as he was, his faceplate was centimeters from her face, and he imagined the dead, flat eyes reproving him.

I hope she didn't suffer.

As his hand reached her hip, it also touched wood. She had been jammed into a large branch that protruded down into the mud bottom. That was what was keeping her from being swept downriver. He gently tried to lift her out of the fork, but she was stuck fast, and he was afraid of damaging her body. Reaching back under her, he grabbed the branch itself. It felt to be a good ten centimeters across: nothing for his PICS. Locking his finger, he pulled steadily back and was rewarded with a loud snap, even from under the water. The tree lurched as if the branch was the only thing holding it in place, and Noah snatched up the body, lifting it free.

The top of the tree swung farther downriver, as if the tree wanted to break free. Noah stepped back, not wanting to get caught up in it.

A soft cry, barely a caress, reached him. He wasn't sure he heard anything over the rush of the water pounding on his legs and the snapping and creaking of the tree. Still holding the dead woman, he blinked up his AI and told it to isolate the sounds. Six lines popped up, one labeled. . . "human voice."

The tree gave another lurch and swung farther around. Part of the trunk, still on the shore, slid two meters closer to the water.

"Get out of there, Noah!" Corporal St. Fyodor shouted out.

Noah looked up at his team leader, then commanded his AI, "Shit! Intensify and run line four."

"Help," came in clear, high pitched and sounding scared.

Noah immediately threw the woman's body up on the bank, her arms and legs windmilling as she rotated.

"Get down here now!" he shouted. "Keep the tree here!"

He grabbed the trunk just as the base slipped free of its hold on the land. A PICS was an extremely powerful piece of military gear, but the river was even a stronger force, and Noah's feet were sliding in the mud under the water, his boots unable to gain purchase. He was sure he'd lost it when around him, big bodies splashed into the water, and three more Marines grabbed hold, stopping the tree from breaking free.

"What's going on?" Corporal St. Fyodor asked.

"There's someone here, alive!"

"What?"

But Noah wasn't listening. With the rest of his team holding on, he started walking his way deeper into the river, along the length of the tree. Waist deep, chest deep, he could feel the power of the water. Without the tree there in front of him, he was sure he'd have been swept away. He turned on his infrared, but he couldn't see anything in the dense foliage.

Am I crazy? Was the call from somewhere on the shore?

His boots refused to gain traction, and twice, they were swept out from under him, and only by grabbing branches, was he kept from being swept away. At the middle of the tree, about seven meters from the bank, the branches were dense, heavy with needles. They formed a barrier to him, so with one gauntleted arm, he broke off the nearest branch—and he saw her.

A little girl, no more than five or six, lay on top of the trunk, one little hand grasping a small branch, the other arm around the trunk. Her bare legs, pink with scratches, straddled the trunk.

She looked at Noah with the glazed eyes of someone at the end of her rope and weakly said, "Help me, please."

"I found her!" he shouted.

But how to get to her? The branches made a pretty formidable barrier, and his legs were almost useless in the current. If he tried to bull rush through, he could either send the tree on its way downriver or knock the little girl off her perch.

"What's your name?" he asked, trying to keep his voice calm.

"Jennifer," she said, her voice weak and expressionless.

"OK, Jennifer. I'm here to help you. Can you come to me? Can you crawl so I can reach you?"

Her face wrinkled up for a moment as if to cry; then she turned her head away.

"Jennifer, Jennifer! Can you hear me?" he called out.

She didn't move.

"What's your status?" the corporal asked.

"I've got a little girl, maybe five years old. I'm trying to get her to come to me, but she can't. And I can't go forward. Maybe we can push the crown downstream to get it closer to the shore?"

"That's a negative. It's all we can do to hold it as it is. If you push the crown, that will free the roots, and then it'll be off to the races. Can't you get in there?"

"Let me try."

Noah reached forward and took a hold of a branch right at the trunk. Applying steady pressure, he pulled until it snapped off. He threw it over the tree into the water on the other side, and it was instantly whisked away. He moved up half a step, and broke off another one.

Only fifty more to go.

Slowly, he broke off branches advancing centimeter by centimeter. First, she was five meters away. Then four, then three. He could cover that in a split second on dry land, but here it seemed like a klick away.

He kept up a conversation with Jennifer, assuring her that he was there. Her body was still. Noah thought she should be shivering, but he remembered that when hypothermia set in, shivering eventually stopped as the body temperature fell to dangerous levels. Somehow, the little girl had held on for hours, but he was pretty sure she couldn't hold on much longer.

"Noah, we've got a problem," his team leader said. "We've got a tsunami heading our way."

What? We're in a river, not the ocean, he thought, turning to look upriver.

It wasn't a tsunami, but a couple of hundred meters away, a wall of water, a half-a-meter high, was rushing down river. Something had let go upstream. Noah couldn't imagine what, but the evidence was right in front of his eyes. Half-a-meter of water might not seem like much, but Noah had no illusion that it would be gentle rise. It would hit the tree and him like a hammer, tearing the tree loose no matter how many Marines held it.

"Hold on,' he shouted, breaking more branches.

"You've got 15 seconds, Noah, then you've got to pull back."

"No, I'll get her!" he shouted.

"You cannot put yourself in danger!"

Heedless of knocking the tree free, he crushed the branches, closing the distance.

"Jennifer, come here," he pleaded.

"Out of the water!" Corporal St. Fyodor shouted to the other two. "Noah, get back!"

With one last lunge, Noah pushed forward, reaching out to grab the little girl. He almost knocked her off as she gave a little cry of fear, but he snagged her cat-dove top, thankful for the strong collar of the style. He pulled back, trying to clear the tree's reach when the water hit.

He was wrong. It wasn't like a hammer; it was like a freight train. Almost neck deep in the water, he barely had any weight, and he was driven under the water, going head over heels. He banged into the tree, which was now free to sweep downriver. Feeling more than seeing the bottom, he pushed off, trying to straighten out, pushing his arms up and holding Jennifer out of the torrent. He fell back down under as he scrambled for purchase, the river keeping him in its grasp. Once more he sprang up, but this time angling for the shore. Once more, he held the little girl high, going under to push off again. Twice, he tumbled, and he lost his grip on the girl with one hand, automatically tightening with the other, mindless if he was doing any damage to her. Better crushed bones than to be lost to the river's might.

He banged against something hard, and that stopped him for a moment. The river was pressing against him, but he found his feet and pushed as hard as he could towards the bank, erupting from the water like a great white shark broaching. Suddenly, he was waist deep, and as he struggled ashore, a body landed beside him with a crash, and strong mechanical arms, grabbed him, helping him reach the bank.

"I've got you," Turtle said.

"Give me the girl!" Tad shouted, reaching down from solid ground.

Dazed, Noah realized he still had Jennifer in his arms. He passed her limp body up to his fellow Marine, who took her and put her on the ground. Corporal St. Fyodor was just completing an emergency molt, and he hit the ground hard before bounding up and rushing to the girl. He immediately started CPR.

"Fucking shit A," Turtle said, his voice subdued. "I thought we'd lost you."

"I. . ." Noah started, before falling silent. His mind was a jumble, but he kept his eyes glued on the little girl.

Come on, Jennifer, come on! he pleaded.

Less than a minute later, five Marines and Doc Eagleton crashed through the trees. Doc immediately went into emergency molt mode, and twenty seconds later, he was kneeling over Jennifer's limp body. After a quick scan, he pulled out a ziplock and told one of the other Marines to get it ready. He stripped off Jennifer's clothes, then gave her an injection. Picking her up, he slipped her into the ziplock and initiated stasis.

Noah's heart fell. Stasis was for seriously wounded Marines—or those killed with hopes of regen.

"Doc?" he asked.

"You pulled her out?" he asked Noah, then before getting an answer, "Good job. She'll be fine."

"But stasis?"

"Just a precaution. We're four hours from anyone, and if we can't get a Stork, that's a long time. She took in a lot of water, most that Corporal St. Fyodor expelled, but still, she's weak, hypothermic, and she has a crushed knee.

That was me, Noah realized.

"That's a lot for her to tolerate, and I don't want an infection to set in her lungs. We're not done here, right?" he said, looking at Sergeant Natakarn, who nodded. "So better put her in stasis. She'll wake up in orbit fine."

He turned back to the readout, watching as stasis kicked in.

"What the fuck, Noah," Corporal St. Fyodor hissed. "I told you to break free. You were *not* to risk yourself."

"Sorry, Corporal," he said, not meaning a word of it as he stared at Jennifer.

Seeing the tiny body in the ziplock, the steady green flashing light on the display, was more than worth any trouble he was in.

WAYFARER STATION

Chapter 26

Esther

*The Third Minister of the United Federation of States takes
great pride in presenting the*

Civilian Protector Medal, Second Class

to

*Private First Class Noah Lysander, United Federation Marine
Corps,*

for service as set forth in the following citation:

*On 19 January 315, Private First Class Lysander was part
of humanitarian operations on Soros Reach to protect and
evacuate civilians. When reports were received about a trapped
family along the rising Petergast River, PFC Lysander's squad was
dispatched to their rescue. Upon arriving at the family's last
location, the squad split up to locate them. PFC Lysander's team
was assigned to search the banks downstream where the body of a
deceased family member was located tangled in the flood debris.
PFC Lysander entered the raging torrent to retrieve the body when
he heard the call of a child. Without regard to his own safety, PFC
Lysander moved into the deeper torrent while the Marines in his
team secured the debris. Able to secure the child before being
struck by a rush of water, he retained his grip on her until he was
able to make his way to shore. Without PFC Lysander's daring*

rescue, the child would have undoubtedly been lost. PFC Lysander's actions saved the life of a United Federation of States citizen and were in keeping with the highest traditions of the Federation, the Naval Service, and the Marine Corps.

For the Third Minister
Brettman Wilks-Otaka
Administrator, Wayfarer Station

Esther watched as the administrator took the silver-ribboned medal and pinned it to Noah's chest. It seemed odd to see a civilian at an awards ceremony. He was obviously uncomfortable with his position, but as the ranking Federation official, the duty fell to him.

The Civilian Service Medal was rarely awarded to Marines or sailors. It wasn't even approved by the Chairman, much less the First Minister. Lifesaving awards like this came under the Third Minister, out of the military chain of command. In all her time around the Corps, Esther didn't know if she had ever seen one awarded to a Marine, and while she'd seen cops and even FCDC officers receive lifesaving awards on the news, she had to look up what the medal looked like.

Now, two Marines in the battalion had the medal. Corporal St. Fyodor had the gold CPM, First Class, for his command of the rescue, from holding the tree in place to then administering CPR, while Noah was awarded the silver-colored CPM, Second Class.

Esther glanced down at the breast of her Charlies at her own BCM3 and her Combat Mission Medal. These were Marine Corps Medals, for combat and distinguishing herself in it. Noah had two ribbons now as well, but the Humanitarian Service Ribbon and now the CPM 2. Technically, his CPM2 was a higher-precedence award than her BCM3 and just under a BCM 2.

It wasn't like he was in danger, she thought. *He was in a PICS, for God's sake. He wasn't going to drown.*

Shit, not jealous, are we? Just be happy for him, she admonished herself.

It didn't really bother her that his award was higher than hers. Most Marines wouldn't even recognize it, and if they did, it was a Third Ministry award, not a First, and so, it didn't carry the same weight. It might mean something to the FCDC, but the Marines' mission was combat, not farting around with civilians. No, people would know *she* had the real award, and Noah's was political.

The station administrator looked to the CO for guidance who motioned with a quick flick of the wrist for him to stand back. The administrator awkwardly took two oversized steps to the rear while the adjutant ordered Noah and his corporal to post.

Come on, Noah! she silently pleaded when her brother took his first step too soon, treading on the back of the corporal's heel. *Get it together!*

The adjutant dismissed the staff, and the officers and senior staff went to shake the administrator's hand. He might be a perfunctory out in the sticks now, but young men in his position had a habit of climbing up the ladder to positions of real authority, and he was drawing Marines to him like flies to shit. Esther unconsciously wrinkled her lip as she watched.

Several junior Marines moved forward from the seats to congratulate the corporal and Noah—many more to the corporal, Esther noted. She didn't have much of a problem getting to Noah.

"Congratulations, Noah. It looks good."

"Thanks, Ess," he said, pulling her in for a hug. "Do you think dad would be proud?" he whispered in her ear.

Esther ignored the "Ess" as she gave in and barely returned the hug. She contemplated his question. Would their father have been proud? Probably, at least to an extent. But their father had been a Marine through-and-through, and Esther had the sneaking suspicion that he wouldn't have placed that much weight on a non-military award. Still, she knew what Noah wanted to hear.

"Of course he would. This is something you'll have after you get out, to prove you did something good. You save that little girl's life."

"Thanks, Ess. I hope he would be proud of me."

Another Marine smacked him hard on the back, hitting Esther's arm in the process. She let go and stepped back.

"Turtle, you know my sister, right?"

"I know of her, Noah. Everyone does," the Marine said before turning to her. "Corporal Lysander, I'm Lance Corporal Gregori de Matta."

"I've told you about him, Ess."

Esther vaguely remembered him mentioning a "Turtle," something along the lines of him being married. That was a rough feat for a non-rate in a high-cost location like the station.

"Ess picked up meritorious corporal. That's PFC *and* corporal meritoriously," Noah said, pride evident in his voice.

"Shit, what's your problem then, Noah? I'm surprised that you're even slated for lance coolie!"

Esther looked up sharply at this Turtle. What he'd said bordered on what she felt at times, that Noah wasn't cut out to be a Marine, but that didn't mean she wanted him to hear it from others. He still carried the Lysander name.

But Turtle was laughing, and Noah put an arm around his shoulders saying that even a blind squirrel could find a nut every now and then. She relaxed. This was only the usual give and take among Marines.

Don't be so uptight!

Esther was so focused on success that she sometimes didn't recognize the smack talk, the joking around, and she had to make a conscious effort to fit in with others outside her inner circle, which was very limited. She had many, many acquaintances, and she seemed popular, but there were only a few with whom she really felt a connection.

I used to be close to you, too, she thought wistfully as she watched her brother and his friend insult each other.

She still wondered exactly what had happened. Noah was still Noah, and he would always have her back. But something had come up between them, something evidently only she could see. She knew she'd rather they be stationed separately. She suspected that she worried that Noah would sully the family name, which could reflect on her, but it would also reflect on their father, something Esther would fight to keep from happening. If Noah had remained a civilian, it wouldn't have mattered much. Their father's legacy started with Ben's death, and now she was determined add to the legacy—and she didn't need to be worrying about Noah when she was trying to accomplish that. A year-and-a-half, and he'd be out of the Corps, and she wouldn't have to worry about him.

She watched Turtle reach out to touch Noah's medal, and then when Noah looked down, flicked his forefinger up to smack Noah's nose—the oldest trick in the book, and she had to smile. She was only nine minutes older than her twin, but he was far, far younger than she was, at least in personality.

But not in all ways, she reminded herself as memories flooded her thoughts. Her mind jumped back four years ago to Luna Station, when she'd absolutely lost it seeing her father appear, ready to sacrifice himself for them. It had been Noah—flippant, loner, sometimes sullen Noah—who had taken over, who had gathered her up and took her to the ship.

She was still ashamed about breaking down like that. She was the strong one, she was the hard-charger. But that had simply been too much for her, and she'd broke, as simple as that. That her father had been later rescued by the Confed team didn't negate her moment of weakness, something she vowed never to repeat.

Noah had never mentioned the incident again, and she was eternally grateful for that.

Esther felt a stirring of affection for him, something she hadn't felt since camp Charles, maybe before. She still resented his presence, and she feared him screwing up big time and tarnishing the family name, but when he was finally out, she hoped they could rekindle the relationship. With their parents and Ben gone, they were all they had left.

"Hey, Noah. I've got to get back to the company. Congratulations on the medal. I mean it."

"It was no big deal, Ess, but thanks. And thanks for coming to the ceremony."

He pulled her in for a hug, and this time, she hugged him back.

Chapter 27

Noah

Noah paused, trying to gather up his courage. He waved the hatch open and entered the exchange.

"Hi, Miriam," he said as he walked back to the geedunk shelves.

"Hey, Noah," she answered, not looking up from her PA.

For the last six months, Noah had been coming to the exchange when he could, supposedly shopping, but really just to spend time chatting with Miriam. He'd tried to time his arrivals when the traffic was slow, so that he wouldn't interfere—and others wouldn't be around to listen, and he'd tried not to be too obvious as to his intent, so he tried to space out his visits somewhat.

There wasn't that much he needed from the exchange to justify so many visits, so he'd taken to buying geedunk. He didn't really like snack food, what with the heavy sugar and salt loads, complete with artificial flavors, but they were a consumable, and he faked having a sweet tooth. In reality, he passed his purchases to his squadmates. He couldn't tell if that endeared him any more to them, but it was better than throwing them in the trash.

And over the six months, he'd gotten to know her, all in bits and drabs. He'd learned about her leaving her family on Nova Esperança. He wasn't still quite sure what had happened to her to make her leave, but he could tell it wasn't good, and that she'd suffered from it. She'd bounced around the Federation for three years, sometimes relying on other Torrites for survival, other times scratching out sustenance however she could. Finally, she ended up at Wayfarer Station, and at the end of her rope, had asked help from Citizen's Assistance. Cleaned up and with new clothes, they got her the job at the exchange, and she'd been slowly getting her life together over the last year.

Three days ago, flush with excitement over getting his medal, and knowing he'd be a lance corporal soon, he'd screwed up his courage to ask Miriam out on a date—a real date, as in out in the ville for dinner. She had immediately refused, saying she didn't date Marines. Noah had been crushed, but years of hiding his emotions allowed him to laugh it off as if he hadn't been serious. He'd gone back to his quarters and into bed, wanting to avoid any human contact—which was pretty much impossible with three roommates. He almost went to see Esther, and in the old days, he would have. Now, he didn't want her to see his failures. He knew she wanted him to excel, and he hadn't given that to her yet.

Noah wanted nothing more than to never go into the exchange again, but he knew that by simply disappearing, he'd be proving he had not only been serious in asking Miriam out, but he'd been crushed by her refusal. It was true, but that was just one more person in a long line of them who'd know he was a failure. So he knew he had to go back at least one more time and make small talk as he'd been doing for six months. He didn't want to, but his pride demanded it.

He picked up a Sizzle Stick, a horrendous concoction of blue sugars. If he was going to act like he had a sweet tooth, at least he could be liking something a little higher on the snack scale, but Turtle loved the things. He sauntered over to check-out and placed the Sizzle Stick on the counter.

"You doing OK? Your roommate situation working out?" he asked as casually as he could.

"I'm fine, but Zoey's still a pig. I took her dirty panties off the dining chair last night and threw them under the sink."

"You did?" Noah said, intrigued despite himself. "She just left them out like that?"

"I think she was 'entertaining,'" she said, leaving no doubt in Noah's mind what "entertaining" meant.

Zoey was also a Citizen's Assistance case, so Miriam didn't have much choice in changing roommates until she saved enough to get her own place. Zoey, from how Miriam described her, was less than enthusiastic about the re-training procedure and routinely ignored the restrictions place on her by CA.

"I doubt she even remembers where she took them off, so. . ." she said, shrugging.

"She'll probably think she put them under the sink herself," Noah said.

He'd never met Zoey, of course, but the woman fascinated him. Not is a good way, though. He just couldn't fathom someone so bluntly ignoring rules, especially when the CA was only trying to help her.

"Maybe. Is that all you have?" she asked, pointing at the Sizzle Stick.

"Yeah."

"I still don't get what you see in them, you being a foodie and all. I can't stand the things."

Neither can I, and I won't be buying any more of them, he thought, tempted to say that aloud.

"We all have our vices," he said instead.

Three lieutenants from Alpha came in, laughing about something. Noah looked up, at them in despair. He wasn't going to stand there chatting with three O's there.

It doesn't matter. You're not going to see her again anyway.

He didn't want to cut it short, though. He wanted a few more minutes, but that wasn't going to happen.

"Well, I've got to get back. I might not be around for a while, so take care."

"You're going off-station? I haven't heard about any deployments," she asked, her eyebrows scrunched together in confusion.

"Oh, no. Nothing like that. It's just our op tempo is rising, and I'm going to be real busy."

At "op tempo," one of the lieutenants looked up and him and frowned.

Grubbing hell. Just what I need now.

Miriam worked in the battalion area, and she knew more about unit deployments and training than most Marines, but that didn't mean Noah was free to discuss them with her. The lieutenant looked like he wanted to say something to him.

"I've got to go!" Noah said quickly, snatching his Sizzle Sticks.

He spun around to quickly leave when Miriam said, "Noah, your receipt!"

Noah didn't want the receipt, he didn't need the receipt. What he needed was to get out of there before the lieutenant got it into his head that some PFC needed immediate correction.

But he couldn't be rude, even to someone who'd turned him down. It wasn't as he was raised. He turned around and reached out, almost snatching the receipt out of her hand.

Why can't we join the modern world? I mean, who else uses physical receipts?

Noah knew it had something to do with the black market which was a problem at the station where outside the base, prices were quite high. He waved open the hatch, and raised his hand to toss the crumbled receipt into the shitcan in the passage. He missed.

Of course, I missed. What else is new? he asked himself as he bent down to pick it up off the deck.

A flash of blue on the receipt caught his eye.

Blue? Receipts use black.

He unfolded the receipt to see a string of numbers. Under the numbers was a short note:

Call me, OK? Miriam.

Chapter 28

Esther

"I had a talk with the lieutenant this morning," Sergeant Orinda told Esther.

The two Marines were on their way back from their annual gender neutrality brief, something Esther thought was a humongous waste of time. Women in the Corps were no longer a new event. Her father had opened the Corps (and Navy) to women almost six years before, and some of the first joins were now sergeants, a handful of staff sergeants, and even some lieutenants. There had been very little overt resistance from the men, and the few cases of gender-based discrimination or sexual aggression had been quickly, and quite publicly, adjudicated. Esther, at least, had never been subjected to anything she felt to be prejudicial based on her gender.

There were rumors, of course, of more than a few cases of harassment and even sexual predation, but only a handful of cases had been reported over the last year. The worst one was probably the young male Marine who'd been hog-tied and had his balls shaved and painted bright pink before being left on the Third Marine Division parade deck. Rumor was that he'd been more than a little pushy towards one of his female fellow Marines, and that several of her fellow female Marines had extracted their own brand of justice. That case may have been the most egregious, but it was roundly applauded throughout the rank-and-file of the Corps.

"What about?" Esther asked.

"Second Squad. Sergeant Jreki's about to rotate out, you know."

"Yes, I know," Esther said, her interest rising.

"We don't have anyone inbound in the near future, and so one of the corporals needs to step up in the interim."

Esther started feeling her face flush. She had hoped to make squad leader on this tour, but to have it actually within her grasp was really more than she could have hoped for.

"And. . .?"

"I recommended you, of course."

Yes!

"The thing is, you are the second junior corporal in the platoon."

Shouldn't matter. The position should go the corporal best able to do the job.

"But the most qualified," Esther said, not caring how that might sound.

"Ha! You don't hold back, do you? But the thing is, Staff Sergeant Ski doesn't think you're ready. He thinks you need more time as a team leader.

Esther felt as if she'd been kicked in the gut.

The staff sergeant doesn't think I'm ready? Who does he think is more ready than me?

"So why are you telling me this, then?" she asked, hoping that maybe Sergeant Orinda was going to tell her that the lieutenant had overruled the platoon sergeant, and that she would still get the position.

Not likely. Staff Sergeant Ski's got the lieutenant wrapped around his finger.

"Two reasons. First, I probably shouldn't have told you any of this, but it'll undoubtedly slip out, and I wanted you to know he thinks you're a kick-ass Marine, but he wants you to develop more."

"And second?"

"Second is that I'm going to take over Second."

Esther thought about that for a moment, and her Marine Corps mind kicked in. It made sense. First Squad was the strongest squad in the platoon. Esther liked to think it was because she was one of the team leaders, but in reality, Sergeant Orinda was a hell of a Marine and a hell of an NCO. The success strength of the squad was due to the squad leader.

But where did that leave First?

"And. . .?"

"Kinder's taking over," the sergeant said.

"Huh," Esther puffed out, a wordless expression of nothingness.

Corporal Kinder was the platoon's senior corporal, just a few points shy on his last cutting score for sergeant. He wasn't a bad team leader, but he wasn't great, and Esther knew she was far better than him. He'd never treated her poorly when she was in his team, but since she'd been elevated herself to team leader, she was positive that she'd far surpassed him.

They'd reached the berthing area, and the two Marines paused outside Esther's quarters.

"And you want to know if I'm OK with that," Esther said, keeping her voice low.

"Yeah, in a nutshell, you could put it that way."

Esther wanted to say no, she wanted to request a transfer, but that was ridiculous. There was only one answer.

"Of course I am. He's senior to me, and I have no problem as my squad leader."

Sergeant Orinda looked deep into Esther's eyes as if trying to read into her soul. Esther stared back, not defiantly, but without backing down, either.

"OK, good, then," the sergeant said, backing down. "I'll see you after chow for the loggy[9] brief."

"Are you still squad leader for now, then?" Esther asked.

"Yeah, until Tuesday. So you're still stuck with me until then."

She turned to leave, hesitated, then turned back and said, "Just hang in there, Lysander. Kinder's got his own strengths. Learn what works for him and what doesn't. You'll get your turn in the breach, and no one doubts that you'll eventually bypass us all."

Esther watched her squad leader cross to her own quarters, trying to absorb what she'd said. She was disappointed, to be sure, but it had been a little much to hope that not even two years into her assignment, she'd be a squad leader. She'd bide her time, polish her skills, and be ready to seize the opportunity when it did arise.

---

[9] Loggy: Slang for logistics.

DX-4

Chapter 29

Noah

"You coming, Noah?" Turtle asked.

"Nah, you go ahead. I want to get this isolated."

"OK, but I'm not going to be able to hold a seat. You know how crowded it is in the messhall."

Noah nodded, turned back, and ran the little scanner over his PICS' fan-plate. The numbers were good, but his knee movement had seemed a little quirky during the last exercise. He looked over to where Mr. Coulter was deep inside another PICS, mumbling to himself.

Mr. Coulter was the lead armorer. He'd evidently been around Wayfarer Station forever, and rumors swirled as to why. The techs tended to go to larger units as they became more senior and experience, and the battalion only had enough PICS Marines to normally justify a less-experienced tech.

There were three levels of armor maintenance. The first level was the individual Marine. Each Marine and sailor was responsible for basic analysis and maintenance. A Marine ran the scans on his or her PICS, and they could swap out components for Class C repairs. The next level consisted of Marine armorers. These were usually second or third enlistment NCOs who received additional training at the Corridor-Epsilon facilities on Anson. Every Marine was a rifleman, but one way to stay in the Corps as Marines became more senior was to move into support-type billets. Marine armorers took care of supply for things such as cold-packs, and they could perform Level B repairs. Any major work that didn't have to be returned to the factory was done by the civilian armorers.

The battalion had only two civvies: Mr. Coulter and Mr. Tarryhand, the younger armorer who'd first fitted Noah for his PICS.

Neither man was what could be called approachable. But with the two Marine armorers having just left for chow, if he wanted to get the knee checked out beyond his meager capabilities, it would have to be Mr. Coulter.

Maybe I should just wait until later.

He didn't want to do that, though. This was only their third day at Dixie, and they had a night exercise scheduled in a little over six hours. He wanted his PICS to be in tip-top shape for that. Noah had been steadily gaining in skill with the PICS, and his performance numbers were continually in the upper third of the platoon. His goal tonight was to have the highest numbers in the squad, if not the platoon, and he didn't want any sort of PICS glitch to slow him down.

No one seemed to consider Noah particularly skilled as a PICS Marine, and even Turtle seemed surprised when the numbers were promulgated, but the facts were that he was developing as a Marine. He may not be a super hard-charger whom everyone looked up to, but he was an effective cog in the platoon.

And, to his own surprise, he was feeling more confident in his own abilities. He did not feel like a liability anymore. Only part of that was his performance, though. He knew dating Miriam was also contributing. It was as if her choosing him validated his self-worth.

Growing self-confidence or not, he was not ready to tackle Mt. Coulter. He tip-toed around the man, to be honest.

Noah looked around the large armor maintenance shed. Over 40 meters long and 20 wide, it was actually an expeditionary hangar; but after some 19 years, it had lost its "expeditionary" or temporary status. Along with its twin that actually function as a hangar, the two looked like a cylinder split in half length-wise, with each half becoming a facility. Neither was fancy or high-tech, but they did the job. With rising O2 levels in the atmosphere, neither even had to be pressurized anymore.

The armor shed housed the PICS storages racks and maintenance bay on one side, and three Mambas and their associated maintenance bays on the other side. The three Mambas were training units that stayed on the planet. When the tank sections of 1/16 or 2/16 arrived for training, they left their Mambas behind and fell in on the training vehicles. Deploying units with the M1 battle tanks brought in their own vehicles when they arrived for training, but they often took the opportunity to train with the smaller, nimbler Mambas as well.

Two people were working on one of the Mambas. Sergeant Phong and Mz. Vitterly were looking at a readout and animatedly discussing it. Some of the basic components between PICS and Mambas were the same, and others worked in the same manner. Noah wondered if either of them might have some input for him, but he didn't want to interrupt them. Looking back at the still mumbling Mr. Coulter, however, made up his mind. He left his PICS in the cradle and wandered over to the two.

"That's a plus or minus .3, right? That's too much!" Sergeant Phong said, her voice rising in her excitement.

"Too much for an initial assessment. But you are forgetting the degradement schedule. One-zero-zero-three's been here for 16 years. Look up your schedule," Mz. Vitterly said.

"Sixteen freaking years? That long? Well, hell," she said as he punching something in her PA. "Damn, you're right. Point-three-four is within tolerance. I guess we're good to go tonight. I've just never seen anything older than five years."

"Most of the M1-5s are newer, but this is one case where the FCDC gets the newer chassis."

Noah had no idea what the two were talking about with the numbers, but he did know that the Mamba was actually an FCDC asset. The Marines had put in a side-buy for some of the assault tanks for units were the larger battle tank did not make sense or were too large for the situation.

Both women looked up as Noah reached them.

"What do you want?" the sergeant asked.

"I. . .well, I know you were in PICS, Sergeant. Today, I felt a slight hitch in my stride, and I'm getting some weird readings on my knee assembly. I was wondering if you might have any suggestions."

The staff sergeant made a pointed effort to look past Noah's shoulder back to the PICS maintenance bay and asked, "And you didn't want to ask Mr. Curmudgeon?"

"Let me see your readout," Mz. Vitterly said, holding out her hand.

Noah gave it to the young woman who barely glanced at it before saying, "You've got a faulty H-23 unit."

"An H-23? But that's in the upper nexus," Noah said, confused.

The upper nexus was located just under the chest carapace, not in the leg.

"And what does in control?"

"Uh, movement synchronicity," he said.

"At least he knows that," the sergeant told Vitterly.

"And. . ." she prompted.

"Ah, this isn't a problem with the leg itself. It's the controls!" he said as realization hit him.

"There you go. That's a Class B repair, so get Sergeant Olov to fix it before you go out tonight if you don't want to ask the Curmudgeon.:

"Curmudgeon." That's pretty good, Noah thought, trying not to smile.

"Thanks. I'll do that."

"If you don't get it done tonight, that's OK. It's not enough to downcheck your unit. But get to it sometime. It'll only get worse over time," Mz. Vitterly said.

"I will," Noah said, his eyes drifting to the Mamba in front of him.

He'd see them, of course. He'd been "killed" by one of them the first time he was on Dixie. But he'd never gotten a really close look at one.

"Sweet machine, huh?" the sergeant said, pride evident in her voice.

"Yeah, it is," Noah said, meaning every word of it. "I got killed by one the first time we were here."

"Really?" Sergeant Phong asked with a laugh. "I think that was my first training operation with the section. It felt pretty copacetic mowing you guys down."

"That was your first time? I figured you'd been in tanks for longer than that."

"Nope. I was with 3/9, PICS, just like you. I'd just gotten here from the Itch a couple of months before, too late for the previous Dixie training."

The "Itch" was Itzuko-2, an arid mining world belonging to the Itzuko Daihatsu. The Marine Corps leased facilities and training areas from Itzuko to train both tankers and pilots and to develop and train units in combined arms operations.

"Why did you switch from PICS to tanks?" Noah asked before realizing he might be out-of-bounds, a lance corporal asking a sergeant like that.

He needn't have worried. Sergeant Phong was more than willing to respond.

"I loved being a PICS Marine. But look at this baby! How could you not love something so powerful?"

She stroked the polycero latticed armor side, like a lover stroking her partner. That struck Noah as weird—but somewhat intriguing.

"You want to see inside?" Mz. Vitterly asked.

"Really? Sure!"

Noah had clambered over an M1-5 during boot camp, but he'd been one of a couple of hundred recruits, and he hadn't really absorbed much. He'd never been this close to a Mamba at all.

Both women hopped up on top the tank. Noah, easily 20 centimeters taller than either, was a little clumsier as he joined them.

"This is our Bambi," the sergeant said, patting the short, stubby gun tube projecting out of a slot in the top armor.

The BMB-60 was a 60mm, smoothbore gun, capable of firing any number of rounds. It was smaller than the 90mm gun on the M1-5, but it packed a big enough punch to knock out pretty much any vehicle on the battlefield. It was a little harder to depress for closer-range shots given that the Mamba didn't have a turret per se, but it was still a wicked-fierce weapon.

The top hatch was on the tank was open, and Noah peered inside. It looked surprisingly simple, almost Spartan, and nothing like the old-time tanks he'd seen in the flicks.

"Can I get in?" he asked hesitantly.

"How tall are you, Lysander?" Sergeant Phong asked.

Noah wasn't sure what surprised him most: that the sergeant knew who he was, that she called him by his last name (no one did that—"Lysander" was Esther), or that she asked his height.

"Uh, I'm 185."

"Ooh, just snuck in under the wire," Mz. Vitterly said.

Noah was aware, in a general sense, that tankers, like PICS Marines, were limited in how tall they could be. He didn't recall what the limits were, though.

"Under waiver, if his legs and torso match," Sergeant Phong said, then to Noah, "The height limit is 182 with waiver to 186 after a fitting."

I just want to see what it's like, not transfer! Noah thought—not that he could even make the choice until he'd had at least a year as a lance corporal, and was approved for the lateral transfer.

"So I can get in?" he asked.

"Sure. Don't hit the red button that says 'Fire!'" the sergeant said.

What? This thing is armed? he thought, looking up in alarm, only to feel his face redden in embarrassment as the two burst out into laughter upon seeing his expression.

OK, OK, you got me, he thought as he lowered himself into the driver's seat.

It was cramped, and with a helmet on, his head would be close to hitting the hatch when closed. Still, it felt right. Noah loved being in a PICS, but this was another level up the pyramid of fun. He'd give anything to be able to take the tank out for a spin.

"Pretty freaking copacetic, huh, Lysander?" the sergeant said, crouching over the still open hatch.

"Yes, sergeant. Pretty freaking copacetic."

REQUIEM

Chapter 30

Esther

"What do you think?" Sergeant Kinder asked his three team leaders as they glassed the processing plant on the valley floor below them.

"Can we get another scan from the *Kearsarge*?" Esther asked.

"I don't know. She's pretty locked tight with the rest of the company."

Well, ask, why don't you? All they can say is no.

Esther knew that they weren't the point of main effort, and the *Kearsarge* would be in full support of the bulk of the company at Lassiter Crossing. Still, even if the ship was only a schooner, she carried much more scanning gear than the company's assets.

With only drones, electronic scanners, and aircraft, the Marines relied heavily on the Navy for intel, both active and passive. Since Esther had been with the battalion, both ships assigned to her two missions had been schooners, the Navy's bare-bones, low-cost men-of-war. It hadn't mattered that much for the re-taking of the *Excavator King*, but here, with an actual ground mission, a more powerful platform would be making things easier for them.

The operation on Requiem was one of those mission-creep assignments that her father had detested. Rio Tinto, the same corporation for whom her platoon had recovered the *Excavator King*, and Excel Sun both held concessions on the planet. The two corporations had split the original terraforming costs, but over the years, their relationship had become contentious, and that had spilled over into open conflict as to mining rights. Both sides had hired "security teams," and when the teams had expanded to battalion-sized forces, that had not surprisingly broken out into violence.

When mercenaries fought, the Federation often turned their collective eyes, letting them achieve their own resolution. That was when civilians wouldn't become collateral damage, however. On Requiem, more than 300,000 civilians were in harm's way on the southern continent, civilians only recently re-located to the planet after Callet rejected its terraforming. Over a hundred had been killed from artillery fire, something both mercenary companies blamed on the other, and Bravo Company had been deployed as a buffer to stop the fighting and allow the FCDC forensic teams to investigate the tragedy.

Normally, when the Corps or Navy was to be interjected into a situation, opposing forces went into a flurry of activity to consolidate their position before the Federation forces took over. And while probably neither side wanted to formally take on the Marines, they wouldn't let small units or individual Marines get in their way in the rush to strengthen their position before a cease-fire was eventually called.

Which Esther expected at any time. A representative of the Third Ministry at that moment was negotiating with Rio Tinto and Excel Sun somewhere in orbit. Like most Marines, Esther didn't understand why the Federation was negotiating. Excel Sun's headquarters was in Alliance space, but it had huge assets within the Federation, its share in Requiem being just one. Esther felt that the Federation should just simply make a decision and demand compliance.

And so, while the negotiations dithered on, First Squad was overlooking an Excel Sun processing plant two klicks away. There weren't any overt signs of activity among the jumble of machinery and buildings, but Esther would have preferred to have the *Kearsarge* conduct a full scan of the place.

Don't be too cautious, she admonished herself.

She'd been nervous as they had approached their last objective, a joint chemical warehouse back along the main highway. Five employees, three from Excel and two from Rio Tinto, had met them and bemusedly watched as the squad had searched the facilities. If the tension between the two corporations had affected the five, they certainly hid it well from the Marines.

Still, something about the processing plant below her didn't feel right to Esther. The warehouse, placed far away from population centers due to the volatile nature of the chemicals, only had five employees. The processing plant, while automated, should have more than a few workers moving about, and there should be some sign of people among the small gathering of buildings outside the front gate to the compound.

"Maybe they all evacuated," Telly Eason said as if he could read her thoughts. "I don't think I'd want to be in there, or anywhere near, if it got caught up in the fighting."

"Maybe," Sergeant Kinder said, his voice not sounding that confident. "But, we're behind schedule. We've got two more places to hit before nightfall, so let's head on down. Squad "V," Second Team back, First and Third up—and watch your dispersion!"

Esther half-listened as the sergeant reported back to the lieutenant, who responded back with a deep-into-the-weeds transmission on keeping alert and staying safe. She tuned him out—not that what he was saying was wrong, but because they all knew the drill.

Esther didn't feel comfortable simply sauntering down the slope, but this was not a fight yet, and hopefully, it wouldn't erupt into one. Appearances mattered. Going in too aggressively could trigger a fight with nervous mercenaries.

In training, she usually knew who was the enemy and simply reacted to the changing tides of battle. Here, in real life, she didn't know if this would be like the chemical warehouse or something more challenging.

"Get ready. We're going on down there," she told Maltese, Yadry, and Wells. "Squad V."

"Just like that? In the open?" Maltese asked.

Despite his less-than-stellar start in the fire team, Maltese had developed into a better-than-average Marine, and his mind was constantly churning. Esther was developing a degree of affection for him that she'd never had for the other two Marines in the team. It wasn't as if she disliked the other two—they were simply part of the landscape in some ways, although she took the responsibility for their wellbeing to heart. But she felt more than that for Leroy. In so many ways, he and she were nothing alike, but in a few important aspects such as considering the ramifications of their actions, they matched.

"Just like that. Let's hope anyone there is as complacent as at the chemical warehouse. OK, let's get ready. We've got the asshole," she said, referring to the position in the rear of the formation.

First and Third teams were already moving over the crest of the ridge, spreading out as they descended. Esther waiting until both teams were a good twenty meters away before she gave the signal to move out.

The hill was covered in the small scrub and grasses favored by terraforming teams to help keep the atmosphere in check. Tough and wiry, the low-hugging plants were not nearly as impressive as trees, but they established quickly and created more biomass given the same amount of land. That didn't make logical sense to her, but too many engineering and nature shows on the holo had driven that piece of knowledge into her brain housing group.

But what the groundcover didn't provide was concealment. To approach the factory unseen, they'd have to be on their bellies low-crawling in some sort of sniper stalk. That wasn't happening, though. They were just walking down as if they hadn't a care in the world. Esther felt naked and exposed.

Her senses were on high alert, and she scanned up and down her AI's meager capabilities. There were a few of what might be ghost images, but nothing substantial. The expected incoming of enemy fire never materialized, however, and the squad entered the small settlement outside the factory's gate.

"First, take the two-story. Second, you've got the pink house, and Third, you take the white and silver buildings," Sergeant Kinder said. "Keep on the alert and give me feeds if you see anything."

Squad leaders could only track one subordinate extra feed at a time, unlike platoon sergeants and higher who could scan and pull up any Marine's helmet feed. Esther had never understood that restriction, but it was something she was used to. Still, it was one of the many things on her list she'd change when she played her private "If I Was the Commandant" mental game.

Excess hubris was not one of Esther's problems.

"Let's go," she passed to her three Marines.

Clearing buildings was something the squad could do in their sleep. With the battalion based in a station, structures were plentiful. It was training in wide open spaces that was at a premium, given they had to catch rides to any planet.

PFC Maltese barely hesitated as he performed a heat scan to make sure there was not a hostile waiting just inside the home's front door.

"Contrary," Esther reminded him.

"Going in right!" he shouted as he kicked open the door and rushed to the left.

It was a simple misdirection, and with the AI's locked on, a big flashing "LEFT" on their face shields reminded each Marine that Maltese was in fact going left, not right as he announced.

"Coming in left," Yadry shouted, darting to the right.

"Clear!" Maltese shouted a few moments later.

"Contrary, off!" Esther ordered, as each AI switched modes.

Esther wasn't too sure the contrary mode was a good idea. Even with the AI displays flashing, in the heat of battle, things could get confusing, and a Marine hearing a shout might react instinctively. The contrary clearing command was fairly new, and even if they'd rehearsed it many, many times, Esther was a little wary of it. With the entry gained, she thought she could switch off from contrary mode.

"Coming in right. Actual right," she added, walking more than darting inside the home, Wells on her ass.

For such a bright pink home on the outside, the interior was rather more subdued. The furniture consisted of a tan, overstuffed sofa, a dining table with mismatched and beat up chairs, and a small, older-model holo projector. Esther took off her helmet, and immediately, she was hit with the unmistakable smell of grissen pounte, the inedible delicacy of the Funden Belt—of which Callet had been part of until its evacuation. Fundens were inordinately proud of their love of the fermented mass of crap they called a delicacy that no one else in human space could stomach. They even insisted that no fabricator in the universe could duplicate it, so it had to be prepared by hand.

Esther walked up to the table where she saw three half-eaten bowls of congealed grissen. She reached out a forefinger and touched the contents of one of the bowls—it was pretty hard. Esther didn't have a clue as to how long the bowls had sat there, but it was clear to her that they'd been abandoned quickly.

"Sergeant Kinder, the pink house is clear," she passed on the P2P. "It looks like there were three people here, but they left in a hurry. They left behind three bowls of grissen pounte, all well-congealed."

"Grissen pounte? Got to be Callet refugees, then," he passed, stating the obvious. "Come on back out."

Esther held her forefinger up and twirled it in a circle, then flattened it out to point out the door. Maltese nodded and led the team out. Esther took one last look around. On the wall by the door, a simple 2D picture hung, featuring a smiling man and women, a grown man-child between them with the obvious features of a regressor. Esther couldn't withhold a shudder. Regressors never grew too large, but the furrowed brows and lower-jaw droop were the primary signs of the genetic condition, one of the few that doctors could not cure. Even with genetic manipulation and then regen, the same symptoms simply reappeared. The unfortunate sufferers live shorter, much more limited lives, and their frequent outbursts made caring for them difficult. Many ended up as wards of the state, but evidently, not in this case.

Esther stepped outside, glad to get out of the house. The parents of the boy had been dealt a rough hand, first with their son, and then losing their home on Callet. They'd arrived on Requiem as refugees, and now, it looked as if they'd been caught up in the fighting. Esther couldn't imagine a life like that, but still, the two had been smiling, and the father's hand on the boy's shoulder spoke of something deep, something vital in their connection.

Esther felt an unexpected pang of loss. She'd been cut adrift herself when her parents were killed. Noah was the only family she had left now, and she'd been more than a little distant to him since

Camp Charles. She still wished he'd never enlisted, but she also knew she needed to rectify that.

All three teams gathered around the squad leader. The little settlement had been abandoned. No one could tell if they'd fled the area or were inside the looming factory taking refuge or being held as human shields.

Esther looked up at the massive facility. Processing ore had become streamlined over the last few centuries, but still, a massive amount of ore was being refined, and the size of the plant reflected that. Esther couldn't even imagine how much the facility cost. It looked quiet, but she doubted that either corporation would simply abandon it to wait out the conflict. The fact that their scanners weren't picking up anything hinted that if there was anyone in there, they were sophisticated enough to be able to block any detection.

Which probably meant the St. Regis Brigade, which had been hired by Excel Sun. The brigade had once been one of the finest, best-armed mercenary units before their ill-fated experiment with creating "super-soldiers" using a "zombie parasite"-based procedure. Stung by their defeat, the brigade hadn't folded but become far more aggressive as it tried to regain its former reputation. Esther's father had even faced them on Gaziantep while a battalion commander, and he'd acknowledged they were a worthy foe.

The brigade had resurrected its reputation through a series of conflicts, but perhaps most by siding with the Evolution, fighting—without pay—alongside the rest of the evolutionary forces. They'd managed to rebuild themselves, purchasing the best gear right up to—and some charging past—the Kiev Limitations. And now, the circle had been completed. Ether's father had fought against the brigade, the brigade had fought with her father's forces, and now it potentially faced the daughter.

Excel Sun was not a powerful as Rio Tinto, but they'd scored a coup in hiring the brigade. MKX was a good unit, but if it came to a confrontation, Esther would rather face the Mixxies than the Regis mercs.

"What's the plan?" Telly asked the sergeant.

"We just go inside and check it out. You take the left. Lysander, you've got the middle, and Dogman, you take the right."

Esther kept a straight face. Sergeant Kinder was a good NCO, but he was a "pantser," as in going by the seat of his pants. He rarely had detailed plans worked out, instead relying on giving very vague guidance and relying on training. Esther was firmly convinced that operations orders, even at the squad level, needed to be more detailed. It was all well and good to shift due to enemy reactions, but there had to be a good solid base from which to shift in the first place.

"OK, let's move out. Keep me updated," he said.

Without a firm boundary, Esther turned to her team and pointed at the front office for the compound. She'd clear that, then coordinate with Eason to the right. With Maltese leading, they simply walked up.

"Actual, no contrary," Esther said as Maltese waved his hand over the pad, and to everyone's surprise, the door whisked open.

"Coming in right," Maltese said as he darted inside, followed by Yadry.

Esther and Wells were right behind the first two. The main office was rather small for such a large facility, she thought as she looked around. A front counter kept visitors from the main office, where four desks with screens stood empty. The Marines vaulted over the counter and spread out to check the side offices, the head, and what looked like a break room. In the back was a long, rectangular room with a window for a back wall that looked over the compound. On the front wall of the room was a bank of monitors, a few showing various spots in the facility, but most were turned off.

"Corporal!" Yadry said, pointing to a rack along the back corner of the room.

Esther walked up. It was a weapons rack, no question. There were slots for ten weapons, slots that were now empty. She couldn't tell what the weapons were, nor if the slots had even been filled, but this was not good news.

"We've got possibly ten weapons out there," she passed on the squad circuit, pushing her helmet cam view to the sergeant.

"What kind?" Sergeant Kinder asked. "Can you see?"

"No. Can't tell. Personal weapons, from the size of the racks, but beyond that. . ."

Many isolated facilities had weapons for security. Most often, they were non-lethal, and Esther hoped that was the case here. But given the situation between the two corporations, she wouldn't bet on that. And these were only company weapons; they would be in addition to any merc weapons, if merc forces were in the facility.

"Anything else in there?" Sergeant Kinder asked.

"A bank of security screens. Most are off," she passed as Wells played with the controls, trying to pull more online.

"Roger. If there's nothing else, move on. We've got to sweep this place as quickly as we can if we're going to get to our next two objectives."

Esther frowned. "Quickly" so as to get to the "next two objectives" was not a course of action, in her opinion. "Thoroughly" was more important. Get the job done, then worry about other objectives. It would be easy to bypass an enemy if they went too quickly, an enemy who could jump up and bite them or the rest of the company in the ass. Third Platoon's mission was to clear the southern approach into Lassiter Crossing. First Squad had been assigned the small valley along Sukiko Ranch Road, clearing four objectives, after which they'd set up a blocking position at the ranch itself. They were to keep individuals from using the road, or if a larger unit moved past, too strong for a single squad to stop, report that back.

If they missed someone in the compound by rushing, whoever that was could have a clear shot all the way to the city if that was their intent. And the huge facility could easily hide even a platoon-sized unit.

"You heard the man. Let's move on," she told the other three Marines.

"But I've almost got this," Lance Corporal Wells said, fiddling with the control panel for the screens.

"Yeah, just another two hours, I can get it," Yadry mocked.

"Now, Wells," Esther ordered. "We need to move."

"I could've got it," the lance corporal muttered as he complied.

The four Marines filed out of the office, automatically moving into a fire team diamond. Esther looked around, then pointed to what looked to be a pipe nexus, a square building, about 15 meters by 15 with pipes of various diameters converging on it and disappearing inside. Maltese nodded and headed in that direction.

At the back point of the diamond, Esther was responsible for rear security, so she was scanning the area. Dogman's team was exiting their first structure, which looked to be some sort of maintenance bay, and looked to be heading to a berthing area, and Sergeant Kinder was in the small common area in front of the apartments, one foot up on a bench and leaning forward, arms on the elevated knee as he watched Third Team. He made a good picture, and if they'd been deemed important enough for the press to be with them, Esther knew they'd be recording him. It was just the kind of image that they loved—the stalwart Marine, defending the citizens of the Federation.

For a moment, Esther wished he'd been standing like that, looking oh so competent, and that the press was there. She might be a mere corporal, but the more anyone was in the public eye, the better it was. Part of her was ashamed for considering politics, but it would be stupid to ignore the realities of life. It wasn't as if she created the system, after all.

She was just turning away to scan to their direct rear when a sharp crack of ionizing air filled the compound as Sergeant Kinder collapsed.

"Run!" she shouted a split second after her feet launched her forward. She'd made it less than ten meters before a cacophony of kinetics reached her. She swept up the other three as they sprinted to the pipe nexus.

That was an energy weapon, she realized as she dug down for more speed. *But from where?*

Something hit her hard on the shoulder, but her bones hardened as designed, and she wasn't hurt. She reached the building and hit the deck behind the wall, finding a space between the other three.

"Hal! You OK?" she asked over the squad net.

She'd seen him drop, and she feared his condition. He had to have been hit by the energy weapon, and as good as the STF armor that made up their bones was against kinetics, it wasn't that effective against the more powerful energy weapons. And from the volume of the sound of the displaced air, Esther was sure the sergeant had been hit with a crew-served weapon.

"Sergeant Kinder's dead!" Telly Eason passed over the net.

Shit!

With the sergeant down, the command AI monitor would have switched over command properties to the next senior Marine, which was Telly. Part of the command avatars was that they went light blue for WIA and gray for KIA.

"I need help!" Dogman shouted over the net. "We're pinned down and taking heavy fire."

Rounds kicked up the dirt and grass alongside the pipe nexus. So far, though, nothing reached them behind the wall. But on the other side of the common area, Dogman was in the shit. Esther superimposed their avatars on an overhead image of the compound.

Sergeant Kinder's avatar, still blue on her face shield, was where he'd fallen in the middle of the commons. Dogman's team was arrayed alongside the apartment building.

Where's the firing coming from?

Without live surveillance, she couldn't get tracking. Looking at the impacts just a few meters away, she thought that at least most of the rounds were coming from the white, flat-topped building on the far side of the commons.

What about that fucking crew-served?

But she'd seen Kinder fall! Esther gave her AI the command, and a moment later, the display was back to just before the weapon fired. Changing the visual mode to compressed spectrums, she advanced the recording. When the weapon fired, she tried to ignore the sergeant as she picked up the beam track, a red streak across the now blue-tinted image.

She pulled up the overhead view and superimposed the track. From this view, she couldn't tell elevation, but the beam came from either the same flat-roofed building as the kinetic firing or one of those behind the building. She wished she knew exactly from where it had fired, but at least she had an axis.

She saved the track, then sent it out to the other Marines.

"Hare's down. WIA. We need help here, guys!" Dogman said.

"Come on, we've got to get fire on this," she told her team, blinking forward the overhead of the building to their AIs.

"Get ready to get the hell out of there," she passed to Dogman. "On my command!"

Maltese and Esther hugged end of the wall, Yadry and Wells the other end.

"And now!" she told her team members.

"Go, Third!" she passed as the four leaned forward to pour fire at the building.

She caught sight of Dogman leading his team into the apartment building, two of them dragging Hare.

Shit! Now you're stuck inside!

A round ricocheted off the top of Maltese's helmet from where he leaned out over her.

"Back!" she ordered, an instant before the whiz of something large-caliber passed where her head had just been.

Whether whatever it was had the power to punch through her armor, she didn't know, but she suspected that it did.

"Telly, where are you?"

She could see his avatar on her display, of course, but no one in his team had moved.

"Esther, I called the company for help, and they just told me to hold on," Telly said, his voice high, his words clipped. "What do we do now?"

There was another crack of ionized air, and a moment later, Woowoo managed to get out, "Dogman's KIA. And me and Luna're messed up something fierce. We're inside the building!"

Esther could hear the outrage in his voice, but she wasn't surprised. Judging from the large displacement of air after the weapon had fired, she guessed that it was a high-powered, man-packed meson cannon, and simple walls were not enough to shield from a beam like that.

"Try and get out the back, Woowoo, if there's any way," she told them. "And take Dogman with you."

Dogman's AI might list him as KIA, but if the walls of the building had absorbed enough of the beam's energy, then his nervous system might not be too damaged to preclude resurrection.

"Telly, you've got to maneuver around. Try and flank them here," she said, highlighting a smokestack.

It was probably sturdy enough to withstand the cannon fire, and maybe they could get up high enough to put plunging fire on whoever might be on the roof of the building.

Esther pulled up her recording again, then timed from the shot that killed Kinder to the one that hit Dogman and Woowoo. Seventy-three seconds. She ran a search, pulling up all energy weapons with a 70-75 second recharge rate. Nothing from the Regis or Mixxie weapons list came up. There wasn't anything close.

What the hell? There has to be something.

Then it hit her. They had to be tied into the grid. She changed the parameters, ran them again, and hit paydirt.

What was facing them was probably a Sylvesterie DR-40, fired by St. Regis mercs. The Confederation-made cannon was a two-man, three-megajoule meson weapon, with a 110-second battery recharge-cycle, a 70-second direct connection recharge cycle. With one battery pack, it could fire between three and twelve rounds, depending on the output setting.

Esther's body suddenly spasmed, every nerve on fire. She barely heard the clap of air that followed. Her mind panicked for a moment before the tingling stopped and she could breathe again.

"You OK?" Yadry shouted as he rushed over.

"Fuck me royal," Maltese said as he shook out his leg.

"Yeah. We're still kicking," Esther said, even if Maltese seemed to be having some trouble.

"You're lucky it was a near miss," Yadry said.

"I don't think it was a near miss," Esther told him. "I think there're enough pipes inside this building," she said, patting the wall behind which they had taken cover, "to deflect most of the beam."

Another round, and the mathematics of the situation or the enemy gunners upping the charge could change just enough to let a lethal shot through. Esther tried to shake off the cobwebs and ran a quick options check. They hadn't located the cannon, for one, and even if they did, their options were limited. The M333 might be able to take out the cannon with a direct hit, but that was about it. With Hare down, that meant they had two of them left in the squad, two to stand up to a still un-located cannon.

"Telly, we need that support from the company. Where are you on that?"

"I told you. They said to hang on."

"'Hanging on' is going to get us all zeroed. We need the Stork or mortars. Hopefully the Stork."

It would be a far reach for the mortar team attached to the company, but it was worth a try. The Stork, though, could stand off and take out the cannon with one of its missiles. The first would be shot down by the gun team, but the second would hit long before the cannon could re-charge.

"But I told you, they said no."

Esther rolled her eyes and took a deep breath. It wouldn't do any good to explode on Telly.

"Look, Telly. This is what you are going to do. You're going to switch over command to me. Then you're going to get your team to the smokestack and provide us with covering fire. Understand?"

There was silence on the other end of the P2P circuit. Esther understood that. She was junior to Telly, and Marines didn't willfully pass command to someone else. After 15 seconds had passed, she was wondering if she was going to have to repeat the request when her face shield shifted to command mode.

"Basker-Three-Six, this is Basker-Three-One. Request immediate fire support to follow," she passed.

"Lysander, what's wrong with Eason? I've got him still blue," the lieutenant asked.

"I took over," she passed, not expounding on the situation. "And we're pinned down by a Sylvesterie DR-40. We don't have the firepower to take it down."

"What about your dunkers?"

"We haven't located it yet. And two dunkers against a DR-40 is a little much to ask. We've got two KIAs and three WIAs right now, and we need help."

"Roger, and I'm trying to get it. You're out of range with the mortars, and the Stork's supporting First Platoon right now. They're heavily engaged. I'm sending over Orinda to your pos now, but her ETA's in an hour minimum."

"Lieutenant, an hour and we'll all be cooked!"

"Corporal Lysander, I'm working on it. Let me get off the hook with you, and I'll be back."

"What about the *Kearsarge*?"

"Staff Sergeant Ski's working on that. Look, do the best you can and let me get something sprung loose to help you."

"Roger that," Esther said, tilting her head back against the wall and closing her eyes.

"Not good?" Maltese asked.

"No, not good."

If it was only the troops, Esther was sure they could hold out until help arrived. The ground situation that kept her from assaulting the enemy position kept them from assaulting the squad. Their body armor wasn't as good as the Marines', and they'd be mowed down if they assaulted. But with that damned DR-40, it was only a matter of time before the gun crew hit the right combination to take them out. Esther couldn't even retreat out of the facility. The cannon had a range of over four klicks against personnel, and they'd be sitting ducks anywhere outside of the compound. To add to the gravity of the situation, tied into the facilities power grid, the gun had an almost unlimited number of charges for all intents and purposes.

Power grid! That's it!

She wanted to smack herself in the head. They had to take out the power grid.

"All hands, pull up the facility schematics. I need the power station or the nodes."

She was going over her own schematics. Immediately, she could tell that the power station was a no go. Situated in the back of the compound, the Marines would have to fight past the mercs to reach it. It was a space-relay, so she couldn't ask the *Kearsarge* to take out the array, which would plunge the entire area into a black-out, Lassiter Crossing included. She rejected two other nodes as only knocking out power to specific areas, and only for a few moments until the power could be re-routed.

"What about the office?" Wells asked.

"There's no node there," Esther said, looking at the diagram.

"No, but there's the meter for the power going to the buildings outside, right by the security cam controls. And there's a system-wide emergency cut-off."

"Can't anyone with a remote turn it back on?" she asked.

"Not if we destroy it. That would block the command signals."

She only thought about it for a moment. It made sense, and Wells seemed awfully sure of himself. Looking over to Maltese, she raised an eyebrow that he could see through her face shield.

"I can give it a try," he said, shaking out his leg once more.

He'd taken more nerve damage to his leg than he was admitting, Esther knew. With her team the closest to the office, that broke it down to Yadry, Wells, and her. Wells knew what to look for, and Yadry had the dunker.

"OK, Wells, it's you and me."

She looked at the avatars for the others, and knew none of them could put out suppression fire.

"Leroy, Pieter, put out massive rounds. Massive. Send a rocket their way, too. Maybe that'll make them keep their heads down.

"Give me a toad," she added to Maltese as Wells scrambled over to them.

"Telly, listen up," she passed on the P2P.

She told him what she had planned and for him to be ready to take over again if something happened to her."

"You two ready?" she asked Maltese and Yadry after she finished.

"Roger," the two said in unison.

"Fire!"

As soon as the two swung around to light up the building, Wells and Esther took off, both going different directions as they left the cover of the pipe nexus. Two rounds hit Esther in the back, and while one stung like a son-of-a-bitch, she kept on her feet.

There was another crack of displaced air, and Wells' avatar immediately went gray. She darted to the left to grab him, but the smoke wisping up from his body told the story. She darted back as the heavy pup-pup-pup of a big kinetic crew-served sounded, the angry wasp-buzz of rounds whizzing past her.

Sorry, Kelten, she thought as she darted back to the office.

A few moments later, she broke around the front, shielded from anything other than the DR-40. She set her timer sixty seconds, then started it counting down. She didn't know if the cannon crew would target her, but she'd put herself on the skyline, so it was a good bet that they would. With the flimsy construction of the office walls providing almost no protection, they could fan out the dispersion to make sure they caught her in a lethal beam.

Wells had said the meter was with the security screens. Esther ran inside the office, vaulted the counter again, and within moments was in the back room. She looked up and out the window and, by pure happenstance, spotted the DR-40 at the far left corner of the roof of the enemy-held building. Almost immediately, stars erupted all along the back window. The mercs could see her, and they were targeting her. The pastiglass was pretty sturdy, though, and it would take lots of hits to break through. The more hits, however, the more the stars would block their view.

And then the glass shattered. Esther hit the deck as the big crew-served put 12.7 mm round after round into the room.

Forty seconds, she noted to herself. *Where's the switch?*

The gunner for the big 12.7 kept shooting through the blown-out window, which was a mistake. He should have been firing through the wall beneath the window. Esther wasn't going to correct him, though, as she scurried forward on all fours, pieces of window fragments and screens showering her. Near where Wells had been standing, she risked raising her head.

Thirty seconds.

At first, she didn't see anything, and she turned to look to the other side of the room. Still, she didn't spot any turn-off switch, and she felt a momentary rise of stress. She jammed her back against the wall, and hoping she'd be out of sight to the gunner, slid her back up until she was standing. And there, right above where she'd been crouching, but on a control panel sticking out of the wall, was a red button labeled "Main Power." She lunged for it, turning it off. The two remaining lights in the room that hadn't yet been shot out turned off.

Twenty seconds.

She wasn't done yet. Wells had said they could remotely turn the power back on. She wasted a couple of seconds looking for access to the space below the control panel, giving up and shooting it open with her M99. Kicking out the splinters, she looked inside, seeing nothing. Her panic surged. How could she cut the line if there wasn't anything to cut?

But Wells never said "cut." He said "destroy." And she suddenly realized that only the lines going outside the facility would be near her. The controls were just controls, not part of the grid itself. If she could destroy them before someone activated it, the power was going to be down for a long time.

Ten seconds.

She whipped out the toad Maltese had given her, thumbed it on, noticing the timer was on five. Esther placed it on top of the control, then stepped back, taking out her own toad. With a practiced move, she thumbed in live, set it at three, and tossed it there for good measure.

Her timer hit zero, and a second later, the small sun that resided in each toad ignited. Without her face shield, she would have been blinded as 1100° C of burning hell burned right through the control, leaving it a smoking ruin. Esther stood there for a moment, watching the destruction.

Shit! The cannon!

Esther might have turned off the power, but the cannon had batteries. She didn't know how long it would take them to realize what had happened and then switch to battery power, and once they did that, how much longer it would take to recharge the cannon, but she was sure she was cutting it close. At a full sprint, she left the burning toads, darting out the door and into the main office as 12.7 rounds chased her. She barely touched the counter as she vaulted it, putting her shoulder down and smashing through the front door. If she turned right, she knew she would be in full view of the building where the enemy were lodged, so she turned left and put everything she had into getting some distance in between her and the office. Going left might not be any better, but it couldn't be any worse.

Her timer was still going, and the now green numbers kept growing: 17. . .18. . .19. . . . For a moment, she thought the cannon wasn't going to fire again, and she slowed down just a bit when she felt the tingle in her back, followed by yet another clap of displaced air. She stumbled, but didn't go down. Looking back, she could see the bits of the office building's spotlights that had been destroyed bounce off the ground. The building had been hit with what had to be a pretty big charge. If the tiny trace gasses in the lights had received enough energy to explode, anything organic inside would have been cooked.

Fire again, suckers!

That shot had to have drained quite a bit of power, and Esther would love to see the cannon unable to recharge.

"Esther, you OK?" Telly asked. "I can't see."

With her retaining the command display, he couldn't tell if her avatar had grayed out.

"I'm still here. Wells is KIA, down hard," she said. "Now, we've got to knock out that fucking cannon."

"But. . ."

"I've got a handle on it. Who's on the dunker?"

"With me?"

"Yeah, of course with you!" she said as she jogged over to where she could move forward concealed from the building.

"Bubba."

"Well, you send Bubba back to see me. I'm heading here," she said, blinking forward a position behind a holding tank of some sort. "ASAP!"

"Yadry, meet me here now," she passed on the P2P after forwarding the same spot.

Her lance corporal beat her to it, but together, they had to wait four minutes and through one more blast of the DR-40 before Bubba arrived.

Despite the name, "Bubba" was one Lance Corporal Delight Fontana, a 1.5-meter, redhead pixie. Esther didn't really know her that well, even if they had adjoining berthing, but she had a decent rep.

"What do yah got?" Bubba asked.

"I got a DR-40, just sitting up there, taking us out piece-by-piece."

"But we don't know exactly where it is," Yadry said. "I looked."

"Ah contraire. You were too close. Here," she said, forwarding the helmet cam capture.

"Not much of a window to shoot at," Bubba said. "And that's a polychrome shield in front. My Airy might penetrate, might not."

"Don't need it to. Look where it's at. Right at the corner. If we take out—"

". . .the corner, London bridge falls down," Yadry said., sounding impressed.

"Oh, that could work," Bubba said, nodding. "Still. . ."

"Still nothing. We've got Airies and grenades. That building wasn't built for war. It will come down."

"So what do you want us to do?" Bubba asked.

"Wait one," Esther said, before pulling up the lieutenant again.

"Basker-Three Six, where we at on that air?"

"Nothing yet. Orinda's 45 minutes out. Can you hold?"

As if on cue, another clap of air echoed off the buildings. Immediately, PFC Warren's avatar went light blue. The DR-40 team had somehow spotted Telly's team moving forward.

"That's a negative. We are down another Marine."

"Roger, I just saw that." There was a pause, and then, "What are you going to do? Can you pull back?"

"That's a negative. We'd be too exposed. We're going to bring down part of the building under the cannon," she passed, forwarding her cam capture.

"Uh, wait one. Let me clear that."

"Lieutenant," Esther said, switching to the P2P. "I'll be damned if I'll get more Marines killed just to save some corporation's credits. We did that once, and we lost your predecessor."

"It isn't that, Corporal. It's, well, we've got a micro-drone within range, and there are ghost signals that might indicate people in that building."

"Of course there's people in there! There called mercenaries, and they're killing us."

"I didn't mean them. Possibly human shields."

That stopped Esther.

"Are you sure?" she asked after a few moments to gather her thoughts.

"No, we aren't. The images are all over the facility."

"So it could be a faulty drone, or it could be spoofing."

"Affirmative, Corporal Lysander."

"So are you telling me not to attack?" she asked, wanting to get his response on the record.

There was a pause, even longer than Esther's had been, before he answered, "Do not initiate anything. However, if it's a matter of life and death, do what you have to do. Paragraph 3b."

Paragraph 3b of the Harbin Accords specifically stated that civilian casualties were not war crimes if the civilians were not specifically targeted and their deaths were a result of lawful engagement of enemy combatants. It was a legal out if the requirements were met.

"Aye, aye, sir. I understand."

She turned to the waiting two Marines and said, "We wait here. If they do nothing, we do nothing. If they act, then the two of you have to take down the corner of the building. What do you think? Rockets?"

"Grenades," Yadry said as Bubba nodded her agreement.

"OK, grenades it is."

She had just begun to pass the word when the DR-40 fired once more. This time, Warren's avatar went gray. Telly and Van

Nustern had moved forward and were out of the direct beam, but Warren was KIA.

"All hands, on my 30 second mark, fire everything you have to the rooftop. We've got to keep them off our dunkers. Mark!"

As her timer counted down, she turned to the two Marines and said, "It's up to you. Fire what you've got until the fucking thing comes down."

They moved to their right, so that they could step out and take the building under fire.

At ten seconds, Esther released her safety. At zero, she shouted "Fire" and jumped forward, spraying the rooftop. Maltese, Telly, Van Nustern, and Woowoo, who'd moved back into the apartment, joined her.

The first dunk of the M333 sounded beside her, followed by the second. Esther kept up a steady stream of darts, but her eyes were on the corner of the building. The first grenade hit, blowing off a chunk of wall as she heard the dunk of another outgoing round. Another explosion erupted, spitting chunks of building like a sideways volcano. Esther could see the projector barrel of the DR-40 swing to take them under aim. Esther realized she should have started firing sooner to give them more time. Twenty or thirty more seconds, and the cannon would be re-charged.

A third, fourth, fifth, and sixth grenade hit, and the main support was cut in two, but still the roof didn't collapse.

"Switching to rockets," Bubba shouted.

A moment later, the flare of the Airy took off, making a beeline for the building. It hit with less of an overt explosion than the grenades, but the roof shook, and Esther could see the muzzle of the cannon projector jerk.

Two rounds hit her, one in the chest, on in the knee. The knee hurt like a son-of-a-bitch, and she took a step back just at Yadry's grenade hit inside the gaping hole. The rooftop lurched, and the DR-40 slid to the side as mercs dived to their left to more solid footing. For a moment, Esther thought the roof would hold, but creaking that they could hear 150 meters away, the roof tilted even more before collapsing with a roar. The DR-40 itself seemed to fall in slow motion until it disappeared, their sight blocked by the pipeline nexus.

Heedless of the enemy, Esther ran to her left until she could see around the nexus. Up ahead, in a cloud of dust, the DR-40 lay upside-down, projector muzzle buried into the dirt, the barrel bent almost in half. Two bodies lay still beside it.

The surrender chime sounded, and Esther jerked her M99 up, noting her 12% magazine fill. She'd forgotten for a moment the other mercs. But the surrender chime was ingrained in every Marine. She hesitantly lowered her weapon.

"This is Corporal Esther Lysander, United Federation Marine Corps. Who are you?"

"Assistant Leader Cody Fuentes, St. Regis Brigade. I've got five, including me, to surrender. One WIA. Do you have a corpsman?"

An assistant leader was roughly the equivalent to a sergeant. As far as Esther knew, the smallest St. Regis unit had a leader, or staff sergeant equivalent in charge.

"We've a corpsman inbound," Esther said as she saw a figure look over the edge of the roof. "Come on down, no weapons."

"Telly, get down and come cover me. I don't expect anything, but still, be ready.

"Woowoo, are you mobile?" she asked, noting his light blue avatar.

"Affirmative. Hurtin' for certain, but alive and kicking."

Esther let out a sigh of relief. She quickly went over her readout. She had seven effectives, including Woowoo. There were four KIA's, of which Wells was far beyond resurrection. Then there were two WIA's who needed immediate medical care.

She called in the medivac, which the lieutenant took without getting in her shit, for which she was grateful. He had to be dying to get her report, but with the prisoners now making their way out of the building, he was letting her do her job. She knew he'd be monitoring her visuals, though.

"Corporal, we are your prisoners. I'd appreciate it if you notify the Red Cross," the assistant leader said, a man in his thirties.

He had 14 operations hashes on his sleeve, so this man had seen some action. He didn't seem upset, which seemed odd to her.

"You are the commander?" Esther asked. "An assistant leader?"

"I am now," he said, tilting his head to where the ruined cannon lay, along with two bodies. "Speaking of which, may we check them?"

Esther nodded, telling Yadry to escort them forward.

She told Telly, who was just arriving, to go tend to their wounded while she reported in. She had just started her report when Yardy shouted out, "Corporal Lysander, I think you need to see this!"

"Wait one," she told the lieutenant.

What does he want?

She walked over to where Yadry, the St. Regis assistant leader, and one more merc were standing at the edge of the rubble. Instead of looking at the dead mercs, though, they were looking inside the half-collapsed building.

Esther hopped up on a chunk of plasticrete and followed their gaze.

She almost threw up. There were at least a dozen bodies, civilian bodies, lying in the rubble. Esther bounded off her perch and bolted forward. Some of the bodies were half-buried, their blood bright, too bright where it ran through the dust that coated every square centimeter of their skin.

Right in front of her, two figures lay together, the man trying to cover the smaller body of the boy as he vainly tried to protect him. His arm was wrapped protectively around the boy's head.

Esther didn't want to look, but something drove her forward. She reached them, knowing what she would see and not wanting to. Slowly, she bent over and grabbed the man's wrist, folding the arm back. The boy's face was covered with dust, just the smallest amount of blood leaking out of his nose, but there wasn't any doubt.

It was the regressor boy from the pink house.

WAYFARER STATION

Chapter 31

Noah

"Alas, I have never found a man worthy of my attention," Bella Montrose said, her famous eyes glaring hard.

"What a bitch!" Sampson said, throwing a sock through the image.

Bella barely flickered as she turned away and strode off, leaving the Copper Knight to stare at her retreating figure.

"The Copper Knight's more than worthy enough for you, you bitch," Sampson added.

Noah agreed with his blunter roommate, but given this was Hollybolly at its best, he figured the Copper Knight would win the lady in the end.

The four roommates were in the racks, and the flick was playing on the small projector platform they'd all pitched in to buy. Most junior Marines watched the holos in the rec center, but with the new projector, the four of them had been binge-watching. "Permian" was the fourth holo in a row that they'd watched, with "Dr. Stumble" next on deck.

Just as the Copper Knight turned to his horse, their hatch chimed.

"We don't want any!" Turtle said.

The hatch chimed several more times, one after the other.

"Better get it, Turtle," Noah said. "Pause the flick first."

Turtle was on the rack below Noah, and with a groan, he got out of his rack and opened the hatch. A newbie from Second Platoon stood outside, a red arm band designating him as the duty runner.

"Oops! The boot's got on his red flag of shame. It must be official!" Sampson said.

"What do you want, boot? We're busy," Turtle said.

"Lance Corporal Lysander, you're needed in the company office," he said.

Me? What for?

That they sent a runner to get him was odd. The company clerk could just as easily have sent him a request on his PA.

"What'd you do now?" Sampson asked. "You sneak your girlfriend into the base again?"

"I told you, she works here! I don't need to sneak her anywhere!"

Noah knew Sampson was just giving him shit. But when the new Alpha Company First Sergeant had seen Miriam and him talking together in one of the supply lockers, he'd turned them both in, not listening to their protests. It had taken 15 minutes to convince him that Miriam worked in the exchange and was only getting new LEDs and that Noah had only followed to help.

He'd received a ration of shit from his fellow Marines, and for a short time, he'd even been nicknamed "Romeo," something that had almost as quickly fallen out of favor. Truth be told, he'd been mortified when it happened, but now, he almost enjoyed the tiny degree of notoriety. His roommates knew the score, but other Marines might give him the slightest degree of street cred now.

He hoped.

Noah put on his boots and utility blouse, said, "Don't start the flick again until I get back," and followed the runner to the company office. A few minutes later, he was outside the company commander's office, knocking and announcing himself.

"Stand at ease," Captain Yule said. "This will be out soon, but I wanted to tell you myself. As you know, Bravo Company's been deployed to Requiem—"

"Is my sister OK?" Noah interrupted, suddenly sure why the skipper had called him in.

"Yes, she's hurt, but OK. She's got minor nerve damage, from the report. Didn't even realize she was hurt at all. She took over when her squad leader was killed. . ."

Sergeant Kinder's dead?

Noah's mind was stunned, first with worry about Esther, then relieved, then hearing that the sergeant, who Noah knew fairly well from the gym, had been killed.

". . .acquitted herself quite well. She's being put in for an award—which one, I don't know. She's scheduled to return at 1515 tomorrow, and we'll be in the middle of MCAATs at that time, so I've asked Captain Loess if you could sit in with Alpha during at 0815. I figured you'd want to meet her when she gets back."

"She. . .she'll do regen here?" Noah asked, not sure what else to say.

"No. It'll be back on Malika. She'll undergo debrief here before moving on, along with six other Marines. I don't know how long she'll be on station, so that's why I wanted to give you the head's up."

"Thank you, sir. I appreciate it."

"If there's nothing else, check with Sergeant Guang on when and where for your MCAAT. And when you see her, tell your sister that we're all proud of her."

"Aye-aye, sir."

Now that he knew Esther was going to be OK, his heart, which had jumped into overdrive, calmed back down. He wasn't sure Esther would be dying to see him when she arrived, but he was glad the captain had worked it out.

Chapter 32

Esther

Esther waved off the corpsmen who met her at the gate. She didn't need nor want transport. Along with Woowoo, she stood to the side while the other four Marines were taken out on grav gurneys. She waved to Cat Weis, a PFC from First Platoon, who'd broken her leg and hip in the fight outside Lassiter Crossing. She's gotten to know the young Marine on the trip back to Wayfarer and felt almost sisterly to her. Weis had a month or two of regen, and Esther was confident that she'd be back strong and ready to go.

Not so with Van Nustern and Dogman. Both Marines had been put into stasis, but Chief Alistair, the independent corpsman assigned to the company for the operation, hadn't been too confident that either would survive. They, along with the other serious WIAs and the KIAs had been sent directly back to Malika. The six of them who'd first been taxied back to Wayfarer Station would be debriefed, then put on a passenger liner to join their comrades at the Naval Hospital. By evening, they'd be gone.

"Ess, how are you?" Noah said, calling past the gate.

The small passenger hopper had docked at A2, a civilian gate, and the staff wasn't letting anyone, even a uniformed Marine, get past them.

Despite vowing to improve their relations, Esther felt the tiniest bit of annoyance upon seeing him. He was like a puppy who wouldn't leave her alone. She made an effort to smile, then waved.

"I'm fine. Just got a tingle. Two weeks at Malika, max, and I'll be back good as new.

"You ready?" she asked Woowoo.

Woowoo had been hit harder than she'd been. He had damage in both legs and up his back, and he really should be in a grav-chair at a minimum. But his pride wouldn't let him, and Esther wasn't going to fight him on that and order him to take a chair. If he could take the pain, then that was his choice.

"You know Lance Corporal Woutou, of course," she said as the two were scanned and let past the gate.

"Yes, we've met," Noah said, hand out to shake. "And this is Miriam. Miriam Seek Grace."

Who? And a Torritite? What's this?

Esther thought the woman looked vaguely familiar, but she couldn't imagine why she'd be with Noah. Maybe she was on some civilian staff who met WIA Marines?

Esther shook the woman's hand, noting that she was not dressed like a Torritite. Her mother's religion was not very conservative in most ways, but they did tend to dress in muted colors. The young woman standing in front of her was wearing a shocking pink baroness top and turquoise thigh puffs.

"I'm so glad to meet you—formally, that is. Noah's told me so much about you," she said.

So we've met? And Noah's been telling you about me? Curiouser and curiouser.

She looked back at Noah, calculating.

"Uh, good to meet you both, but we've got to get going. We don't have much time," Woowoo said, the strain in his voice snapping Esther back.

"Yes, we've got a debrief, then we're on to Malika," she said, ashamed that she'd stood there when Woowoo, despite his insistence that he was fine, was hurting.

"OK, we'll walk you back," Noah said.

Esther's leg was aching by the time they made it to battalion, and she was happy to say goodbye to Noah and his good-natured questions on the operation. She gave him a hug, and then she and Woowoo entered the S2 office.

Top Worrel, the S2 chief, looked up as they entered, then said, "There you are. The lieutenant's down at sickbay looking for you."

"We're not there," Esther said. "We walked."

"Yeah, I can see you're not there. I've got eyes, Corporal. But you will be there, as soon as your legs can carry you. Am I right?"

"Right, Top. We're on our way."

Esther had assumed that the debrief would start with the S2, in his office. She hadn't considered that the other four Marines wouldn't be as mobile.

A minute later and a deck below, Esther and Noah were entering sickbay. A couple of Marines were sitting in the seats, awaiting routine sick call. Lance Corporal Fratelli was one of them, and she perked up at the sight of Esther.

"Oh, hi! Corporal Lysander! How're you doing?"

"Can't talk," Esther said as the S3 motioned her over.

Esther was glad of the interruption. She didn't like Fratelli, who was less than a stellar Marine. A sick-bay commando, she seemed to spend more time trying to get out of work than performing it, and she had taken a liking for Esther, as if the gender-sisterhood would somehow make up for her being a shitbird.

It didn't.

"Yes, sir?" Esther said as she and Woowoo reached him.

"Corporal Lysander, these are Mr. Van Ploft and Morales. They've got some questions for you, and I'd like for you to go with them. When they're done, Lieutenant O'Hare and I will take care of the rest of the debrief," he said before turning to the two men and adding, "Gentlemen, please remember that they've got a ship to catch. We need to be done by 2045, and both of these Marines need a few moments to gather up some gear."

Civilian debriefers? What's going on?

Esther and Woowoo followed the two men back up a deck and into the S3's office, right next door to the S2's office where they'd been three minutes prior. One of the men motioned for Esther to enter the major's office. She didn't know what was going on, but she gave Woowoo a pat on the shoulder before leaving him.

"Corporal Lysander, I'm Mr. Van Ploft with the NOI," the man said after Esther had taken a seat.

NOI? Naval Office of Investigation? Why?

"Sir, is something wrong?"

"Oh, no, Corporal. And I'm not a sir. You can call me Mr. Van Ploft or Agent Ploft, whichever you prefer. We've just some routine questions for you, strictly routine."

"But why, sir?"

"Mr. Van Ploft, please."

"OK, why, Mr. Van Ploft."

"Just routine, Corporal. We need to ask questions any time civilians are killed."

Esther's heart fell. She felt guilty, and the sight of the dead boy had been haunting her for the last three days, invading her dreams when she had been finally able to nod off. But the lieutenant had assured her that she'd done nothing wrong. Assistant Leader Fuentes, as the surviving unit commander, would probably face charges for using human shields, but the Marines, and of course, her, would be held blameless.

"I didn't know they were there, sir," she said, not that she really felt that was an excuse.

"Of course. I've read the preliminary report. But you know, after the Evolution, we're trying to heal any rifts within the populace, so we need to gather the facts. It's just one huge cover-your-ass.

"Richard Van Ploft, Agent 33485, Wayfarer Station, 19 April 408. Interview with Corporal Esther Lysander, United Federation Marine Corps," he spoke into the room before turning back to face Esther again.

"So beginning when you first started to approach Excel Sun Processing Plant #4, please tell me what happened. Don't leave anything out."

Esther took a deep breath, calmed her nerves, and started talking. She tried to remember everything as she related each event, each observation. Mr. Van Ploft rarely interjected, rarely asked any questions. Still, it took much longer than Esther would have imagined. She included being relieved by Sergeant Orinda, reporting to the FCDC police team which was with the Marines, and at Mr. Van Ploft's prodding, all of her conversations with the lieutenant before she left the planet to return to Wayfarer. Finally, exhausted and wrung through the wringer, she was done.

"I want to thank you for your cooperation, Corporal Lysander. You've been most forthcoming."

He opened the door, and a worried Master Gunnery Sergeant Quiero-Smith immediately poked his head in and said, "Corporal

Lysander, you've got 34 minutes to catch your ship. Do you need anything from your berthing? I can get Sergeant Johnston to fetch it and bring it to you.

I've been in there that long? she wondered, looking at Mr. Van Ploft. *How high up the food chain are they that they can push aside a major?*

"No, Top. I'm OK. I can grab my bug-out bag and make the ship in time."

"Well, I'll get out of your way," the civilian investigator said. "You need to go get taken care of."

"Did I. . .I mean, did I do anything wrong? You know, with the civilians?" she asked hesitantly, not able to voice anything more specific.

"Oh, I'm here just to gather information. But I wouldn't be too worried. You showed a lot of courage, Corporal, in cutting the power. Courage and ingenuity both. Your father would be proud of you."

Esther felt a partial wave of relief flow over her. She knew on an intellectual level that she had acted within the bounds of warfare, and from conversations with her father throughout her life, she thought the investigator was right, her father would have been proud of her.

The only problem was within her. She wasn't proud of what happened, and she wasn't sure she'd ever be able to forgive herself.

Chapter 33

Noah

"Sergeant Phong, do you have a moment?" Noah asked.

The sergeant looked down from the top of her Mamba where she was holding some sort of calibration equipment against one of the tank's sights.

"Ah, my PICS friend. Sure, climb on up."

That was easier said than done. The three Mambas were jammed in tight in their tank pool with barely enough room for him to slide in between two of them. He ended up pushing against the one behind him with his back, then crawling up a meter or so until he could reach over to the main gun, grab it, and pull himself up. At least the tank motor pool was on the same level as the PICS closet, so the overhead was a full four meters high, and he could stand on top without hitting his head.

"Nice job your sister did. The whole battalion's buzzing about it."

"Thanks," Noah said, automatically.

He was proud of Esther, but to be honest, he was getting a little tired of everyone constantly harping on it. Four Marines had died, and while he didn't blame his sister for that, he thought the general feeling of excitement should be muted in light of their losses. He'd known two of them, Sergeant Kinder and Kelten Wells. Even if they were in different companies, Noah thought Kelten was a close acquaintance, if not an actual friend.

"So what brings you down to our dungeon?" she asked as she looked at her readings.

"I was wondering what the demand will be next year for tankers," he said, trying to keep his voice casual.

"Why, you want to join the dark side?"

"Well, I don't know. My enlistment'll be up in eleven months, and yeah, I was thinking about it."

"Really? You do know this is sort of a dead end. It's hard to advance in the pipeline," she said, looking up at him.

"I know, I read that. But I think I'd like to see what it's like."

"But, I mean, with your family background. . ." she trailed off, breaking eye contact and looking down at her fingernails as if something had just sprung up on them.

Not this again, Noah thought with an audible sigh, which brought the sergeant's gaze back up.

"Sergeant Phong, with all due respect, I'm me. I'm not my father. And I'm not my sister, either. I enlisted for my own reasons, and I can assure, you, Commandant of the Marine Corps in not one of my goals. I want to serve where I best can, period."

The sergeant gave him a piercing, lingering stare before she shrugged and said, "OK, my mistake. Sorry for assuming."

Noah had been a little sharper than he'd intended, and he understood her assumption. It wasn't a secret that Esther was a go-getter with huge potential—and had a huge drive as well. It wouldn't be a reach to assume that he had the same goals and drive as her.

"You going to make E4 before your contract's up?" she asked him.

"Probably in four months. Six months for sure."

"And your MCAAT?"

"Ninety-six."

"Oh, a smart young lad, aren't we? Well, we dumb trackheads only need an 88, so you've got that in the bag."

She put down her calibrator and sat on the gun tube.

"Look, if you really think you'd like to try tanks, that's fine with me. But it's a big step. We've got another Dixie exercise in three weeks. Why don't you see if your platoon commander can spring you for a day or two while we're there, and I'll clear it with the staff sergeant. We'll get you in one of these bad boys and see how it feels. Then, if you're still interested, we can see about getting a package in for the lateral transfer. How does that sound?"

"That would be great, Sergeant! I'd love that!"

"Well, I'm about done here now. You let me know first if they'll spring you, and then I'll clear things here."

She jumped off the tank, turning to fit in the narrow space between it and the next one.

"See you around, Lysander."

Noah waited until her back was to him before he pumped his fist in the air. He jumped off the tank, not caring that he bruised the crap out of his shin on the next tank over.

It wasn't for sure yet, but he had a pretty good feeling that he was going to be a tanker!

Chapter 34

Esther

"Welcome back, Corporal," Pokky Opparell said as Esther entered the brain shack.

"Thanks, Pokky. Good to be home," Esther said.

"Good to be on this floating can? After the bright lights of Malika? I thought you were smarter than that."

"Not much chance of getting out of the hospital when going through regen, Pokky."

"Yeah, I guess there's that. Anyway, good to see you in one piece."

The diminutive woman was one of the MIS engineers, with the battalion for 34 years, making her the dean of the civilian support personnel assigned to the base. No one really knew much about her, but if the full-body tattoos were any indication, she'd lived a wild life in her youth. She could be somewhat of a nosy busybody, but Esther was rather fascinated by her.

"I read your proposed citation. Pretty impressive. You'll have to stop by and see me sometime and give me the real story."

Of course, you read the citation, Pokky. You read everything.

Still, Esther's ears perked up. She knew she was getting written up for something; she just didn't know for what. That was probably why the lieutenant wanted to see her. She hadn't even gotten off the passenger liner when she received the message to come to his office before she did anything else.

"Sure, Pokky. I've got to see Lieutenant Markopoulos first, though. Maybe after chow if you haven't gone home yet."

"Oh, you know me, Corporal. I live here."

Not quite, Pokky. You live at the Pelican Beak, Lana's, or whatever dive bar strikes your fancy. Your party-girl reputation and love of stout precede you," she thought as a smile creased her face.

Esther passed the company offices. She almost stuck her head in the first sergeant's hatch to tell him she was back, but the lieutenant had sent word to see him first.

She knocked on the jamb of the open hatch and announced, "Lieutenant Markopoulos, it's Corporal Lysander," into the platoon commanders' space.

The lieutenant popped his head above his cubical partition, spotted her, and said, "Corporal Lysander, come in, please." He tapped on the top of his partition, and said, "Wyatt, can I have the office?"

Lieutenant Andres said "Sure thing," and stood up. "Welcome back, Corporal," he added before leaving the space.

All four lieutenants shared the same small space, each with a tiny cubical, but they were used to ignoring whatever other platoon business was being conducted, so Esther was mildly surprised that the lieutenant asked his fellow lieutenant to leave.

"Take a seat, Corporal," the lieutenant said, and Esther slid into the small chair, her knees touching her platoon commander's desk. "How did your regen go? Any issues?"

The lieutenant seemed as if his question was perfunctory, but Esther said, "Fine, sir. Three weeks. I've got a little ghost ache, but the techs said there's no lasting damage. Lance Corporal Woutou's doing great. Just another two weeks."

She didn't mention Van Nustern or Dogman. Both had been resurrected, both were still in their regen coma, but the techs and doctors couldn't make any prognosis yet.

"Oh, that's good. Um, I wanted to talk to you personally. It's about Excel Sun #4."

Esther's heart gave a lurch. He didn't sound like he wanted to talk about an award.

"The. . .when. . .the investigation into the civilian deaths has been kicked up. It's a formal Section Five now."

Esther's mouth dropped open in shock.

A Section Five? But the investigator said everything was OK!

Esther was still having dreams about the fight, and she kept second-guessing herself, but she didn't expect a Section Five.

"But Paragraph 3b!"

"Yes, I know, Corporal. It's clear to me, and it's clear to my lawyer."

"Your lawyer, sir? Are you under investigation, too?"

"The both of us, Esther. You and me. I called my dad's lawyer this morning. He can't do anything official yet until. . .unless. . .they level charges, but I thought it'd be a good idea."

Esther tried to take it all in. She didn't have a lawyer to call. She could probably find one easy enough, but she thought that might look like she felt she was guilty.

"Why, sir? What happened? I was told everything was fine."

"And it was, from all I can tell. But a buddy of mine at Division told me Admiral Blankenship is involved."

And the fog that had taken over Esther's mind coalesced into clarity.

Admiral Blankenship was her father's appointment as the First Minister, an olive branch to the loyalists after the Evolution. Her father hadn't been chairman long enough for him to be a problem to him, but the admiral had been a constant thorn in the side of Chairman MacCailín. And he represented more than a few powerbrokers who while they had to accept the facts of the Evolution, they resented the new situation.

And General Ryck Lysander, even in his death, was their boogeyman.

It didn't take a detective to understand that politics had reared its ugly head here. There was a faction that would love nothing better than to pull down Ryck Lysander's daughter.

And the lieutenant was collateral damage.

She looked up at him, his finger drumming nervously on his desk.

It might not be her place, but she said, "I'm sorry, sir, to get you dragged into this."

"It's not your fault, Corporal. . .Esther," he said as if their situation had drawn them together. "I gave the order, so if anyone is to fall, it should be me. Not you."

Esther couldn't tell if he really meant that or if he knew that was what he had to say. She appreciated it none-the-less.

"I'm sorry to be the one to tell you about this, but I thought it should be me," he said. "Now, we need to check in with the skipper, then the CO. Division is sending an SJA, and we'll meet with him tomorrow. So if you're ready?"

"Yes, sir."

"OK. The skipper's waiting for us."

For a brief moment, Esther wanted to run to the comms shack. She knew any number of flags, both retired and still on active duty. But a rising swell of indignation swept through her. She'd done nothing wrong, and her pride would not allow her to beg for help. She had to face this head-on and let the chips fall as they may.

Chapter 35

Noah

"It's just. . .oh, I don't know. I thought he'd be proud," Princess Mayhem said, a tiny tear forcing itself from the corner of her eye.

Noah, his arm around her should, gave her a hug, pulling her into him.

"But are you proud? That's what's important."

"Yes, of course, I am. Making corporal. Being approved for re-enlistment."

"Not everyone gets that far, Dora. You *should* be proud."

"But that's why I thought he'd be, too."

Princess Mayhem's father was a police chief on Knight's World, and over the last two years since he'd joined the battalion, bits and pieces of her relationship had slowly come out. It wasn't a close relationship, that much was clear. But the degree of how much she wanted to gain his approval had only become clear after the Princess had come into his berthing space 20 minutes ago and opened up to him.

The thing is, Noah knew exactly how she felt. He'd always craved his father's approval, he never felt he'd received it, and now that was out of reach forever. Sometimes, when other Marines came to him with their problems, he could empathize, he could sympathize, but he didn't know exactly what the other Marines felt. This time, Princess' troubles had been his own. He understood her intrinsically.

"Sometimes, you just have to think of yourself," he said as Princess laid her head on his shoulder. "If you're proud, then wear that on your chest. You're Princess Frigging Mayhem, and no one else has ever earned that title. Marines quake when you tread, they worship your footprints!"

"Shit, Noah," she said, straightening up and punching him in the shoulder.

She laughed and brushed the tear from her face.

"Yeah, they all worship the ground I walk on, huh?"

"That, or they're afraid you'll have them for dinner."

"Eat me, Noah, eat me," she said, her voice much more relaxed. "You sure have a way of speaking to the girls, telling them what they want to hear."

"Just trying to serve, Ma'am. Just trying to serve," Noah said, glad that his weak attempt at humor seemed to have struck a chord with her.

"You're a good bloke, Noah. Miriam's a lucky girl."

Noah felt his face flush, and he knew he was as red as a beet. He seemed to know what to tell others to cheer them up, but he felt embarrassed when others complimented him.

"Well, thank you for listening to me go on about my old man. I'd better get out of here before someone sees us and thinks we're going at it like dogs in heat."

Noah flushed even harder, if that was possible. One moment, Princess was meek and vulnerable, the next she was back to the earthy Marine he'd come to know.

"It might do your rep some good, but I wouldn't want Miriam to think I'm moving in on her property."

"Property? You think we're, like, uh, like that?" Noah asked.

"Think so? No shit, Sherlock. It's pretty obvious that she's latched onto you, Noah. Not that anyone understands it," she said with a laugh.

She must have seen the shocked look on his face, because she hastened to add, "Just joking, Noah. We understand it. Hell, I understand it. If you weren't claimed property, maybe I'd take a shot at you."

Noah's look of shock had nothing to do with her jab about no one understanding it. It had to do with the idea that Miriam considered them a "thing," that he was her property. Things had been going well between them, and they spent a lot of time together, but she had never said anything to him that might indicate she thought more of him than just a good friend.

Dora came here to get a pick-me-up, but she just returned the favor! This is good intel!

There was a chime as someone wanted entry. Normally, the hatch would be open and whoever it was could just lean his or her head in, but Princess had shut the hatch when she came in.

"Speaking of not starting rumors, I guess it's too late now. Should I open the hatch?" Princess asked.

"Go ahead."

Pokky Opparell stuck her head into the hatch, keeping her body out of the room as if she was afraid to enter.

"Noah, I need to tell you something," she said looking pointedly at Princess Mayhem.

"Uh, I can take a hint, Pokky," Princess said.

She got up, then bent back down to plant a kiss on Noah's forehead.

"Thank you, my brother," she whispered before leaving the space.

"What do you want?" an embarrassed Noah asked after Princess had left.

"It's about your sister."

"I know. She should be back by now. I'll see her later."

The first sergeant had told Noah that Esther was being put in for the Navy Cross. That was a pretty big deal. With the battalion missing most of the fighting during the Evolution, it has been a long time since any Marine or sailor from the battalion had been recommended for such a high award. Pokky, with her nose into everything, must not know that the first sergeant had already told him about the recommendation.

"I think you need to see her now. They're convening a Section Five on her, her and Lieutenant Markopoulos."

"What?" he asked, confused. "No, she's been recommended for the Navy Cross."

"That, too, but now there's a Section Five going being convened."

"No, Pokky, you've got to be wrong. Who ever heard of both of those going on at the same time?"

"I'm not wrong. I saw the convening order myself. It's happening. Your sister is with the lieutenant now seeing the SJA.

And get this: the investigation officer is a Navy captain, appointed by Admiral Blankenship."

It all suddenly fell into place. Admiral Blankenship was no friend of their father. This was payback, pure and simple. Noah felt the heat of anger rush from his toes to his head, taking over.

"Where is she now?"

"Like I told you. She's with the lieutenant. They're with the SJA."

Noah put on his utility blouse as he marshaled his thoughts.

"You're going to do something about this, right? I mean, this is bullshit, and you know people."

"Thank you, Pokky. And yes, I'm going to do something about this. But first, I have to see Ess."

He brushed past Pokky, and headed for CC level, two below his and where Bravo Company was berthed. Marching into the NCO wing, he chimed his sister's door. There wasn't an answer, so he pulled out his PA and hacked the hatch—the app for that was an ill-kept secret that exploited a system-wide flaw in the programming.

Noah had never been in his sister's quarters, but there wasn't a question as to who's side of the space was who's. The lower rack had a pastoral view-screen over the head, an image of the morning sun lighting up a mountain meadow. A purple zebra, the kind you could win at a carnival, sat enthroned on a bright orange pillow. The top rack, on the other hand, was made with precision and lacked any degree of personalization. The desk along the other bulkhead was equally stark in contrast. A synthetic flower was attached to the bulkhead over one-half of the desk, a small chain with a heart hanging from it. Several print novels were lined up against the wall. On the other half of the desk, a coffee cup with styluses was the most prominent item. On the bulkhead over that half of the desk was a small plaque with the words "Pain is Weakness Leaving the Body."

Noah pulled down the seat on the far bulkhead and waited, brooding as his anger simmered. Twenty minutes later, the hatch whisked open, and Corporal Gnarson, Esther's roommate, came in. She saw him and froze.

"What the he—"

"I need your room," Noah said, his tone brooking no discourse.

She looked at him a second, her posture wary.

"Is something wrong? Is Esther--"

"I need to talk to her in private."

She stared at him for a few moments, her thoughts almost visible as they crossed her face, before she said, "OK. Let me get my PT gear, and I'm out of here. Uh, any idea how long you'll be?"

"Don't know, Corporal. She's tied up at the moment."

"OK, then," she said with a shrug. "I'll just make myself scarce."

"Thank you, Corporal Gnarson."

Noah settled in for a wait, his thoughts churning. He tried to arrange what he should say, but he couldn't concentrate. To his great surprise, though, he nodded off, only to jerk awake when Esther burst into the room.

"What the hell are you doing here," Esther asked, her voice tense with stress as she put her cover on the top rack.

"Is it true, Ess? Are you getting a Section Five?"

She spun around to face him, asking sharply, "Where did you hear that?"

"Pokky Opparell. She came to see me two hours ago."

"Hell, Pokky. Of course. She knows everything before they even happen," Esther said bitterly. "Yeah, it's true."

"What the heck, Ess? How can you be getting a Navy Cross and a Section 5?"

"A Navy Cross? That's what I've been put in for? That's just precious," she answered. "And so fucking appropriate."

She flopped down on her roommate's, rack, the purple zebras falling over. She absent-mindedly reached over and pulled it into her lap, her eyes unfocussed.

"Did you do it?" Noah asked, straining to keep his voice emotionless and non-accusatory.

"Did I do what, Noah? Did I order my Marines to take the building under fire? Yes. Did civilians die there? Yes. Is that what you wanted to hear? Does that make you feel better?"

"Ess, stop that! No, it's not what I wanted to hear, and no, I'm not feeling better. I'm pissed, royally pissed. I just need to know for sure so we can figure out what to do next."

"So 'we can figure?' Who's this 'we?' You my lawyer now?"

"I'm your brother, Ess, and that more important than any lawyer."

Esther pulled her roommate's zebra into her chest, dropping her chin until it rested on its head.

"I know, Noah. And I appreciate your concern. Yes, I gave the order, but I didn't know any civilians were in the building. I had approval from my lieutenant. Paragraph 3b covers me."

"You know that, Ess, and I know that. But you know who initiated the Section 5, right?"

"Admiral Fucking Blankenship."

"So you know what's happening here."

"No, I'm an idiot, Noah. Why don't you explain it to me because my poor little old brain can't connect the dots."

"So what are you going to do?"

"I'm waiting for my lawyer to arrive. And we're going to present the facts."

"Which isn't going to do much with a Navy captain, one of Admiral Blankenship's buttboys, running the investigation. We need to go higher with this."

"What, call up General Simone and ask him for help? 'Hi, Jorge, this is Esther. You know, you worked for my father. Can you just call up Admiral Butt-for-shit and ask him to drop the investigation? Please?' Noah, it isn't going to happen. Even if a Lieutenant General could overrule an Admiral, the First Minister at that, what the hell are we saying? I did nothing wrong. Oh, I have nightmares, and I regret it, but I am *not* guilty. But I need to be proven not culpable, not that I got off because I know someone."

"And if you do nothing, you're going to burn, Ess. And you know it."

"So be it."

"Come on, Ess. You're a shooting star, here. You're going places. You're getting a Navy Cross, and a commission is within your reach."

"The thing is Noah, a shooting star burns out."

She pulled down the zebra and looked at its face for a few moments before she tossed it back onto her roommate's pillow.

"We know more than General Simone. More than retired generals." Noah said.

"Who?"

"The chairman."

"Oh, that's even better. I go out of the chain of command to get cleared. That will go over well. If I ever had a career ahead of me, that would sink it."

"And if you do nothing, your career is sunk, too."

"So I'm screwed either way."

"No, one of those ways and you're still a Marine."

"Tarnished. No, this has to go through the process, without interference. I can't pervert my honor."

"You're making a mistake. I want you to contact the chairman. Just talk to her."

"Yeah, just call her up."

"It might take a bit of time, but she'll take your call. She owes father, and she said she was there for us."

"No, Noah. I'll let the system play though."

"And you'll dishonor father?" Noah blurted out, standing up. "You'll let his name get dragged through the mud?"

Esther jumped off her roommate's rack and stood face-to-face with him, her eyes centimeters from his nose.

"Who the fuck are you to say that, *Lance Corporal*? You haven't been doing much to honor him, have you? And you really think running to the Chairman of the Federation Council is honoring him? Get the fuck out of here, Noah. I don't need to listen to your crap!"

Noah stood silent for a moment, his nostrils flaring, as he stared down his sister.

"If you're too stupid and too proud to take care of yourself, then I'll have to do it myself," he finally said, steel in his voice.

"YOU. . .WILL. . .DO. . .NOTHING! Now get the hell out of here, Lance Corporal."

At that moment, Corporal Gnarson opened the hatch.

"Oh, are you two still busy?" she asked, taking half a step back.

"No, my brother's leaving now," Esther said, her voice firm with determination.

Noah waited a few long seconds before he said, "My sister's right. I'm leaving. Thank you for giving us your room."

Noah wheeled around and strode out the hatch. His heart was pounding, his vision narrowing. He knew his sister was stubborn, but this was going too far. If she was guilty, that was one thing, but she was innocent of the charges, and to let the Admiral get revenge on their father this way was a travesty. If she wouldn't reach out for help, well, the chairman would take his call, too.

Chapter 36

Esther

"It's been dropped," an obviously relieved Lieutenant Markopoulos said.

"Sir? Dropped?"

"Yes. I just got the word now, and I wanted to be the one to tell you."

"So Captain San Delgado found for us?" she asked.

Her meeting with the captain had not gone over well, Esther had thought. He seemed to have already made his mind and was only fishing for enough so-called facts to back up his conclusion. She'd been expecting a release of findings any day now, but she also expected them to refer her to a court martial.

"No, the captain didn't find us innocent. He never had the chance to release his findings. This came from somewhere on high. Someone finally realized what was happening to us and put a stop to it."

"So we were not cleared, sir?"

"Cleared? From Captain San Delgado, no I guess not. But cleared, yeah, I'd say so. No charges. No misconduct. No court martial. I'm calling that cleared."

"So we were never technically cleared? Someone just ordered the investigation stopped?"

"Well, yeah. But so what?"

"Sir, that means this is hanging over us. Unless we were formally cleared of misconduct, other Marines can assume the worst, and that it was politics that stopped a court."

"I. . .well, maybe, but really, Esther, I don't think that's a problem. Everyone knows what was what here. We didn't do anything wrong. You're Navy Cross is still in the pipeline, and that would have been pulled if you'd screwed up."

"Some Marines know, sir, but with all due respect, not all. The word will go out that you and I were protected, that we had friends in high places who did what they had to make this all go away."

"Friends in high places? Hardly. You, maybe, but not me," he said, then hurriedly added, "I didn't mean, that. It's just that I don't know anyone high up the chain of command. And from what you've said, I don't think you asked for any favors."

"No, sir, I didn't. I wanted us to be found not at fault, that we did what we had to do. I wanted full exoneration, not getting off on a technicality."

"Corporal Lysander, I understand what you're saying, but I think you're putting too much into this. The bottom line is that we've got nothing on our records. I can look forward to captain, and you can re-enlist. As far as I'm concerned, that is a victory to me.

"I probably shouldn't tell you this," he said in a conspiratorial voice, "but seeing as it's OBE, I guess it doesn't matter. Word is that Captain San Delgado found us culpable. He was going to release a finding of misconduct. You and I were heading to a court, so given the alternative, I'm embracing the events."

"He found us culpable?" Esther repeated, not surprised.

"Yeah. I heard that two days ago. I didn't tell you because it wasn't confirmed, but I got it from a reliable source. In fact, today, when the SJA asked me to contact him, at first, I thought it was to give me the bad news. So right now, I'm feeling pretty good.

"Now this isn't confirmed at all, but my source says our guardian angel was none other than the chairman herself."

"Chairman MacCailín? She intervened?"

"Looks like, yeah. I mean, who else could? It was the First Minister who signed the convening letter, after all."

Esther stomach roiled with bile, and she had to swallow down the vomit that threatened to burst up.

Noah!

She knew with certainty that Noah had gotten involved. He'd contacted the chairman and somehow convinced her to intervene. That was the only thing that made sense.

A tiny part of her was relieved that it was over, but anger blossomed that overwhelmed any relief. She was not being righteous when she told the lieutenant that she wanted to be formally cleared of any wrongdoing. She needed to be cleared. Having suspicion placed on here was bad enough, but having a rep of getting heavy hitters to intercede for her was the kiss of death with regards to her aspirations in the Corps. She couldn't afford that reputation. Having a court martial and being found guilty would almost be better. At least then, her career would be over now while she was still young enough to forge a new career. Now, she could serve years before the consequences would have any effect on her. She'd invest years of time and effort only to be sunk later.

That is why she'd forbade Noah from contacting anyone on her behalf. If she couldn't get cleared through the system, then she needed to accept that and find a new purpose in life.

But Noah, in his brotherly protective mode, screwed that up. He'd placed her in career limbo, where she could still hope to achieve her goals only to fall short later.

Why can't he just leave me alone?

Esther barely knew what she said to the lieutenant over the next few minutes, only that at last, she was standing outside his office.

She pulled out her PA and sent Noah a simple, "Get to the waftball court, now!"

She strode with a purpose, eyes locked ahead. No one stopped her. The waftball court was in the rear of the weightroom. When the base was built, waftball was popular; now, sixty years later, the sport was mostly forgotten, and the odd pentagonal shape of the court was useless for most anything else. Marines had been known to use it to settle disagreements the old-fashioned way, and Esther was in a fighting mood.

"Hey, Lysander!" someone shouted out from the bench presses as she stormed through, ignoring whoever had called out.

She kicked open the door to the court, which had a habit of sticking, then paced back and forth, waiting for her brother. On the fourth time to the front of the court, she kicked out, slamming her toe onto the bounder board.

Shit! She thought as she hopped up and down, her foot on fire.

"Ess," Noah said from behind her.

Esther turned around, put her foot down, and asked, "Did you contact Chairman MacCailín?"

"Oh, so that's what this is," Noah said. "I take it I was successful?"

She strode up to him, trying not to limp, and hit him high in the chest with the flat of her hand.

"I told you not to," she shouted, hitting him again.

He took half a step back, but didn't raise his hands to protect himself.

"I did what I had to do because you are too stubborn."

"It was my choice, not yours!"

"Your choice to drag dad's name into the dirt? Your grubbing choice?" Noah asked, his voice getting louder.

"What the hell do you care about that? You never loved him anyway, and he never loved you, you, freak."

Noah went still, then said, his voice level and even, "The Lysander name's my birthright, too. And whether Dad loved me as much as you or Ben, that doesn't matter. Mom is a Lysander, too. And I wasn't going to let you shame either one of them. Or me. I wasn't going to let you shame me."

"So now, you think you saved our name? Saved me? You think having the fucking Chairman of the Federation Council step in to protect me is saving our benighted name? Do you have any idea how the world works?"

"I know that Admiral Blankenship opened the Section 5 to get back at Dad. I know you didn't deserve that. And I knew I had to act. I waited, Ess, until I knew what the results were going to be before I moved, so grant me that. But with you getting a court martial, I knew it was time to act."

"You knew about the court? Before me?"

"Yeah, I knew. It was kind of important, you know? So I kept informed. Like you might have wanted to do if you could have gotten off your lofty perch."

"And how did you find out?"

"I've got avenues. I had the copy that went up to the Admiral for his approval."

"Fuck, you were hacking accounts? You can't do that yourself. Who helped you? Lieutenant Fairhold? Pokky?"

Noah's eyes gave him away, and she said, "Pokky, then. Risking her retirement. That's frigging precious."

"It doesn't matter how I got it. I did, and I acted. To save your ass, you're welcome."

"I never asked you to do that. In fact, if I remember my words, I told you not to. Did you forget that?"

Noah stared at his sister for a full twenty seconds as her chest heaved with each breath.

"I didn't forget. But you needed help, even if you're too pigheaded to realize that. And I had to protect the Lysander name. Mom and dad deserved that, at least. And Ben. Did you forget them in your pride?"

"I haven't forgotten anyone! But I'm going to forget you. We're done, Lance Corporal. Done! Do you understand that?"

Noah stared at her once more time. He opened his mouth as if to say something, then closed it.

Finally, he said, "As you wish, Corporal."

He pushed past her, his shoulder hitting hers as he left the waftball court.

Esther was fuming, and she wanted to shout out at Noah, but with him now in the weightroom, she didn't want to air the family's dirty laundry.

Not family anymore! I'm finished with him.

Hidden in her righteous anger at Noah, though, was a hole in her heart, one she feared would never be filled.

Epilogue

Noah

"Hey, Noah, I just heard. That's pretty copacetic," Jessie Rose said as Noah walked down 4B to the Mamba maintenance bay.

"Thanks, Jessie," he answered, wondering how Jessie knew about his orders.

He'd just received them 25 minutes before, and he didn't think they were important enough to be spread about.

"So, are you going to have to salute her?" Jessie asked as he came to an exaggerated position of attention and executed a flamboyant, palm-out salute.

Of course. He's taking about Ess, not me.

Esther had been selected for a commission and would be leaving the battalion for NSA Annapolis in a month. Noah hadn't spoken to her since then—he hadn't spoken to her since their blowup in the waftball court. He'd sent her a brief congratulations on his PA, but he'd received nothing in return.

Amazingly, most of the battalion hadn't noticed their rift. Sampson, Princess, Pad-Man, and a few others close to Noah knew, but he was pretty sure Esther hadn't told anyone. That wouldn't be her style.

"You better believe it," he said, forcing a smile onto his face. "You know those butter bars. They need their fragile egos stroked."

"Damn right!" Jessie agreed.

"OK, see you. I'm heading down to the bay," he said.

Noah walked to the end of the passage, then took the elevator down to the logistics deck. He stuck his head into the tank section's office, but it was empty, as he'd expected. Sergeant Phong was not a desk jockey—as a motorhead, she preferred being with her babies.

And sure enough, as he entered the bay, he could see her legs poking out from under 213.

"Sergeant Phong, you go a second?"

"Hand me a cross-spanner, Lysander" she shouted from under the tank.

"Cross-spanner, cross-spanner," he muttered as he looked over the maintenance table. "Oh, this one."

Noah had spent quite a bit of time with the section over the last year, but he was hardly an expert. He was relieved that he recognized the correct tool. He handed it to her and waited patiently while she grunted and groaned under the Mamba. It took at least a minute for her to finished whatever tasked he had before she scooted out from under the tank.

"What's up, Corporal of Marines," she asked, brushing her cheek, but leaving even a greater smudge of black across it.

Noah smiled. He'd been a corporal for only three weeks, and the title still seemed fresh and new to him.

"Just thought I'd let you know I got my orders. I've got 42 days and a wake-up."

"And. . .?"

"Camp Ceasare," he said, his tone nonchalant while he was brimming with excitement on the inside.

"Son-of-a-gun, Noah. The Itch! That's phantasmagorical, Marine! You, a tanker!"

She jumped up, wiping her hand on a dirty rag before thrusting it out. Noah took it, giving as good as he received from her firm grasp.

"You're going to do real well there. I've got full confidence in you."

"Well, I've got a head's start, thanks to you. And the staff sergeant, of course."

"Eh, no big deal. We're always looking out for good Marines. Everyone wants to be a grunt, but someone's got to pull their asses out of the fire, dontcha-know."

"I'm looking forward to it. Something new."

"How's your girlfriend taking it?" she asked. "Nine months at school's a long time, and I doubt you're coming back to the station here."

Jeez! Is that all anyone wants to know?

Noah had already told the Princess, Sampson, and Pad-Man, and the first thing anyone wanted to know was about Miriam. But now even Sergeant Phong? Was his personal life common knowledge in the battalion?

"I haven't told her yet," he admitted.

"Don't put it off, Marine. And don't lead her on."

"But hell, I know you won't. You're one of the good guys, right? You know what you have to do," she said, clapping him on the shoulder—and leaving a smudge of black on his utility blouse.

I guess I'm going to have to get used to that, he mused.

"I'm on my way to the exchange now, Sergeant. She's on her shift."

"Well, then, I'm not going to keep you. Anyway, congrats. You'll do well, I know."

"And thank you, Sergeant. You were a big help."

"My pleasure."

Noah left the maintenance bay, took the elevator to AB, and headed down the passage to the exchange. His heart-rate started to rise and she tried, for the hundredth time, to formulate what he was going to say.

He'd only just now received his orders, but both Noah and Miriam had known that he was approaching the end of his tour. Once, they'd even discussed Noah getting out and staying on Wayfarer, but that was really a non-starter. It had taken Noah some time to find his way within the Corps, but now it felt like home. With his parents and Ben gone, and now with Esther not speaking to him, Turtle, Princess, Pad-Man, Sampson—they were his family now.

Noah paused in front of the hatch, took a deep breath, then waved it open. Miriam was with a new private, patiently explaining to him how to hack his rack with Springtime Air.

"But won't that make the blanket, like, uncomfortable, ma'am?"

"What do you want, Private? Hospital corners that the gunny will love or a baby soft blankie?" she asked, catching Noah's eye and winking.

"I guess the hospital corners, ma'am."

"You guessed right. Let me ring you up."

Noah watched her, the girl without a direction in life, now Mz. Marine, knowing all the tricks on how to get by in the Corps. She finished up with the boot, then waved Noah over.

"And how're you today? I didn't expect to see you until this evening."

"I know, but I wanted to, well, I mean. . .uh. . .I've got something to tell you. I, uh, I got my orders to today. To Camp Ceasare. Forty-two-days-and-a-wake-up."

He stopped, waiting for a reaction, just staring into her big brown eyes. Miriam said nothing, he said nothing.

Finally, she asked, "And?"

"Well, uh, we've been, you know, we've been together for almost two years. But Camp Ceasare's a long ways from here, and tank school's nine months long. I don't even know where my next duty station's going to be yet," he managed to get out.

"And?" she asked, no emotion showing on her face.

"I know you've had a hard life, and I know you've found yourself, sort of, ending up here. This is your home now. You fit in here."

"And?" she asked for the third time.

"And, and, I don't want to lose you. I want you to come with me to Camp Ceasare. I'm not a sergeant yet, so we can't get housing or anything like that, but we can figure out something. I know we can," he spit out in a rush.

"What are you asking, me, Noah Lysander?"

"I want you to marry me!"

Miriam looked at him as Noah had a sudden need to hit the head as a spasm wrenched his gut.

Why isn't she saying anything? Shit, I knew this was going to happen.

"Noah, I already turned in my notice. Forty-two days and a wake-up."

"What? Whu. . .why?"

"Why? Because I found out about your orders, of course."

"How?" he asked, totally confused as to what was going on.

"How do you think? Who's the camp gossip? Pokky, of course. She told me an hour ago."

And it dawned on him what she'd just said.

"So you quit? To be with me."

"Yes, to be with you, Noah. And yes, I will marry you," she said, jumping up on the counter and sliding her legs around to straddle him.

She gave him a big kiss.

"Uh, PDA,[10] young lady," Noah gasped as he came up for air.

He didn't' let go of her waist, though.

"What're they going to do, Noah Lysander? Fire me? I already gave them my notice."

"So, you resigned your job. How did you know I was going to ask you?"

"Really? You have to ask me? I've known you for two years. I know you couldn't survive without me. Besides, you really had no choice. If you hadn't asked, I would have come anyway. Like it or not, you're mine."

She leaned in for one more kiss. And she was right, Noah knew. He didn't have a choice in the matter.

Not that he wanted one.

---

[10] PDA: Public Display of Affection

Thank you for reading *Legacy Marines*. If you liked it, please feel free to leave a review of the book in Amazon.

This is the first book of a planned series detailing the life and times of Esther and Noah. Please stand by for the next book of the series, *Esther's Story*.

If you would like updates on new books releases, news, or special offers, please consider signing up for my mailing list. Your email will not be sold, rented, or in any other way disseminated. If you are interested, please sign up at the link below:

http://eepurl.com/bnFSHH

Other Books by Jonathan Brazee

The United Federation Marine Corps' Lysander Twins

Legacy Marines
Esther's Story (Coming Soon)
Noah's Story (Coming)

The United Federation Marine Corps

Recruit
Sergeant
Lieutenant
Captain
Major
Lieutenant Colonel
Colonel
Commandant

Rebel
(Set in the UFMC universe.)

Women of the United Federation Marines
Gladiator
Sniper
Corpsman

High Value Target (A Gracie Medicine Crow Short Story)

The Return of the Marines Trilogy
The Few
The Proud
The Marines

The Al Anbar Chronicles: First Marine Expeditionary Force--Iraq
Prisoner of Fallujah
Combat Corpsman
Sniper

Werewolf of Marines
Werewolf of Marines: Semper Lycanus
Werewolf of Marines: Patria Lycanus
Werewolf of Marines: Pax Lycanus

To The Shores of Tripoli

Wererat

Darwin's Quest: The Search for the Ultimate Survivor

Venus: A Paleolithic Short Story

Secession

Non-Fiction

Exercise for a Longer Life

Author Website
http://www.returnofthemarines.com

Made in the USA
Coppell, TX
11 November 2019